W9-AQU-187

01/24
STRAND PRICE
$ 5.00

Also by RM Johnson

Dating Games

Love Frustration

The Harris Family

Father Found

The Harris Men

The Million Dollar Divorce

A Novel

RM Johnson

SIMON & SCHUSTER

New York   London   Toronto   Sydney

Simon & Schuster
Rockefeller Center
1230 Avenue of the Americas
New York, NY 10020

This book is a work of fiction. Names, characters, places,
and incidents either are products of the author's imagination
or are used fictitiously. Any resemblance to actual events or locales
or persons, living or dead, is entirely coincidental.

Copyright © 2004 by R. Marcus Johnson
All rights reserved,
including the right of reproduction
in whole or in part in any form.

Simon & Schuster and colophon
are registered trademarks of Simon & Schuster, Inc.

For information about special discounts for bulk purchases,
please contact Simon & Schuster Special Sales:
1-800-456-6798 or business@simonandschuster.com

Manufactured in the United States of America

7   9   10   8   6

Library of Congress Cataloging-in-Publication Data
Johnson, R. M. (Rodney Marcus)
The million dollar divorce : a novel / R. M. Johnson.
p. cm.
1. Separation (Psychology)—Fiction.
2. Millionaires—Fiction. 3. Divorce—Fiction. I. Title.

PS3560.O3834M55 2004
813'.54—dc22   2004049145
ISBN 0-7432-5816-9

The
Million Dollar
Divorce

1

Monica Kenny awakened and without opening her eyes reached across the bed to feel for her husband. He was not there.

She rolled over, barely opening her eyes to glance at the clock. The glowing red numbers flashed 4:37 A.M.

Monica sighed, peeled off the blankets, and threw her legs over the bed. She sat on the edge of it, wondering, should she really pursue this with him? But something had to be done. It had been almost every night for a week that she had woken up and found her husband gone.

She stood up from the bed, grabbed her robe, and ventured out to find him.

She walked slowly through the huge downtown penthouse, pulling her robe on and tying the belt around her waist. She took the stairs down from the upper level, not bothering to turn on the lights.

When she made it halfway down the flight, she could see a great deal of the first floor, the huge open living room and dining room, and the entrance to the kitchen.

It was all dark down there, but light from the towering skyscrapers just outside their balcony doors, on the sixty-fifth floor, made it possible for Monica to see her husband, Nate. He was sitting amazingly still in one of the dining room chairs he had pulled away and set facing the windows.

His back was to her as he stared out at the illuminated buildings.

He did not turn around, even though Monica was certain that he heard her come down the stairs, was certain that he could feel her as she walked up and stopped just fifteen feet behind him.

"Nate," Monica breathed, almost afraid to say another word. "Why are you doing this?"

There was no reply, nor any movement from Monica's husband.

"Nate."

"Go to bed, Monica," he finally said, his voice low.

"But every night you get up and you come down here. I just want to know—"

"Monica, please. Go to bed," he said again, without turning in his chair. "Just leave me alone."

Monica opened her mouth to say something, but thought better of it, and stopped herself. She turned and headed back for the stairs, grabbing the rail, pulling herself up four or five of them; then she stopped.

"Don't stay down here too long, okay, Nate? You'll be tired in the morning." Monica stood there at the banister waiting for a response, but when one didn't come, she continued climbing the stairs.

❦

It took forever for Monica to fall back to sleep, but when she finally did, she felt as though she had been out for only five minutes when her alarm clock started screaming beside her head.

It was 7:30 A.M., and still Nate wasn't beside her. She doubted if he ever came back.

Monica showered, dressed, and figured she would make her and her husband breakfast, considering she didn't have to be at the store until 9 A.M.

She walked down the stairs, hoping that what was so heavy on Nate's mind had been resolved. She needed to talk to him, work on getting things back to the way they used to be. But when Monica got halfway down the stairs, she heard the front door quickly open, and then close again.

She hurried to the front door, threw it open, and stepped out into

2

the hallway, only to hear a "ding" from the elevator and the doors slide to a close.

She stood there, unable to believe that her husband, it seemed, not only could no longer sleep an entire night with her in bed but now couldn't stand the sight of her in the morning.

❦

Monica skipped breakfast, for she had no appetite, and headed on to work. She walked, as she did every morning, because where she worked, an exclusive Italian men's clothing store on Michigan Avenue, was just minutes from where they lived on Chestnut Avenue.

She was the first to arrive every morning, because she was the manager, one of the rewards she received for attaining her M.B.A. She could've quit long ago. It wasn't like she was hurting for money, considering her husband was a millionaire. But she liked the independence, having something more to do than just have spa treatments and shop all day. Besides, she enjoyed what she did, and didn't have to run to her husband every time she needed spending money.

Monica unlocked the store, made her way in across the hardwood floors, and disabled the alarm. The store was made up like a very wealthy man's town home. Exposed brick enclosed the area; the second floor was an overlooking loft. Sofas and chairs were placed about, very expensive clothing intricately strewn over their backs as though someone actually lived there and had just left after hurriedly dressing.

Racks and racks of other ridiculously priced suits, shirts, slacks, and jackets stood all about the store. And in the back, shelves of shoes costing up to a thousand dollars a pair were neatly stacked.

Monica had worked in retail clothing all her life, but made the jump from working in the lower-paying South Side stores to downtown when a girlfriend who also worked in retail suggested it.

"You never know. A girl looking like you might snag herself a rich man," Monica's friend said.

She was twenty-seven years old at the time, and it seemed as though all her girlfriends were either getting married or engaged. Monica was nowhere near that point, was stuck dating clowns who approached her on the street.

She was ready to throw in the towel—considered buying house cats for those lonely Friday nights—when a man walked into her store.

"Girl, do you see what I see?" Tabatha, Monica's associate and best friend, said, pulling on Monica's arm as though she were alerting the girl to a fire in the next room.

"I see him," Monica said, yanking away from Tabatha. "I'm looking right at him."

They were both in one corner of the store, admiring the tall, broad-shouldered, brown-skinned, wavy-haired man.

"So, what you gonna do?" Tabatha said.

"I'm not doing nothing."

"What! Why not? The man is fine. Obviously, he got money, or he wouldn't be here, buying this overpriced stuff. And there is the fact that you ain't got a man, and ain't had one in, like, eons."

"Shut up, girl. Who asked you? Just go over there and ask him if he needs any help."

"I'm not asking him," Tabatha said. "I have a man, and I'm afraid something like that over there could tempt me into leaving his behind tomorrow."

"Just go over there," Monica said, pushing Tabatha in the back. Tabatha stumbled forward, shooting Monica an evil glance, after making sure the man didn't see her trip. "Fine, but don't say I didn't try to give him to you first."

Monica watched as Tabatha walked over, feeling that maybe her girl was right. Maybe she should've gone over there herself, because, like Tabatha said, Monica was terminally single. And then, the man was gorgeous. But looking like that, he had to be married, Monica told herself.

She got a glance at his wedding finger, saw that it was bare, and wanted to kick herself. Really wanted to, after Tabatha threw her head back laughing, dropped a flirtatious hand on one of his broad shoulders, then shot a look back at Monica that said: Told you. Shoulda came over here yourself.

Oh well, Monica thought, disappointed. She'd been single forever, so what difference did it make?

Tabatha bounced her narrow behind back over to Monica, a huge giddy grin on her face.

"So what did he say?" Monica said, less than enthused to hear the answer.

"He wants to impregnate me . . . Naw, syke! He said he wants to talk to you."

"What?"

"Yeah. He said he wants you to be the one to help him with his suits. Now *you* go over there," Tabatha said, shoving Monica forward, just as Monica had done to her. Monica stumbled as well, but when she looked up to see if the man had seen her trip, he had.

Monica blushed with embarrassment as she walked up to the man. "Yes sir. How may I help you?"

The man appeared slightly bewildered. "I don't know," he said. "Your associate said that you'd know what I'd need."

"Oh, oh, yes sir," Monica said, waiting for the man to turn and continue looking through the suit selection before she turned to see Tabatha in the corner of the store, her hand cupped to her mouth, laughing hysterically.

Monica helped that man for more than two hours, and when he left, he had walked out of the store with four suits and Monica's phone number.

He was a sweet man, attentive and very eager. "I'm going to call you tomorrow, is that okay?" he asked after she had written her home number on the back of a card and passed it to him.

"Yes, I'd like that," Monica said.

And that was the beginning.

Nate and Monica started dating, saw each other at least three times a week for dinner, drinks, movies, or the theater.

They slept together after two weeks, and after that, Nate seemed as though he couldn't be in Monica's presence without making love to her, for he was a very passionate man.

"So, dude got money?" Tabatha said one day while they were folding and reshelving some sweaters, a month after Monica and Nate got together.

"Yeah, he has a small condo down here on Wacker, and drives a Mercedes of some kind or other," Monica said, as though it was no big deal. "He's trading stocks for a firm downtown, but says he wants to break away and start his own company soon. And then he said something that kinda freaked me out."

"What, girl, what?" Tabatha said, leaning in close.

"We were laying in bed last night after—" Monica paused, seeing Tabatha's eyes bulge some—"well, you know . . . after. And he was telling me about his plans. Then he said he was going to start his own company, but he was just waiting for the right woman to come into his life so he could marry her, and they could pursue his dream together."

"What!" Tabatha said, screaming at the top of her lungs. "He said that!"

"Yeah," Monica said. "And I don't really know how to take it."

"Take it like he's trying to marry you, girl!"

"We've only been seeing each other for a month, though. Don't you think it's too soon to be talking like that?"

"The man is thirty-six. When do you expect him to talk about it—when he's fifty? Maybe he wants kids or something."

"He does. That's all he seems to talk about," Monica said.

"So you're saying, he proposes to you a month from now, you're going to turn down a successful, handsome man that will probably just become more successful? A man that's about marriage, family, and is certain of that. So certain, that he wants to do it with you. You gonna turn that down?"

"I guess that would be pretty crazy, hunh?"

"Oh, yes. Crackhead crazy."

Six months later, Nate did propose, and Monica found herself happily accepting. The wedding took place six months after that, and Monica thought there wasn't a way that she could've ever been happier.

Nate was a beautiful, successful man that loved her like crazy and wanted nothing more in the world than to immediately start a family.

Unfortunately, that's when she and Nate had their first disagreement.

She had known how eager the man was to start a family, had known that from practically the first date they had, but she didn't inform him until the night of their wedding that she had no intention of rushing into having children.

"I'm only twenty-seven, baby. I want a few years just to enjoy us."

Nate was disappointed, probably more than she had ever let herself realize, but he seemed to accept it, and things once again were perfect between them.

Without the children to slow them down, for the first three years of their marriage Monica and Nate traveled all around the world. They spent nights out on the town, would come in at whatever time they chose, and then make love for as long and as loud as they wanted to, which happened quite often.

It all seemed like a dream back then, Monica thought now, four years later, standing in the same store she had met her husband in. Everything was perfect, until the day she gave her husband exactly what he had been begging for, and got pregnant.

2

Nate finished painting over the last of the room he had just painted baby blue not two weeks ago.

He looked around him, shaking his head at what he had just done.

Nate set the paint roller in the corner, held his hands before him, looking down at his brown skin covered with splotches of black paint.

He had painted the entire room this dismal color.

Early this morning, like every morning for the past week, he found himself in bed unable to sleep because of everything that was going on in his head. He pulled himself up, wandered downstairs, and just had to think, try to sort things out, make sense of it all.

He remained there till the dark skies in front of him began to lighten, until he heard the alarm clock above him, in their bedroom, go off, and heard the shower water running. At that time, he ran upstairs, slipped on some jeans, a T-shirt, and walked out of the house, just as he heard his wife descending the stairs.

He went to a home improvement store, bought supplies, and once home, called his secretary, Tori, and told her to cancel all his meetings because there was something important he had to do today.

Nate took the black paint and covered every inch of what was supposed to be his child's nursery with it. This was his way of putting the past to rest, of never having to be reminded of what he once was so sure was going to happen, but never did and never would. This was Nate's way of mourning for the child he thought he and his wife would have, but did not.

It took him all day, and by the evening, Nate found a place on the floor of the room and had a seat on one of the sheets of plastic he had laid down.

His wife, Monica, would come in the house, see the room, and be furious, Nate told himself, rubbing the splotches of black on his hands. But she would have no right, because if there was anyone that should've been angry, it was him.

Nate met his wife four years ago while shopping for a suit. She was beautiful and intelligent, and he proposed to her after only six months. In Nate's mind there was no reason to wait. He was thirty-six, had fallen in love, had been anxious both to settle down with a good woman so he could concentrate on his business, and to start his family before he found himself getting too old.

Since he was a child himself, he had always wanted children. He remembered all the good times he and his brother had coming up, remembered how he practically idolized his father. He remembered the man telling him, "When everything is gone, when a man has nothing else, he realizes that family is all that matters." That day he knew he would have one of his own.

So Nate married Monica, but getting his wife pregnant was farther off than he had thought, because Monica all of a sudden wanted to wait three years before trying to conceive.

"I want you all to myself for a little while," Monica said the night of their honeymoon, when Nate walked into the bathroom and caught her trying to down a birth control pill with a glass of water.

"You'll have me to yourself for the rest of our lives, honey. That's why we got married." Nate extended his palm. "Just give me the pill."

Monica slipped the pill into her mouth, kicked it back with a swallow of water. "Too late." She grinned.

She wanted to build a strong marriage foundation, she told him after they had made love that night. She wanted them to travel, be able to go to a movie, dinner, or just shopping without first having to call a baby-sitter or packing up everything relating to the baby and dragging it along with them.

It all seemed odd to Nate, because she had never mentioned any of that to him until that night after they had gotten married. When he asked her why that was, she said, "You wouldn't have agreed with me if I had told you then."

There in the bathroom, he looked away from her. She touched his face, turning his attention back to her.

"I'm right, aren't I? You wouldn't have wanted to wait."

"I don't know," Nate said. But he did know. She was right. He wouldn't have agreed with her on that, and given how strongly he felt about his plan for a family, he probably would've had the woman agree to a premarital deal—either they start having babies once they get married or they end their relationship that very moment.

That night, in their honeymoon bed, his wife falling off to sleep peacefully at his side, Nate felt betrayed. He wondered how Monica could keep something so important to herself without realizing just how damaging something like that could be to their marriage.

Nate grabbed his pillow, doubled it, stuck it under his head, and forced himself not to think about it any longer. He was married now, he had a wife, and whether she wanted them or not, Nate told himself, they were going to have children.

He smiled mischievously to himself, looking over at his beautiful wife sleeping beside him. He would just have to continue pushing her till she conceded.

Every month afterward, he mentioned them getting pregnant, but was always met with the same answer. "Not yet."

There were times at night, when he stood in the bathroom over the sink, after brushing his teeth, that he would eye Monica's little clamshell birth control case, and he thought of stealing it. He would flush the tiny tablets down the toilet, or chuck the whole thing out the window. Maybe he could get some replacement pills. Something much weaker, or possibly even sugar pills. He had a close doctor friend. The idea wasn't too far-fetched.

But he didn't want to trick his wife into having his children just because she was able to trick him into waiting.

He would just continue asking, and Monica would eventually agree, Nate was sure.

It happened exactly as he had thought. He did finally convince her to have his children . . . only three years later, as Monica had said from the very beginning.

After Nate was given the free-and-clear signal, he was ecstatic, and joyfully tried getting his wife pregnant for eight months, but nothing happened. Nate began to worry if there was something physically wrong with him, thought of making a doctor's appointment to make sure everything was okay down there.

Thankfully, the week he considered this, Monica told him that she was pregnant.

To say it was the happiest day of his life was an understatement.

All he could think about was the child he would soon have.

Nate dragged his wife shopping immediately for maternity clothes, for baby clothes, toys, and anything else he thought the child might need in nine months.

"We don't even know what we're having," Monica said.

"We'll buy both girl and boy stuff, and whichever one we don't have, we'll donate the other to charity."

Every night, Nate was in bed, sitting up with the lamp burning, reading through baby name books, saying names softly to himself, determining whether or not they would fit his child.

Two weeks after Monica announced she was pregnant, Nate had found the exclusive nursery school their child would attend. Two weeks after that, Nate had set up the child's college fund. And at a month and a half into her pregnancy, he decided it was time to clear out and paint that extra bedroom in their penthouse they were using for storage, and transform it into a nursery.

Everything was going wonderfully till, at the two-month mark, Nate found out his baby had died.

3

Work for Monica was hard today, not because of the effort she had to put forth but because of how much her husband was on her mind. She tried calling him a couple of times at his office, but his secretary told her that he would be in meetings all day.

Whether or not that was the truth, or just a message Nate told his secretary to relay to Monica, she wasn't sure. After work, Monica dutifully made her way to the gym, not feeling like it, but knowing that it would help relieve some of the stress she had been feeling.

Once she was there, her mind was not on what she should've been doing, but still on Nate, so she cut her routine short, telling herself that she needed to get back, hoping to straighten things out with her husband.

After returning home, she stood frozen just outside their front door, her key in her hand, ready to insert it into the lock but unable to.

It was almost seven o'clock, so she figured Nate was home, and she wondered what he was doing in there—that was, if he hadn't left. Nate had her questioning their situation so much that on any given evening, upon walking into their house, Monica was prepared to find him gone. Not just gone for dinner, or down to the store, but gone for good—his drawers yanked from the dresser, hanging out empty, his home office cleared of all the things he couldn't work without, his favorite sculptures pulled off the mantel and shoved into a box.

It was just so hard living like this, Monica thought, feeling weak all of a sudden and leaning against the frame of the door, dropping her face in her hands, trying not to cry.

She had done everything in her power to try and make things right between them, but he would not hear her when she spoke, would not relax and let himself be held when she tried to wrap her arms around him, and would not even make love to her when she told him that she needed to feel him inside her just to feel as though everything would someday be the same again.

But she knew why he was behaving that way toward her. She had lied to him when she knew she shouldn't have, and he had found out.

❦

After a week of her period not showing, Monica had gone to the drugstore to buy a pregnancy test.

Upon getting home, she took the test and stood over the sink, the little wand trembling in her hand. She waited, holding her breath, staring intently into the little box that would display one line if she wasn't pregnant, two if she was.

She just had to be, she told herself, and felt a droplet of sweat fall from her forehead and run down her face.

A moment later, the results of the test magically appeared before her eyes.

The test read positive.

That moment, everything seemed fine. Monica and Nate were in love, the company that her husband had started a year after their marriage was thriving, and they would finally have the family that he wanted so dearly. At least, Monica thought that until the day of her doctor's appointment six weeks later.

All during the morning while her doctor ran tests on her, Monica felt something wasn't right. It seemed it took forever for the doctor to come back with the results, leaving her in the cold white-walled office, trembling, and worrying about the outcome.

When Dr. Ferra finally returned, she said, "Mrs. Kenny, you took a home test to confirm your pregnancy. Is that correct?"

"Yes."

"And how long do you think you've been pregnant?" Dr. Ferra asked, opening a folder in front of her, looking down at it.

"What do you mean, think?" Monica said. "I am pregnant. The test was positive."

"Mrs. Kenny," the doctor said, looking up sadly from the folder, "is your husband out in the waiting room? Did you bring him with you?"

"No, I didn't bring him with me."

"Do you think you'd like to try him at work, or maybe arrange to come back tomorrow?"

"Dr. Ferra, what I want is for you to tell me what is going on, because you're really starting to scare me," Monica said, feeling a great deal of anxiety now. "Is everything all right with the baby?"

"Mrs. Kenny, I'm sorry to inform you of this, but there is no baby."

Monica could not believe what she had just heard. All of sudden she felt as though she could not breathe.

"I'm pregnant. The test I took confirmed that."

"Home tests can be wrong."

"But I missed my period. It's been two months. I've been sick, I felt my body changing!"

"Mrs. Kenny—"

"I'm pregnant!" Monica said, breathing heavily, sounding on the verge of hysteria. "Maybe *your* test is wrong!"

"Mrs. Kenny," Dr. Ferra said in her most soothing voice. "It's not wrong. All the tests we ran, on your blood, your urine, they confirmed what I was suspecting. You haven't had a period in two months, and you felt those changes in your body, because you were going through premature menopause."

Monica sat up in her chair, shock on her face.

"I'm only thirty-one years old. That can't be! How can I have not known that?"

"Have you felt fatigued, depressed, irritable lately?"

"No."

"Have you had trouble sleeping at all, felt moody, or experienced hot flashes?"

Monica thought, and said, "I've been feeling warm sometimes, been sweating a little at night, and sometimes I can't get to sleep, but—"

"Those are some of the symptoms."

"So what are you saying?" Monica asked, afraid to know the answer. "If I'm not pregnant now, what do I do to get pregnant?"

Dr. Ferra looked at Monica oddly, concerned that she seemed to not understand what exactly was being said to her.

"I'm sorry, Mrs. Kenny. There's nothing you can do. You cannot get pregnant."

Monica all of a sudden gasped for air, felt light-headed, then saw everything start to darken around her. Her body fell limp, and she would've fallen to the floor if the doctor had not rushed to her side and grabbed her before Monica completely fell from the chair.

"Mrs. Kenny." Monica heard her name being called.

She opened her eyes, saw Dr. Ferra's face slowly coming into focus.

"You've almost fainted. Sit here, and I'll get you something," the doctor said, quickly rushing away from her.

But Monica could not sit anywhere. She had to get away from there, away from that place, away from the woman who told her that all that Monica believed true was not.

Monica found herself bursting out of the doctor's office, running down the hallway, tears streaming from her eyes as she sidestepped and bumped into people.

She crashed through the doors of the office building, bright sunlight hitting her in the face, the doctor's last words, proclaiming that she would never get pregnant, never carry a child, ringing in her head.

Monica ran toward the edge of the long flight of concrete stairs, preparing to run down them two or three at a time, get as far away from this place as possible. But she misstepped, twisting her ankle, and was knocked off balance, her body falling forward, plummeting, tumbling down the flight of jagged stairs—the sky, the ground flipping over and over again—until her body landed hard and flat on the cement sidewalk. Her eyes were open, her arms and legs spread out wide. She did not want to move them. Didn't know if she could.

"Outside of some deep tissue bruising, you've escaped that fall without injury," a graying ER physician had told her two hours later. "You're fine," he said, writing out a prescription for Tylenol 4, tearing it from his pad, and handing it to her.

Monica took the slip of paper and thought, no, she wasn't anywhere near fine.

She cried all the way home, continued to cry once she got there. It was mourning for the loss of the baby that she knew was growing within her. The baby that she and her husband had spoken about every night and every day. The baby that she had grown to love, but a baby that some doctor said was just a figment of her imagination.

When Nate got home that evening, regardless how much Monica tried to pretend she hadn't been, he could tell that she was crying.

"Baby, what's wrong?" Nate said, after setting his briefcase down, rushing over to her, and placing an arm around her.

Monica had been preparing for this moment for hours, trying to find the strength to say to him what she had practiced over and over again in the mirror. She knew it was wrong, but she would lie to him. She had no other choice.

"Sweetheart. Please tell me," Nate said. "It didn't have anything to do with the doctor's appointment today, did it?"

How she didn't want to, but she had to lie to him, Monica told herself. If for no other reason than to buy herself time, prove that doctor wrong. They'd get pregnant again, and he'd never find out about any of this, Monica had to trust. And then with as much sincerity as she could manufacture, Monica said, "I didn't get to the appointment. I had an accident."

"Are you okay?" Nate said, moving closer to her, grabbing her by her shoulders.

A tear spilled from her eye. "I'm fine. But our baby . . ."

Nate's eyes widened, his grip tightening on her.

". . .our baby died."

Now, as Monica stood outside her door, wiped tears from her face, she told herself that she and her husband would get through this. It would take some time and understanding, but they would make it through.

Monica unlocked the door and walked in.

Her nose was immediately assaulted by the smell of paint fumes, and she wondered what was going on.

She set her purse on the table by the door and called out her husband's name.

"Nate," she said, taking the stairs, after looking around on the first level and finding nothing. Maybe her husband was getting some work done, but she couldn't imagine what kind of work, and why.

On the second floor, Monica turned the corner, the smell even stronger now. She walked down the hall, saw the nursery door open, and when she walked in, she could not believe what she saw before her. Everything was painted black, the floorboards, the crown molding, even the ceiling.

Nate sat in the center of the room, wearing old jeans and a torn T-shirt covered with paint. His back was to Monica, his knees brought into his chest, his arms roped around them, his face lowered.

Monica just shook her head and wondered how much more of this could she endure—*they* could endure.

"And this is what, Nate?" Monica said, walking into the room.

Nate did not turn around, just continued to stare at the floor like a first-grader sent to stand in the corner for misbehaving.

"I said, and this is what, Nate!" Monica said, raising her voice.

Nate didn't respond, just pulled himself from the plastic sheet that covered the floor, stood, turned, and without acknowledging Monica at all, proceeded toward the door. He passed her as he had been doing for the last two weeks since he had found out all she had lied about. But it had all become too much for Monica now.

As Nate passed her, Monica reached out, grabbed his arm, spun him around, hauled off, and slapped him hard across the face.

Nate stumbled two steps back.

"Don't you just fucking walk past me as though I'm not standing here," Monica cried. "Two weeks! Two weeks I've been apologizing to you, explaining to you why I did what I did. But it's just all about poor Nate," Monica said, tears streaming down her cheeks. "Just the pain you're experiencing, everything you're going through. But what about me? I wanted children too. I wanted the family. But you won't hear any of it. You won't look at me. You won't talk to me. You won't even fuck me. Is it that bad, Nate? Is it that fucking bad!"

Nate said nothing, just stood there, the expression on his face mostly blank, save for the bit of pity Monica thought she had read.

"Do you want a divorce, Nate? Is that what it is?"

"And what if I said I did?" Nate said.

Monica was shocked by his response, but knew she could not show her alarm. She simply said, "Then I'd sue your ass for everything you're worth."

4

Nate Kenny pressed a palm against the glass of the newborns' nursery, lowered his head, feeling a deep depression cover him. The night he found out about the death of his baby was the worst night of his life. After his wife gave him the news there on the living room sofa, he cried, wanting to know the reason, wanting to know how she fell. Why didn't she see the stair? Why didn't she watch where she was going?

It all sounded very accusatory to him, looking back at it now. It sounded as though he blamed her for the death of his child. A child that he had been waiting all his life for. But accidents happen. He knew that, and he told himself that he would have to apologize to her for how he acted.

He remembered shedding tears with her for what seemed like hours, and on that couch she held him, telling him it would all be all right.

Upstairs Nate and his wife showered together, standing in a tight embrace as steaming water crashed against them.

In bed, Monica asked if he wanted to talk. There was nothing he had to say to her. He was angry with her. She moved close to him, but he rolled over, turning his back to her. He knew it wasn't her fault, but still, something made him feel that she had allowed his child to die.

Now in the nursery, Nate raised his head to look at one of the babies. It was a little girl, one that looked just like he imagined his child with Monica would've looked.

Nate would come to the nursery every couple of days after his wife told him that they were pregnant. After work he'd stop here and admire all the beautiful babies. Every now and then, one would smile up at him, and he would smile back, tap on the window, and wave.

Occasionally a father would come by, look through the glass smiling, and Nate would ask him, "Which one is yours?"

The man would inflate with pride, and point to the beautiful child that was his baby.

Nate would tell him how his day was coming soon—"My wife is pregnant right now!"—and how they should be expecting in about six months.

Every man that he had spoken to told Nate that seeing his child for the first time was like a religious experience, like being reborn himself.

Nate would ask if they could further describe that feeling, and they would make meager attempts, but they always said something like, "It's beyond description. I can't explain it. But you'll see for yourself."

Nate would nod his head in anticipation, knowing that was true.

But that wasn't the case anymore. His wife would never have children, and Nate would never experience that feeling.

He remembered her telling him that night that everything would be all right. That they would get pregnant again, that she would give him the children that he always wanted. But that wasn't true either.

It was all a lie.

He remembered coming home after lunch two days later, feeling sick. He lay across the living room couch, trying not to think of his dead baby, but he could not stop himself.

He shut his eyes tight, tried to focus on something more pleasant, when the phone rang.

"Hello," Nate said, sounding annoyed. "Yes, Monica Kenny lives here." He stood up from the couch, concern on his face, after hearing what the woman on the other end asked him. "What do you mean? Appointment for what? Are you sure?"

The woman gave him some personal information.

"Yes, that is our address. Tomorrow, with Dr. Michaels. Yes, I'll be sure and tell her. Thank you," Nate said, hanging up the phone. He grabbed a pen and scrap of paper, and wrote down the information he was just given.

He waited till Monica got off work, until she walked in the door. She appeared startled, finding him there, standing by the sofa.

"Sweetheart," Monica said a bit shaken, "I didn't think you'd—"

"Who is Dr. Michaels?"

"Dr. who? What are you talking about?" Monica said, acting as though she had no idea.

"Dr. Michaels," Nate said, walking toward her, the slip of paper in his hand. "At the Ravenswood Fertility Clinic. Someone from there called today, wanted to confirm your appointment for tomorrow at nine A.M.," Nate said, holding out the paper for her to take.

Monica took it, looked at it as though the information there meant nothing to her.

"Tell me why, if you just had a miscarriage, would you be making an appointment to see a fertility specialist?"

Monica tried to continue like she didn't know what he was talking about, but Nate would not allow that.

"Fine," he said, walking to the phone, picking it up, putting it to his ear. "If you don't tell me, I'll call and find out from them."

Monica stood there, watching him as though he was bluffing.

"The number for the Ravenswood Fertility Clinic, please," Nate said, after reaching information.

Still Monica said nothing.

"Thank you," Nate said, jotting a number down on the pad next to the phone.

He looked over at his wife as he dialed the number for the clinic.

"Yes," he said. "May I speak with a Dr. Michaels, please?"

"Okay!" Monica finally said as she ran toward him, pulling the phone from his ear.

Tears ran down her face as Monica admitted that she did really fall, but she didn't have a miscarriage. The doctor told her that she was never really pregnant. She said that she would never have children, that she could never get pregnant again.

Monica was sobbing so much that Nate could barely make out what she was saying.

He felt as though he wanted to put his arms around her, comfort her, but he was far too angry because of the lies she had told him.

She smeared the tears from her face, looking up sadly at her husband.

"I knew she wasn't right. She couldn't have been. I felt our baby inside me. I had to get a second opinion, and I didn't want to tell you anything until I knew the truth. That's why I lied to you," Monica said, tears still streaming down her face as she reached out to Nate. "I'm so sorry. I just needed to know the truth."

Nate leaned away from her attempts to hug him. He was infuriated. He looked down at his wife angrily. "We'll go to your appointment tomorrow, and then we'll find out," he said, before walking away from her.

❧

They had spent practically the entire day there, Nate waiting outside the lab, outside one doctor's office after another, as tests were run on his wife.

At the end of the day, both he and Monica sat in Dr. Michaels's office. Nate had not spoken a word to his wife since they had arrived at the clinic early that morning, outside of informing her that he was going to the rest room, the vending machines, or that he was stepping outside to make a call to his office.

Now, as they sat in the cold, quiet doctor's office, there was a heavy silence. He looked at his wife sitting beside him, and she looked on the verge of tears, as she had looked all day.

"Are you all right?" Nate had to force himself to ask.

Monica turned to him, looking grateful that he had spoken to her, and she was about to answer when the office door swung open and Dr. Michaels stepped in.

"What your doctor told you about your condition is correct, Mrs. Kenny," he said, sadly.

Nate heard his wife gasp, then moan painfully as if the man had physically assaulted her.

"Tell me exactly what it all means. Explain it to me," Nate said, hoping it wasn't as bad as Monica had told him.

"A woman is born with a finite number of eggs," Dr. Michaels said, "which are stored in the ovaries. The ovaries also produce the hormones estrogen and progesterone, which regulate menstruation and ovulation. Menopause occurs when the ovaries are totally depleted of eggs and no amount of stimulation from the regulating hormones can force them to work. When this happens to women before the age of forty, it is called premature menopause. Unfortunately, the prognosis is the same. Women can no longer produce eggs, so they can no longer become pregnant."

"Then what about other methods? Isn't there any other way that—"

"I'm sorry," Dr. Michaels said. "Without the eggs . . ."

Nate heard Monica crying now, beside him.

"How could this be?" Nate questioned. "How could she just have gone through this, without any notice, without any symptoms?"

"There may have been. Insomnia, hot flashes, and mood swings. What alarms most women is the absence of their period, but since you were trying to conceive, and she thought she was pregnant, your wife mistook the symptoms as symptoms related to her pregnancy. It's a mistake that commonly occurs, and even though this runs in her family, it affected her mother and sister much later. So there was no way that—"

"What did you say?" Nate said, stopping the doctor before he could finish.

Nate saw his wife look up at Dr. Michaels as if to scold him for what he had said.

"Dr. Michaels, what did you just say about my wife's sister and mother?"

The doctor paused, looked at Monica as if trying to apologize, say that he didn't know that was supposed to be private information, then he hesitantly continued.

"Your wife informed me that her sister and mother both had gone through premature menopause."

"But my mother was forty. My sister was forty-three!" Monica said, turning to Nate. "I'm thirty-one years old. This was not supposed to happen to me this early."

Nate turned away from his wife, faced the doctor, feeling an extreme anger start to build within him.

"So you're telling me that two or three years ago, we could've gotten pregnant? That we would've been fine as long as we had done it before this happened?"

Dr. Michaels looked regretfully at Monica. "That's correct, Mr. Kenny," the doctor finally said.

And there it was, Nate thought, stepping away from the nursery's glass. His wife had not only lied to him about miscarrying their child, but withheld the fact that she knew she ran the risk of not being able to have children after a certain age.

What enraged Nate more than anything was knowing that she made him wait. She said she hadn't expected it to happen that early, and was even hoping that it wouldn't happen at all. But that was no excuse, Nate knew. He wanted children. He had told her that from the very start, and now she was the only reason why he could never have what he'd always wanted.

5

Lewis Waters was angry as he walked down the street toward the Ida B. Wells Housing Project, where he lived with his girlfriend in her apartment.

His anger was apparent on his face, in the hard steps he took, in the way he clenched his fists at his sides. He had been at the barbershop all morning without cutting a single head. He didn't want to sit around a moment longer wasting his time, so he just left.

Lewis walked up to the door of the street-level apartment and sank his key in, and walked into the run-down apartment he shared with his girlfriend, Selena.

The place was a mess as it had always been. Not dirty with trash, but run-down with wear, cluttered with dirty, dilapidated furniture. Bedsheets hung over the windows because curtains cost too much. Iron bars were affixed to the outside of the windows, for fear that if Lewis or Selena could afford something nice, it would be stolen the same day by any of their so-called neighbors.

He hated this place, but it was better than nothing. That's what he had when he had met his girlfriend. Lewis was twenty-five years old, felt as though he had been fired from or quit more jobs than he had actually worked, and had nothing to show for it.

He had met Selena on the street, thought she was cute, ran the usual line on her, and a week later found himself in her bed. He asked if he could stay the night, which turned into several nights, and then the few belongings he owned were permanently thrown in her hallway closet.

It was a transition point, Lewis told himself. It was somewhere to crash, until he was able to get back on his feet again. He had no idea he would still be with Selena after two years.

Lewis walked across the soiled carpet of the one-bedroom apartment, throwing his bag of haircutting supplies in the direction of the sofa that he had rescued off the curb a few months ago.

The place was quiet, which surprised Lewis, considering it was only noon. Selena wouldn't be at work, because she had no job, and he knew she wouldn't be out, because her favorite show, *Judge Joe Brown*, came on at that time.

Lewis stepped in front of the closed bedroom door, listened for the TV, then carefully pushed the door open.

Selena was there as Lewis had expected, but she was asleep, stretched out on the mattress that lay across the small bedroom floor.

He walked around the mattress to the corner of the room, where there was a baby crib.

Lewis reached down into the crib and stroked his nine-month-old daughter's back.

She was soundly sleeping, so he was careful not to wake her as he made his way back around the mattress and lowered himself to the edge of it, beside Selena.

The AC was broken, and it was a hot day outside, but when he looked down at Selena and saw that only a bra and panties covered her dark skin, he wondered why she was sweating like she was.

Lewis quickly scanned the area around the bed, looking for what he hoped he wouldn't find, then jumped when he heard Selena say, "Hey. What you doin' back here so early?"

"Nobody wanted a cut. Why you sleep? *Judge Joe Brown* is coming on. The TV broke again?"

"Uh-uh. I was tired," Selena said, rolling onto her back.

"It's late. Why you sleepy? We went to bed early last night."

"Because I just am."

"And why you sweating like that?" Lewis reached out, wiped a hand across Selena's forehead, and pulled back a sweat-covered palm. "You sweating like crazy."

Selena sat up, suspicion in her eyes. "Why you asking me this stuff?"

"Just because."

"Because what?"

"If there's something that you need to tell me, Selena, then why don't you just come out with it?"

"I don't believe you," Selena said, whipping the sheet off her legs and jumping out of bed. "You just gonna assume that I'm . . ." She marched around the mattress, placing her thin frame in front of him. "What are you trying to say?"

"You sweating like crazy. I know the AC is broke, but you sweating like crazy."

"Say what you have to say."

Lewis lowered his eyes, knowing that Selena would be upset about being asked this, but he had to know. "You using again?"

Selena shook her head, disappointment on her face, then simply turned, went to her dresser, and started pulling clothes out. She stuck her legs into a pair of worn jeans, slid them up, then pulled a T-shirt over her head.

"Where are you going?" Lewis said, still sitting on the mattress.

Selena did not answer, just swung open the closet door, sunk her feet into a pair of slip-ons, and headed out the bedroom door.

Lewis got up quickly from the mattress, followed behind her.

"Where are you going?" he asked again.

She did not stop, nor did she acknowledge him.

"Selena!" Lewis yelled, just as she was turning the front-doorknob. She stopped, slowly turned, and looked over her shoulder, appearing more hurt than moments ago.

"I care about you, Selena. But I got to know."

"If you really cared, you wouldn't be asking me no shit like that. You should know that I ain't ever gonna start using again. You should know that!" Selena opened the door, hurried out, then slammed it hard behind her. The walls shook, a picture fell to the floor, the glass in its frame shattering.

Lewis heard his daughter start to cry in the bedroom.

"Damn!" Lewis said, running into the room, lifting Layla out of her crib, and sitting with her on the mattress.

Maybe he shouldn't have asked, he thought, rocking his baby in his arms, trying to put her back to sleep. But just like he told her, he had to know, and just because she said he should've known the answer, that didn't mean that he did.

He couldn't trust himself just to know, because he could remember how he had initially found out that she was using.

He was in barber school at the time, had just walked in from school when he saw Selena, her head in her hands, sitting on the sofa. He asked her what was wrong.

"I'm telling you this, not because you got a say in it, but because you should know. I'm pregnant."

Lewis felt his heart skip. "What do you mean, pregnant? We use something. We always use something."

"Maybe it broke. But ain't nothing to worry about, because I'm going to the clinic tomorrow and get it taken care of."

"Taken care of?"

"I'm gettin' a abortion. So everything is cool."

Lewis stopped his brain from racing for a moment. He wasn't sure he wanted a kid just then, but it was there already, probably growing inside her as they spoke. It was too late to change their minds.

"Hold it. I ain't say I wanted you to get rid of it," Lewis said.

"Lewis. We can barely afford to live here ourselves. How we gonna provide for a child?"

Lewis was quiet. He had no answers. Selena stood up, walked around him, and headed for the bedroom, seeming to take his silence as him agreeing with her.

The following morning Lewis quickly followed behind Selena as she marched toward the clinic.

Later, he sat in the exam room with her, wringing his hands, angrily staring at the floor, searching for the right words to say to save their baby.

When the doctor returned to the office after having examined Selena, he pulled up a stool, sat down before both of them, a grim expression on his face.

"I'm sorry, but there's a tough decision you're going to have to make."

"I told you already. I want the abortion," Selena said.

"I'm aware of that. But if you do, the chances of you getting pregnant again aren't good."

"What! Why not?" Selena said.

"This would make your sixth abortion. I told you last time you were here you ran the risk of not being able to have children if we performed this procedure again."

Selena cried all the way home from the clinic, Lewis walking behind her again, trying to comfort her as they went. She just shrugged off his attempts.

Selena made the decision to keep the child, but Lewis knew it wasn't because she loved it, but because she had no choice.

She'd had five abortions in the past, five abortions that Lewis knew nothing about, but as time continued on, he realized there was a lot more he didn't know.

A week later, Selena seemed to have come down with something terrible. She was sweating in the bed next to him, and shaking so bad from cold that he could not give her enough blankets.

He tried giving her every type of medication they had in the cabinet, but she would not take them.

"Come on," Lewis said, peeling back the blankets, preparing to scoop her up out of bed and carry her with him.

"What are you doing?" she said, her voice sounding increasingly weaker.

"I'm taking you to the emergency room."

"No."

"Yes," Lewis said, sliding his arms under her neck and legs, ready to lift her.

"No!" she said, fighting with what little strength she had left.

"Why not!"

"Because I ain't sick!"

"You ain't sick!" Lewis said, pressing his hand to the side of her face. "You burning up. We gotta—"

"I'm fiending, okay?" Selena blurted out.

Lewis didn't know what she was talking about, looked at her as though she might be hallucinating. "I don't know what you saying to me."

Selena curled into a ball on the bed, wrapped her arms around her, shivering. "I ain't getting my baby sick. She ain't gonna be addicted to heroin just because I am."

Lewis stood there, his mouth open, because that was the first he had heard of any of this.

He couldn't believe it. The woman was on drugs. Not alcohol, not a little weed every now and then, but motherfucking heroin, and how in the hell didn't he know that!

Selena said she wanted to quit, said that's what she was doing at that moment. Lewis said he would take her to a clinic, get her on a program, but she refused.

"I ain't getting on no list, have them giving me more drugs to get me off of this one. I'm quitting my way."

"Selena, maybe—"

"Are you gonna help me, or not?" she yelled, seeming to expend the last little bit of energy she had left. She looked up at Lewis, her face wet with sweat, her eyes red, her body still trembling.

"Yeah," he said, feeling defeated. "I'll help you."

Help consisted of three days of Selena locked in her bedroom, kicking at the door, crying, screaming, and cursing him for doing what he was doing to her, but she had gotten over it.

It was something that he never wanted to go through in his life again, and she said the same, and that was why, when he walked in today, and saw Selena sweating like that, he needed to know if she had gotten back to using again.

She had told him, back then, that she was going through some really rough times, and that was what got her started, looking for something to help her cope.

Things weren't going so great for the two of them now, either. Lewis had been barely making enough to pay for his chair rent at the barbershop, let alone bring any decent money home, and Selena didn't want to start working, because she would have to give up welfare if she did.

So Lewis was fearful of all of that pushing Selena back to the drug again, because if that happened, he had always warned her, he would leave. But he knew leaving Selena also meant leaving his child, and that was the last thing he wanted to do.

6

"That bastard," Monica said to Tabatha once things slowed down around the store. "Do you really think he meant what he said about wanting to divorce me?"

"If you only knew how much of what men say that they *don't* really mean. I wouldn't worry about it. And if he does really want to divorce you, go right ahead, girl. You know how paid you'll be?"

"I don't want his money," Monica said, sadly.

"You're just saying that. You're entitled to it, you know," Tabatha said. "You've been his wife for four years. You went from living in a South Side one-bedroom apartment to a downtown penthouse. From driving an old Toyota Corolla to that little clown-car thing you drive."

"It's called a MINI Cooper, and it's not a clown car."

"Whatever. What I'm trying to say is, you've become accustomed to a much better lifestyle. It's his responsibility to make sure you don't fall from that, just because he wants to divorce you for not being able to have kids. That's not your fault. You couldn't control that," Tabatha said. "Don't let him get out of his commitment with you and send you back to living check-to-check like I'm doing. There's nothing fun about that."

"I'm not worried about that," Monica said, trying to be hopeful about the situation, "because we're never getting divorced. He's upset. We're going through something right now, but we'll be all right."

"Famous last words," Tabatha said, walking away from Monica to check on a customer. "Famous last words."

At home that evening, Monica continued to think about whether there was truly a chance that her husband was considering divorcing her.

She had set the table, made dinner, served it, and now was sitting down, Nate sitting across from her, not eating, but picking at the food Monica had made for him.

There was silence, as there always seemed to be now, and she wished she had turned on some music or something so it wouldn't seem so obvious just how bad things were now between them.

Monica looked up at Nate.

He continued staring down at his plate, pushing his food around with the tip of his fork.

"I didn't mean what I said last night," Monica said. She was met with no response.

She lowered her head, deciding whether to pursue this or not, but realized she had to. "I want things to be the way they used to be. When all we did was laugh and have fun. When, if we had an argument or a disagreement, we'd talk through it, find a solution, and things would be all right."

"It can't be like that again," Nate said, looking at Monica for the first time since they sat down to dinner.

"Why not?"

"Because you lied to me. Because you withheld things from me that I needed to know."

"But I told you, I didn't think that would happen so soon."

"Monica," Nate said, slamming down his fork against his plate. "It wasn't about just you anymore! That decision affected me too. You know how much I wanted a family. How much I want one still. And you didn't tell me something as important as that. No," Nate said, pulling the cloth napkin from his lap, tossing it onto his uneaten food, and standing up from the table. "Things will never just go back to the way they were."

He turned, was about to walk away from the table, when Monica said, "So what does that mean?" There was obvious worry in her voice. "Are you saying you really want a divorce?"

Nate's back was to Monica, and he just stood there, not saying a word.

"Nate, please tell me."

It took more time, another couple of seconds, as though the question was really something he had to think over.

"No. I don't want to divorce you," he finally said, then headed for the stairs.

When Monica finally crawled into bed beside her husband, he was soundly sleeping. She was thankful that he really didn't want a divorce, but she knew there were still problems that they had to work out.

Monica rolled over on her side, away from him, tried to fall off to sleep, but couldn't. She flipped onto her back, then her stomach, but she felt wide awake, and she knew what was keeping her that way.

It had been two weeks since Nate had made love to her. Before all of this happened, they would be together every couple of days.

She had often thought that having sex again would help them in getting past this problem, but now her thoughts were selfish.

She needed to have sex; her body demanded it.

Monica rolled over again, this time facing her husband, thinking about trying to awaken him. She thought better of that, knowing that if she asked him, he would most definitely turn her down. So she would not even get consent from him. She didn't need him to be awake.

Monica reached under the blankets for her husband, felt him practically pulsating under his thin pajama bottoms, and she wondered why, if he was in this condition, he had not approached her with it. She would've understood if he didn't want to say a word to her, just allow them to physically satisfy themselves. She would've taken care of him, and herself too.

Monica slid her hand under the elastic waistband of his pajama bottoms, wrapped her fingers around him. She squeezed him firmly, heard a faint moan escape him. She quickly looked up, loosening her hold some, careful not to wake him. If he knew what she was doing, what she was trying to do, he would stop her, jump out of bed, start ranting about her deceiving him yet again.

But she was careful. She continued stroking him, his soothing groaning letting her know that although he was still sound asleep, he was responsive to her touch. And she felt it too, her body warming all over, the place in between her legs preparing itself to take her husband in.

Monica managed to get her husband's pants down below his hips and straddle him without waking him. She grabbed him, and from behind, gently inserted him.

He slid in, perfectly, almost effortlessly, but with just enough resistance to almost make her orgasm that very moment. She fought it, wanting it to last as long as possible.

Keeping her eyes on her husband, she slid herself all the way down on him, her eyelids falling closed over her eyes, Monica softly biting the corner of her lip as she felt all the tension from the past two weeks start to melt away from her.

She felt his body stir, and quickly her eyes popped open. He was still asleep, but she knew he wouldn't be for long. She wanted him to come, wanted to remind him of how good she felt, remind him of all that he had been missing. But first, she needed to get hers.

Monica raised up from him some, feeling his tip just inside, and there she narrowed her muscles around him, started up and down, feeling every inch slip and slide into her. With each backward motion, she felt the sensation building, the tingling that her husband seemed to deposit within her starting to spread, envelop her entire body.

Monica felt her muscles tightening, her lips numbing, the characteristic precursors to an inevitable orgasm, and she welcomed it, tried to hurry it, because it had been so long.

She shortened the length of her movements, focusing on the spot that gave her the most pleasure, knowing it would come any second now, and just when she felt she was about to—

"Monica," she heard. There were fistfuls of bed linen in her grasp, her face was covered with sweat, contorted in a painful, pleasureful snarl, as she quickly opened her eyes, looked up, to find her husband staring back at her.

"What are you doing?" Nate said, Monica hearing none of the pleasure she thought she was was giving him.

The intensity of the impending orgasm had dropped just slightly, but she could still feel its presence.

"Please. Let this happen," Monica struggled to say, still holding the sheets, still concentrating short slides up and down the length of her husband's penis.

"Monica, stop it," Nate said, trying to slide out of his wife. Monica held on tight to him, clamped her legs around him, securing him there.

"Just let it. I'm almost there, and I want to feel you. I want you to come inside me," she moaned.

Now Monica was hopeful, because it looked as though Nate was giving it a second of thought, had seemed to relax his efforts to toss her off him. Then all of a sudden, with no emotion, he said, "Why? What good will it do? Nothing will come of it."

It was amazing. All the effort Monica had put in to get that feeling, her husband was able to wipe away with just a few words. The tingling, the numbing, all of it was gone, and she just lay there atop him.

A tear spilled from her eye, clung to her cheek a moment, then dropped to the bed.

Monica raised herself up, still straddling her husband, he still inside her, but could feel him quickly shrinking within. More tears came, but she did not bother to wipe them away, just looked down at Nate as they dropped down on his bare chest, making sure that he acknowledged them.

After testing words in her head, Monica found the courage to speak.

"I just thought that maybe this would help us."

"You were wrong," Nate said, and then she felt him pulling out of her.

7

Classic Clippers was the name of the barbershop Lewis had worked in since he finished barber school six months ago. It was a small shop that housed his chair and six others, where half a dozen other barbers worked. Mirrors lined the walls behind the other barbers' chairs; snapshots of their babies and their baby's mamas hung there as well.

Jet centerfolds from as early as 1980 to the present clung to every wall, and hip-hop music blared from a boom box the size of a compact fridge in the corner of the shop.

Lewis sat slumped in his chair, wearing his barber smock, staring up at the muted color TV that sat in another corner.

He had a frown on his face, and in his fists he bent a plastic comb close to the point of breaking it.

Every moment of the day, it seemed, every other barber had someone in his chair but Lewis. He sat there, looking stupidly, enviously at the other barbers as they tended to their clients, received tips, then brushed off the chair for another patiently waiting client to jump in.

All the other barbers in Classic Clippers had been there from five to ten years. The old fat guy in the front of the store was the owner. He was named Beasly. He'd been cutting heads from that same chair for thirty years, he always said.

So when a man walked in the shop and Lewis eagerly jumped out of his chair and asked, "Need a cut, sir?" the man would oftentimes look at him like he was begging for spare change, then say, "Naw, I'm waiting on Tim," or Ricky, or Kevin, or Mike, or, of course, Beasly.

The only time that Lewis would get a client was when someone new came in, and all the other chairs were full, and clients were waiting. Then and only then would the newcomer venture into Lewis's chair, where Lewis did his best to give his client a cut he'd never forget.

But just like the man that stood up from Lewis's chair ten minutes ago, after receiving and paying for his cut, many clients did not tip Lewis a dime.

This happened more times than not, and it was starting to anger him more than he could stand.

Beasly pulled the drape from around his client, got paid, and Lewis saw the man give him a five-dollar tip.

"See you same time next week," the man said to Beasly, a smile on his face, then walked out of the shop.

Another man quickly jumped in Beasly's chair. After Beasly had tied the drape around the man's neck, he looked up across the room at Lewis, as if knowing he had been watched all this time.

Beasly leaned down, whispered something in the man's ear, then dragged himself over to Lewis.

"Come with me, boy," Beasly said.

Lewis followed him through a curtain tacked over the doorway that led to the dimly lit break room.

"Want a pop?" Beasly called out to Lewis, as he stood at the open fridge door.

"Naw," Lewis said.

Beasly sat down on the other side of Lewis, popped the tab on his soda, and said, "It takes time, boy. You a good barber. I seen the heads you cut walk out of here, and you do good work. But you don't just come straight outta barber school and have folks waiting on you. You gotta develop a client list. People gotta get to know you, feel comfortable, then they start coming back and telling they friends."

"I been here six months," Lewis said.

"And I been here thirty years, so I know what I'm talking about. Don't rush so much. It'll come."

"I got a girl. Got bills. Got a daughter. I can't afford to wait for it to come. If you could only see the way we living. My daughter shouldn't have to live in conditions like that. All I want to do is make enough to be able to raise her somewhere nice."

"How many heads you cut today?"

"Three," Lewis said. There was frustration in his voice.

Beasly looked down at his watch. It was already 6 P.M.

"Most of the day is gone, and I only cut three heads," Lewis said.

"Any of them tip?"

"Naw."

"So you got forty-five dollars in your pocket, which I'm figuring you saving to pay for your chair rent."

"Got to."

Beasly took a long swig from his soda, got up from his chair, sunk his big hand into his slacks pocket, and pulled out a decent-size wad of bills. He peeled off three twenties and tossed them on the table before Lewis.

"Handle the stuff at home, and give it back to me when you can."

"You know I can't take this, Beasly."

"Then where you gonna get it from? What's gonna happen with your girl, the bills, and your daughter then?"

Lewis had no answer.

"Take it, boy. You got three more hours till closing. I'll try and send some of my clients your way, and maybe you can make some money before you leave, and you won't have to take mine. All right?"

"Thanks, Beasly."

"Somebody did the same for me when I first started, so don't think nothing about it."

The last three hours were even less productive than the first six. Beasly said he would try to send some of his clients Lewis's way, but whenever Lewis saw Beasly pointing them in his direction, they just shook their heads and had a seat, probably saying that they'd rather wait.

Lewis even went as far as stepping outside like he sometimes did, and when he saw someone with a bush on their head, or just in bad need of a trim, he would ask them if they'd want to step inside for a haircut. He asked ten people, and was turned down by every single one of them.

After work, Lewis parked in front of Selena's apartment. He pulled the key from his ignition, thankful that his old, raggedy car had managed to get him home yet another day.

Lewis got out of the car, thankful that Beasly had given him the sixty bucks. He definitely needed that, and figured he could buy a little food for the house and still have enough to hold him through the rest of the week.

When Lewis got to the front door, he wondered why all the lights inside were off.

He thought about the accusation he had made to Selena yesterday. How she stormed out of the house, and when she came back in late that evening, she didn't have a single word to say to him.

She had probably turned out all the lights, gone to bed early so as not to have to speak to him again.

Lewis unlocked the door, pushed it open, and realized he must've been all wrong about Selena, and by what he saw before him, figured now that she must've been trying to make up for some reason.

Candles were lit all around the living room, and she was sitting on the sofa, looking up at him.

He was shocked, but so happy that he didn't have to deal with any of that nonsense from yesterday.

"Getting romantic, hunh?" Lewis said, smiling, setting down his bag with his supplies in it on the floor. "Got the candles going. This is nice," he said, moving toward her.

"I'm glad you like it, because we don't have no other choice. The lights been cut off."

"What! I thought we had—"

"We ain't had nothing. I told you we had gotten the last notice last week, and this came today." Selena handed him the bill that she had been looking at by candlelight.

"Disactivation Notice," the pink slip read. "Damn!" Lewis said.

"And Layla is trying to get sick again. We need to get some more of the pink stuff, and you know how much that cost."

"Layla always getting sick," Lewis spat, starting to feel overwhelmed.

"You can't blame Layla if she's not feeling well."

"Who said I'm blaming her?"

Selena gave Lewis a look that made him sure that she knew what he was trying to imply. "I was clean when I had her. You know that."

"And what about now? You never answered my question from yesterday."

"Fuck you, Lewis. I ain't using. I was sweating because it was hot yesterday. Believe it if you want to, or not. I don't care. But we got other things to take care of. If her fever break by tomorrow, then Layla probably won't need the medicine. But we got to get the electricity back on, or what little food we got gonna spoil."

Lewis looked back down at the bill. "It's two hundred and forty dollars. We can't pay that."

"We don't got to pay it all. Just some, and they'll turn the lights back on."

"And how much is that?"

"Sixty dollars. Do you got that?"

"Yeah, I got it," Lewis said, and now he was extra grateful for Beasly's kindness. But as Lewis dug into his pocket, pulled out the three bills, and handed them to Selena, he knew that they could not continue on like this. There had to be a better way. There just had to be.

8

At 8:30 A.M. Nate stood in the parking garage of the high-rise he lived in, wearing a gray Versace suit, his briefcase in one hand and an umbrella in the other, for it looked as though there could be rain approaching.

He waited for the valet attendant to bring around his car, which was taking a little longer than it should've, even though Nate had pressed a fifty-dollar bill into the middle-aged white man's hand upon seeing him.

He could've as easily arranged for a limo to pick him up for the short trip to work in the mornings. It wouldn't have cost him anything; he could have just written it off as a business expense. But Nate enjoyed driving himself in what he considered one of the most beautiful automobiles ever made. Two years ago, he had purchased the '62 Bentley, which of course was now a classic. Only ten or twelve were still running in the world. He had bought it at an auction for the very nice price of $150,000, but he was sure that now, with the added work he had had done to it, it was worth almost a quarter of a million.

Nate turned his head to see the valet attendant finally driving up with his car. The man came around the corner very slowly, pulled up to the curb cautiously, making sure not to brush the whitewall tires. He threw the car in park, then quickly hopped out and held the door open for Nate.

"Sorry for the delay, Mr. Kenny. One of the other valets had parked very near to your car, and I didn't want to take a chance in pulling yours out until the other one was moved. It won't happen again, sir."

"Thank you, Collins," Nate said, slapping the man on the shoulder, then lowering himself into his car. "I can always depend on you to take care of my baby."

When the elevator doors opened, Nate stepped around the wall of people that had crowded in after him, and exited onto the floor that was solely dedicated to his business.

The words KENNY CORPORATION, in huge silver letters, were fixed to the wall above the reception area, where two beautiful women, wearing headsets, took and directed calls.

"Good morning, Mr. Kenny," both women said, almost in unison.

"Good morning," Nate said, his words barely audible, as he walked past them.

He walked through cubicles on his left, consultation areas on his right, where his employees worked busily at their stations, making phone calls, checking stock quotes, and following up on leads that could be profitable buys.

"Good morning, Mr. Kenny." "Morning, sir," more of his employees said as he quickly passed them. There were ninety-seven of them in all, from the lowest entry-level employee to his highest senior vice president. He interviewed, hired, paid the salaries of each one of them, and fired them if necessary. He was the reason they were here, could make a living, provide for their families and themselves.

Nate continued walking, down the corridor that led to the executive offices, and out the other end, which led to the lounge. He stopped there, stood in front of the large flat-screen plasma television, which aired financial news reports twenty-four hours a day.

He walked to the back wall, which was made entirely of floor-to-ceiling windows, looking out upon the northwest side of Chicago.

There was a beautiful view of the skyline, Lake Michigan, and the far North Side.

He stood there, very close to the glass, looking out. He hadn't appreciated this view in so long, hadn't really appreciated his success in quite a while as well, and it was a shame it took someone threatening all of it for that to be brought to his attention.

One year after his marriage to Monica, he decided to venture out, leave the brokerage firm he was working for, and open his own. When he had told Monica that he was waiting to find the right woman and settle down before he took that risk, he was not lying to her. He needed that stability; he needed a woman that he knew he could trust, that would allow him to take care of his business at work and assure him that everything would be fine at home. Monica did that for him.

But over the four years they had been married, Monica was more to him than just a supporter. She was his partner, his best friend.

He remembered the times they had had before she lied to him about the baby. They used to have so much fun together, just sharing each other's company, and then Nate thought about the last time they made love. It was two weeks ago, and as he gazed up into her face, he couldn't believe how fortunate he was.

Afterward, she hugged him from behind, kissed the nape of his neck, and told him how much she loved him. He smiled, feeling perfect contentment, knowing that he had done the right thing by marrying this woman.

But now, Nate realized, the woman he married, the woman that knew how much family meant to him, had sabotaged his opportunity to have what he'd always wanted, and now, because he told her that divorce had entered his mind, she wanted to take everything he had.

That would not happen, Nate thought, stepping away from the window and walking purposefully back toward the entrance to his offices. That would never happen. If it was the last thing he did, he would stop her.

9

Monica was unable to go in to work the morning after her husband had refused to make love to her. After he had forced her off him the night before, Monica carried herself, tears streaming down her face and all, into the bathroom.

She tried quieting her sobbing as best she could, turned on the water faucet, making it more difficult for her husband to hear how badly she was crying, but she doubted it did much good.

She stood at the mirror, leaning hard on the sink, her legs feeling almost too weak to support her. The tears were still pouring from her puffy eyes, her body continuing to tremble from emotion.

She had not thought it would be this way, had not expected anything to stop her from being a mother, and she had never thought that her husband would react to it the way he had.

Why me? was all she could ask herself, and she wondered just how bad her situation with her husband really was.

He had practically thrown her out of bed, after waking up and looking at her as though she repulsed him. Where did they stand? It was a question Monica could not begin to answer.

After washing her face with a hot cloth and stopping her crying as best she could, she quietly moved back out into their bedroom. The light had been turned off, Nate sleeping on his side. Monica slipped in the bed beside him, wanting to move closer to him, wrap her arms around him, regardless of what he did, but she just remained on her side of the bed.

When she awoke the next morning, the first thing she did was call Tabatha.

"I won't be able to make it this morning. Something happened."

"Are you all right?" Tabatha asked, and Monica could hear the concern in her best friend's voice.

"Me and Nate are at it again, that's all."

"Is there anything I can do?"

"No," Monica said, needing to hurry off the phone for fear that she would start crying again. "It's up to me to find out what needs to be done."

Monica had spent all morning in her darkened bedroom, the drapes drawn closed, the blankets pulled up over her head. She stayed there, curled in a ball under those covers, trying to find some solution to the problem she was facing, and after almost four hours of racking her brain, she told herself there was only one answer.

When she reached this decision, automatically she started to feel a little better. She climbed from bed, not bothering to slip on a robe or slippers, because with each step she took, she felt her excitement regarding the idea building a little more.

By the time Monica reached the middle of the long hallway that led to her husband's office, she was almost running across the long expensive Persian rug under her feet.

Nate's office door was closed as it always was, but she threw it open, rushed around the huge old oak desk, and plopped down into the leather executive chair.

Monica quickly surveyed the wide desk. It was cluttered but organized, and she would try not to disturb any of the papers he had stacked on different areas of its surface.

She reached over and clicked on the banker's lamp, noticing the snapshot of her and Nate smiling during their trip to Australia.

That seemed like another life, Monica thought to herself, as she swiveled around to the far side of his desk, where her husband kept

47

his laptop. She lifted it open, waited for the screen to refresh itself, then she grabbed the mouse and clicked the Web icon.

Monica was still excited, but she was also starting to worry a little as she clicked to open a search engine.

When she told herself that this was the only chance that her marriage had left, she was not kidding herself. If this didn't work, she was almost certain nothing would.

Monica closed her eyes, said a tiny prayer, then, in the box provided, typed in the word "adoption."

10

The day was a beautiful one. Nate squinted against the bright sunlight warming his face as he walked alongside Tim, his younger brother by two years. Oftentimes when Nate was bothered by a problem he could not seem to solve by himself, he would go to his brother for advice. He had been doing this since he was eight years old and Tim was six, and things had not changed a bit.

"Tim, what are you doing?" Nate asked him over the phone this afternoon around lunchtime.

"I'm trying to write, but nothing's coming. Why?"

"Because I need to talk. Can you meet me at the park around the house in about half an hour?"

"Yeah. I don't think I'll be getting anything good down today, anyway."

Tim was a writer. He had published in a number of small periodicals, had a story published in an anthology or two, but he had not yet scored a novel. That was what he really wanted, what he devoted the last ten years of his life to, and he was fortunate enough to have a wife like Robin, who allowed him to pursue such a lofty goal.

Nate and Tim walked side by side, slowly, down the center path of the park. Children laughed, yelled, and played as their parents sat on benches, conversing, admiring their children.

"What are we doing here, Nate?"

"Told you. I wanted to talk," Nate said, looking ahead as though he was entranced.

"We could've talked at a bar, had a beer or something. We didn't have to come here."

"What's wrong with here? It's gorgeous out here. I thought you'd want to get out, enjoy the day a little. Besides," Nate said, stopping in front of a bench, sitting down, "don't you like to come out here and watch all the kids playing? I mean, look at them. All of them smiling, running around, not a thing to think or worry about. It reminds me of us when we were their age. Do you remember?"

"Yeah, I remember," Tim said. There was reluctance in his voice as he sat beside his brother.

"Remember when Dad used to bring us here every weekend? You don't miss that?" Nate said, turning to his brother, a wistful smile on his face.

"Not really."

"That's probably because you're out here every weekend yourself, tossing the football to Kevin."

"Nate, I don't really want to talk about this."

The smile fell from Nate's lips, because he knew why his brother didn't want to talk about it. Tim's wife, Robin, had given him two beautiful children, an eight-year-old boy named Kevin and a girl, ten years old, named Michelle.

Nate spent so much time with his niece and nephew that Tim often kidded him by asking him was he really their father.

"It's all in preparation for when I have my family. Just want to make sure how to do it right," Nate said, always so happy when he was speaking of his future family.

But one night, past 1 A.M., Tim's phone rang. When he picked it up, it was Nate.

"What are you doing?" Nate asked. His words were badly slurred.

"I'm sleeping." Tim's voice was groggy, barely over a whisper. "What do you think I'm doing?"

"Meet me. I want to talk."

"Where are you?"

"I don't know. At a bar."

"Which one, Nate?"

"Don't know. Just a bar. It says 'bar' outside on the door, I guess."

After Tim convinced Nate to pass his cell phone to someone in the bar so that Tim could get directions, he hurried out.

When Tim arrived at the bar half an hour later, there was an ambulance out in front, red-and-blue lights flashing.

Tim hurried out of his car, rushed to the door of the bar to find paramedics hauling his brother, Nate, out on a stretcher.

"I'm his brother. What's wrong with him!" Tim yelled over the shoulder of one of the EMTs.

"Alcohol poisoning," the paramedic yelled back to him.

Tim rode with Nate to the hospital in the back of the ambulance, and after he was taken in the emergency room, had his stomach pumped, and had sobered up some, Nate had told Tim why he had gotten so drunk that he could've died.

"I'll never have any children," Nate remembered telling Tim.

And now, Nate knew this was why his brother didn't want to talk about anything dealing with kids. He was obviously afraid his big brother would flip out again, go and try to hang himself from the swing set out there in the center of the park or something.

"I'm sorry for bringing this all up again," Nate said.

"No. It's nothing to be sorry about. I just don't want you getting all down again about it."

"I understand. There's just some stuff that I've been thinking about." Just then a football landed and rolled toward Nate's feet. There was a young boy running in Nate's direction. Nate picked up the ball from the grass.

"Hey! Go out!" Nate yelled to the boy, holding the football behind his head like a quarterback and waving him farther out, as if he were about to throw a touchdown pass.

The boy did as he was told, and Nate threw the ball. It was a perfect spiral, and it landed softly in the running boy's arms.

"Thanks, mister!" the boy called.

Nate sat down with a huge grin on his face.

"Now what stuff did you say was on your mind?" Tim asked.

Nate still looked toward the boy. "That stuff. I wanted a son, a family. I still want one," Nate said, turning to Tim, seriousness on his face.

"You're going to adopt?"

"No. I want my children to be biologically mine."

"But you said Monica can't—"

"I'm not talking about with Monica," Nate said, cutting his brother off.

"How, then?"

"I'm thinking about looking into divorce."

Tim looked at his brother, his mouth slightly open, astonishment on his face. "You're going to divorce her," he gasped.

"I didn't say I was going to. I said I was going to look into the possibility. I have an appointment later this afternoon," Nate said, still eyeing the boy across the park, tossing the ball. A slight smile came to his face as he saw the boy run for a touchdown and spike the ball.

"Nate, I can't tell you all the reasons why you would be wrong to even consider that."

"Then don't. I didn't really ask you here to get your opinion anyway. I just wanted to let you know what I was thinking," Nate said, standing.

"You know how I feel about Monica," Tim said. "I thought she was perfect for you the first day you introduced me to her. She doesn't deserve this. Just think it over before you do something you'll regret."

Nate didn't respond to his brother's warning, just went into his shirt pocket, pulled out a folded personal check, holding it out for his little brother to take.

"I don't want that," Tim said.

"I know you don't. But since you want to continue to pursue your writing, and won't come and work for me, I think you probably need this."

Tim was standing now, looking at the check being held out to him.

"Go on, take it," Nate urged. "If not for yourself, for Robin and the kids."

Tim reluctantly did what he was told.

Nate grabbed Tim by the shoulders, pulled him in and gave him a hug, and clapped him twice on the back.

"Thanks for meeting me out here. And don't worry about things on my end. Everything will be fine."

11

After three hours of searching adoption agencies, both locally and nationally, Monica felt she had all the information she needed to go to the next step. She just didn't know when she would take it.

She had mentioned adoption to Nate the same day that it was confirmed that she would never have children, but her husband quickly disagreed with the idea. Nate probably was far too distraught to have actually been able to rationally think it through. She knew now she should've waited a little longer, till he recovered from the shock of it all.

Time had gone by, though, and she figured if she just went about things the right way, presented it to him in such a manner that he understood they had no other recourse than to adopt a child, he would go along with her.

Out of the three adoption agencies in the Chicago area, one stood out. The True Home Adoption Agency. Monica read all the pages of information available to her from their Web site, even printed out some of the information.

She pulled a manila folder from her husband's desk drawer, made a file, then shut the machine down.

She leaned back in the chair, the folder resting on her knees, a content smile on her face, feeling as though she had found the solution. Everything was in the file before her. She'd do some further investigation in a couple of days, and then, maybe even go down there.

But then again, Monica looked at the clock. It was only three in the afternoon. She could throw on some things in fifteen minutes, and . . . Monica flipped open the file, checked for the address . . . She could make it to the adoption agency in nothing more than forty minutes.

Monica found the phone number, called the agency, and made sure it would be okay if she visited today. Afterward, she quickly ran to her bedroom, preparing to take a shower, when the phone rang.

Monica grabbed the phone as she was adjusting the water temperature.

"Hello," Monica said, trying not to get wet.

"Monica, it's Tim."

A smile came to Monica's face. "Hey, Tim, what's going on?"

Tim didn't answer right away. "I don't know. Nothing. Everything okay with you?"

He knew something, Monica thought, turning off the shower water. In the almost four years she had known her very attentive, caring brother-in-law, she was always able to read him like an open book. Even when she could not see the expression on his face, she could tell what he was thinking.

"You spoke to him. He told you about the argument," Monica said.

"Who else would he tell?" Tim said. "As always, I was just calling to make sure that you're all right."

"Yeah, I'm fine."

"Are you sure?"

"Yeah," she said, then paused, and thought for a moment. "Tim, we've had conversations just between the two of us that you've never told my husband about, right?"

"Of course. Why do you ask?"

"Because I'm about to do something that I think is right, and I really want to get your opinion."

"What is it?"

Monica was about to go into the situation, but caught sight of her bedroom clock, and knew she was pressed for time.

"What are you doing right now?" she asked Tim.

"I was trying to write, but nothing's really coming right now."

"Can you be ready to go with me in twenty minutes or so?"

"I guess. Where we going?"

"Just be ready, Tim. I'll honk twice, and then I'll tell you when we're on our way."

It was four o'clock when Monica parked her car in the parking lot of the True Home Adoption Agency.

She cut the engine off, then looked over at Tim, who had not unbuckled his seat belt yet, just gazed up at the building from his passenger window.

"So you don't think my brother should be the one sitting here, and not me?"

"I told you, I'm not bringing home a baby today, we're just coming to get some information. But you still haven't told me if you think it's a good idea or not."

Tim turned to Monica. "If you think it's a good idea, then I think it's a great one." He smiled hesitantly. "But Nate is the one you should be concerned with."

12

"So, I want to know, how much would I have to pay if I were to divorce my wife?" Nate asked.

He had to consult his attorney regarding this matter. Getting divorced from his wife wasn't something that he could just do based on the fact that she could not give him a family.

Nate was worth way too much money to allow his emotions to make that type of decision for him, so he called his attorney, Jeremy Tolbert, to arrange for a consultation.

Tolbert had been Nate's attorney for the past ten years, since the first day Nate ever needed an attorney. He trusted the man like a father. He had handled all of Nate's past legal matters, including matters regarding his marriage.

"Over the phone you sounded like this was an emergency, but I didn't think it would be this," Jeremy said, appearing saddened by this discovery. "I'm so sorry. I really liked Monica. I thought things were going well between the two of you."

"Things aren't always as they seem," Nate said.

Shaking his head, still seeming distraught by the news, Jeremy opened a file in the center of his desk and looked over some of Nate's papers. He looked up and said, "The business, Nate. That was started after you were married, correct?"

Nate bit down on the inside of his lip, knowing that would be the first question Jeremy would ask. "That's correct," Nate said, regret-fully.

"And giving me an estimate—roughly, how much do you think it's worth?"

"Sixty million or so, last time I checked."

Jeremy looked up at Nate. He breathed in deeply, then sighed.

"Just right off the top of my head, Nate, I'll tell you she's going to be entitled to about half that."

"Thirty million dollars!" Nate said, shooting up from his chair. "That's insane. There's no way. There's no way I'm going to give her half of everything I'm worth!"

"Calm down. Having a fit won't make things any better."

Nate sat back in his chair and tried to calm himself as best he could.

"That just doesn't make sense to me."

"There was no business before your wife," Jeremy said. "Her attorney will argue that while you were busy at work, Monica was at home, cooking your food, washing your clothes, providing the type of environment that would allow you to succeed, all while working a job herself. She will argue that your wife's efforts were vital to the success of your company, and with that argument, she will win."

Nate leaned forward in his chair, dropping his face into his hands. "And that's it?" Nate said.

"Well, there is one thing."

Nate quickly looked up.

Jeremy pulled a sheet from the file, placed it in front of Nate.

"This is your prenuptial agreement. You do remember having Monica sign this form, don't you?"

Nate nodded.

"It states if your wife breaks this agreement by committing adultery, then she forfeits any money entitled to her if a normal divorce were filed."

"So what you're saying is, if my wife cheats on me, then she gets nothing."

"Basically, yes."

Nate stood up from his chair, extending a hand to Jeremy.

Mr. Tolbert stood as well, taking Nate's hand and shaking.

"Thanks, but that's not going to happen."

"I didn't think that it would. Monica's a good woman," Jeremy said. "But I'm obligated to bring that to your attention."

And there it was, Nate thought, standing just outside his attorney's office. If he divorced Monica she would be entitled to half, and although, after what she did to him, she truly deserved to be divorced, he couldn't do it. He would not reward her with millions of dollars of his money for lying to him.

He would just have to think of another way out, or accept the fact that he would never have a family of his own. But until then, unless he wanted her to go out there and start talking to divorce attorneys herself, find out just how much she was truly entitled to, he knew he had better start treating his wife a hell of a lot better.

13

Another long day at the barbershop, and Lewis had cut only four heads. He had $60 in his pocket, and along with the forty-five from yesterday, he had a little over a hundred. His $200 chair rent was due at the end of next week. He'd probably have the money, but after he had paid that, he would have nothing to live on, and nothing to give Selena.

He didn't know if it even made sense, him going to work, spending eight to ten hours a day just to make enough so he could spend it on his stupid chair, in the stupid barbershop, that nobody wanted to sit in anyway.

Lewis left the shop around six, telling himself it didn't make sense to sit around another three hours, when he knew nothing would happen. Besides, this would give him time to go to the YMCA and work out all of the stress that had been building in him over the last few days.

At the gym, he pulled off his T-shirt, slipped on some weight gloves, and worked out in his jeans and wife-beater tank top. He bench-pressed till his chest muscles were on fire, curled till his biceps felt as solid and heavy as cannonballs, and squatted till he was barely able to walk without wincing.

By the time he drove home and walked into the apartment, he felt better.

The front room was dark, but Lewis was immediately relieved

when he saw a strip of light across the floor coming from the cracked bedroom door.

He walked in the bedroom, then toward the bathroom door, heard the water going, and figured that Selena was taking a shower, something that he had to do when she was finished.

Lewis set his bag of supplies down in a corner of the bedroom and saw that his daughter was standing herself up in the crib, both her fat little fists wrapped around the bars, helping to support her.

"Whatcha doin' over there? Hunh? Whatcha doin'?" Lewis said, baby-talking her, walking over there and lifting her out of the crib.

Layla laughed and smiled in her father's arms.

"How you been today? Daddy missed you. Have you been feeling better?" Lewis placed his palm to her forehead, under her chubby chin, and on the side of her face. Her fever had gone down, and Lewis was thankful for that, because that meant no expensive pink stuff was needed, at least right now. But Lewis knew that time was just around the corner.

Layla got sick quite often, and Lewis wasn't absolutely sure, but he believed it had something to do with the fact that Selena had been doing those drugs. Yeah, she got clean when she found out that she was pregnant, but what Lewis didn't know was, did she ever go back and use while she was carrying Layla? Or even if she didn't, did the fact that she was ever on the drugs have something to do with lowering Layla's resistance?

Lewis really didn't want to think about it, because when he did, it just made him so mad at Selena.

If she would've told him that she was into that stuff when Lewis had first met her, he would've walked away from that situation that very moment.

When she told him that she was pregnant, he was pretty certain that he didn't want Selena to kill the child, but he didn't know if he wanted to stick around to raise it.

He had initially walked up to Selena because the girl was sexy, had a nice body, and he could see himself sliding up in that. He had never planned on being with the woman indefinitely, going through the crap he was going through with her, and especially hadn't planned on fathering her child.

There were times when Selena was walking around the apartment, her belly hanging out in front of her, and Lewis would be planning just how and when he would leave. He was trying to decide if he would tell her he was going—or would he just pack his things, and while she was sleeping, or at the store, take off and never come back?

He thought seriously about that for a long time, till Selena finally gave birth to his daughter, and instantly, the second after he saw her face, Lewis felt more love for that little girl than he ever thought imaginable.

After that, he had no choice whether he would stay or go. His daughter was here, so he would stay here. Regardless of how hard things got, how much he and Selena disagreed or argued, Lewis would be there for his little girl. But now, he started questioning things again.

Lewis held his daughter in front of him, kissing her on her cheeks, then holding her higher and rubbing his nose into her bare belly. The baby cried out in laughter, kicking her little legs, and Lewis couldn't help but laugh himself as he brought her back into his arms.

Selena walked into the room barefoot, a towel wrapped around her still-wet body.

"Can you take her?" Lewis said, holding out Layla toward Selena. "I want to jump in the shower too."

Selena took the baby.

Lewis leaned down and kissed Selena on the lips. "How was your day?" he said.

"Like every day," Selena said, turning her back to Lewis and placing Layla back in her crib. "But I don't want to talk about it."

Lewis just stood there, wondering if he should feel offended by her dismissal of him, then decided to pay it no mind.

He took his shower, a very hot one. One that relaxed his tightened muscles a great deal and allowed him, if only momentarily, to get his mind off what normally troubled him: bills, his job, the baby, what was going to happen with him and his woman.

Lewis stepped into the bedroom, a towel wrapped low around his hips, beads of water still clinging to his heavily muscled arms and back. Selena lay in bed, the lights off, the TV playing something Lewis had never seen before.

Selena lay on her back, naked, a pillow bunched behind her back, the bedsheet pulled just below her breasts.

Lewis tossed his towel to a chair, lowered himself to the mattress on the floor, and slid under the sheet with Selena, pushing his body very close to hers.

Selena's eyes were lazily set on the TV, giving no attention to Lewis.

Lewis rested his chin on Selena's arm, then started kissing the outside of her left breast. He stuck his tongue out, touching it lightly against her nipple.

Selena still ignored him.

He moved closer to her, brushing his erection against her bare leg, taking her entire breast into his mouth and sucking it.

"Stop, Lewis. I'm watching TV," Selena said.

Lewis ignored her, sucking her breast more, then moving down, baby-kissing her stomach, the crest of her pelvic bone, and then her inner thigh.

He tried parting her legs, was planning on making her feel as good as she had ever felt, but she had stopped him.

"What are you doing!" Selena said, seeming much more disturbed than Lewis thought she should've been.

"What does it look like I'm doing?"

"Why? What's the point?"

"Ain't no point. Just to do it."

"You ain't even move Layla out the room."

"She's sleep."

Selena looked in the direction of her child; the faintest sound of snoring could be heard from the crib.

"I still don't want to do nothing."

"Why not?"

"Because we got bills due, Lewis. Medicine that you know we gonna have to buy one of these days, and I had to walk around the block twice today before walking in the house, just so I could avoid the damn landlord, 'cause you know he looking for the rent." Selena looked at Lewis pathetically. "And you talking about having sex."

"It'll give us something else to think about instead of bills all the damn time."

"That's our problem. We don't think about bills enough. You ever thought of that? You ain't making no money at the barbershop. Maybe you need to find a second job."

"I'm there almost ten hours a day. What about you?"

"I need to get a job too," Selena said.

"But you'd lose the welfare check."

"There's something I could do that the government wouldn't know about." When Selena said this, she was looking very intently into Lewis's eyes, as if she was trying to inform him of exactly what she was talking about without actually coming out and saying it.

She was successful in that, because just by her tone, the look that said she didn't want to do what she was suggesting, but she had to, Lewis knew exactly what she was talking about.

Outside of the fact that Selena once was a heroin addict, there were other things that she chose not to tell Lewis until she felt he was ready to hear them.

She was physically and sexually abused by her stepfather when she was a child. Her mother would not believe her, would not come to her rescue, so Selena ran away when she was sixteen. She made the money she needed by turning tricks, walking the streets at night, eyeing the drivers of slow-moving cars till they stopped and let her in.

"Nothing those men did to me ever affected me," Selena told Lewis the night she dropped this bomb on him, "because my stepfather took whatever feelings I had away from when I was fourteen years old."

That was how she survived then, how she had gotten pregnant

five times, she had told Lewis. Some men had condoms, some didn't. After a while, it didn't really matter anymore. If she got knocked up, she'd go to the free clinic and get rid of it. And once she started using drugs, nothing really seemed to matter. She needed money, and selling her body was a sure, fast way to make it. It worked for her then, and Lewis could tell that she was talking about trying the same thing now.

"I know you ain't talking about going back on the street?"

"I'd be careful. I'd carry condoms. I'd make sure that—"

Lewis sprang from the bed. "I can't believe you even talking this shit!" he practically yelled. "You're talking about going out there and selling pussy!"

"We need money, Lewis. How else we gonna get it?"

"You got a child."

"That's why I'd do it."

"You my woman."

Selena paused. "Really? When I told you I was pregnant, I could tell you was relieved just a little bit when I told you I was getting rid of it. Every day I was walking around here carrying that child, I could tell you was on the verge of leaving."

"But I stayed."

"For who? Layla," Selena answered for him. "Tell me I'm wrong."

Lewis thought of lying, but couldn't bring himself to do it, so he remained silent.

"Do you even love me? Do you even care? Or are you just here because it's somewhere you can sleep?"

"I care," Lewis said, under his breath. "Care too much to let you go out there and do what you're talking about. Just give me a little more time, and—"

"We ain't got a little more time."

"Just give me a few more days, and I'll make some more money. I don't care if I gotta force people to sit in my chair, I'm gonna take care of this. Can you wait?"

Selena sighed heavily. "We'll see, Lewis. We'll see."

14

At the adoption agency, things had gone even better than Monica had imagined they could've gone. They had sat in the waiting room only twenty minutes before a kind, middle-aged woman by the name of Mrs. Wolcott came out and introduced herself.

"Are you Mr. and Mrs. Kenny?" the woman, wearing glasses and a flower print dress, asked.

Monica laughed. "Yes, but no. This is Mr. Tim Kenny, but he's not my husband, he's my brother."

"Well, welcome, Mr. Tim Kenny," Mrs. Wolcott said, shaking his hand. "Maybe if you like what we have to say, you'll want to adopt a child as well. We have many of them here."

"I would, but my hands are full already with a boy and girl."

Monica and Tim were taken back to Mrs. Wolcott's office, a small space with a single square window on the left side of the room. Her desk was crowded with folders, files and papers, but in the center there was a space cleared for her to rest her folded hands as she spoke to Monica and Tim.

"So," Mrs. Wolcott said, smiling the grin that never seemed to leave her face. "What brings you in to us today?"

Monica told the woman about the premature menopause, about never being able to have children, and how much both she and her husband wanted a family.

"And where is Mr. Kenny today?"

"Oh, he's at work. He owns his own financial consulting company. It's very successful." Monica smiled.

"I don't doubt that," Mrs. Wolcott said, taking a quick glance at the huge diamond wedding ring Monica was wearing. "And so he's interested in adopting as well, he just couldn't make it today?"

Monica paused before answering. She felt Tim turn toward her, felt his eyes resting heavy on her. "Yes," Monica said. "More, actually. A family is all he's ever talked about," Monica said, looking back at Tim as if to warn him not to say a word.

Mrs. Wolcott quizzed Monica for another half hour, then seeming satisfied with what was told to her, she said, "All right, then. Let's go on to the fun part?"

She stood up from her desk, and told Monica and Tim to follow her. She walked them into a large white room with a number of long tables, chairs pushed under them. Computer monitors sat at the corners of each of these tables.

There were bulletin boards hung on every wall of the room, notices of all kinds hung from them, along with black-and-white photos of children.

"This room is where a lot of what we do happens," Mrs. Wolcott said, walking over to a desk, pulling out chairs for Tim, Monica, and herself. "It's normally a lot busier than this, but the day is winding down." She scooted her chair up in front of a computer keyboard, and started tapping away as she spoke.

"We facilitate the adoptions of children locally, across the country, and even internationally. We deal with children as old as twelve, all the way down to children who haven't even been born yet."

"Wow," Monica said with a sort of wonder.

"I don't want to wrongfully assume anything," Mrs. Wolcott said, stopping her typing for just a moment to look at Monica, "but I imagine it's a little African American child you're looking for?"

"You imagine correctly," Monica said, smiling.

"Good," Mrs. Wolcott said, continuing to input information into the computer. "It's so unfortunate, but there are many, many African American children who are in need of homes." Mrs. Wolcott grabbed the computer's mouse and slid it in front of Monica. "This is a database showing pictures of many of the children who are up for adoption. Click here to scroll up, click here for down. And if you want more info on any particular child, just double click on that child's photo, okay?"

"Okay," Monica said, feeling more excitement running through her.

"And Mr. Tim Kenny, would you like anything to drink? Pop, water?"

"No, thank you," Tim said. "I'm fine."

Monica waited till Mrs. Wolcott stepped out of the room, then turned to Tim, the mouse tightly in hand, a huge smile on her face. "Something tells me that everything is going to work out all right."

Tim nodded his head, displayed a slight smile. "I hope you're right."

By the time Monica dropped Tim off at his house and was standing in front of her door, it was almost eight o'clock. She hadn't expected to be gone that long, but she had gotten carried away with the search for children on the adoption agency's database.

Every child imaginable was there—so many that she couldn't make up her mind as to which she had the most interest in, until she saw the photo of the little boy. He was not even a year old, and was the cutest little brown baby, with dimples, bright eyes, and curly hair.

Monica sat and stared at that photo for a couple of minutes straight, finally pulling her eyes away to turn to Tim and say, "Doesn't he look like Nate?"

Tim didn't respond at first, but then after scooting his chair a little closer, he said, "Okay, maybe after another thirty-nine years, and a zillion dollars, maybe he would look like my brother."

If Monica had any reservations about this child being the one, they were all resolved when she double clicked on the photo, and found out the boy was in Indiana, only four hours away. But what had even a more profound effect was that the child's name was Nathaniel.

"Just like my husband's!" Monica said excitedly to Mrs. Wolcott after the woman came back in and offered to print out a copy of the child's photo for her.

"I guess you'll have yourself a junior," Mrs. Wolcott said, handing Monica the photo, an application form, and all the other literature she would need to get the process started.

These papers were now tucked under Monica's arm as she slid her key into the front door.

She still didn't know how she would bring all this to Nate, exactly what she would say to make him want to listen to her, because she was sure that he was still mad about the other night, when she practically tried to steal some sex from him.

He would just have to get over that, Monica thought as she turned the knob and pushed the door open. Pissed or not, he would have to get over it.

When she closed the door behind her and stepped just inside, Monica noticed that all the lights were dimmed, and a single candle was flickering on the center of the dining room table. Monica set her folder from the adoption agency down on the table next to the door, set her purse on top of that, and ventured toward the dining room to see just what was going on.

Beside the candle sat a huge bouquet of two dozen roses in a beautiful crystal vase. What is this? Monica said to herself, a smile spreading across her lips.

Monica lowered her face into the bouquet, smelling the rose's fragrance.

Leaning away from them, she noticed an envelope propped against the base of the vase, her name written across it.

She pulled the card out, opened it, and read it.

Sweetheart,
I'm so sorry for last night. I've been behaving like a fool.
You deserve so much better than this. I promise, I will make it all
up to you.

Love, your husband. Always and forever.

It was those last words that jarred the tear lose. The words that truly confirmed he really didn't want a divorce, but was just angry, upset; that he had said and done some things that he didn't really mean, but now was sorry.

Monica wiped the tear from her cheek, brought the card up to her lips, and softly kissed it.

Just then, the lights brightened a bit in the room, and when Monica looked up, she saw Nate standing by the dimmer switch, looking like a child needing forgiveness.

"Do you think you can ever forgive me for how foolishly I've behaved?"

"It's not you who should be asking for forgiveness. I'm the one that lied to you about our baby. I'm the one that made us wait those three years, even though you wanted us to get pregnant right away. If there's anyone that needs forgiveness, it's me," Monica said.

Her husband walked over to her, wrapped his arms around her. "You know I still love you, don't you?"

"Of course I do, baby," Monica said. "How could I not know it?"

"Because how I've been treating you."

"It's in the past, sweetheart. That's all in the past."

15

The next day at work, Lewis was determined to make some money. He couldn't believe that Selena was talking about going out on the street, selling herself, and not thinking anything of it. He knew she said that she could separate giving sex to some strange man from the times she would be making love to him, but Lewis couldn't. Even the thought, the image of her spreading her legs, opening her mouth for another man, made him nauseous.

That was why he had to be busy today, do whatever he had to do in order to get paid.

But regardless of how many times he asked men walking in that door if they wanted their hair cut, no matter how many times he marched up and down the sidewalk, politely asking people if they would step in and sit in his chair, he was most often rejected.

It was noon, and Lewis had had only one client, when the other four barbers that were there today had a steady stream of people wanting cuts, along with men waiting.

Beasly walked slowly over to Lewis's chair.

Lewis didn't bother sitting up, just remained slumped, wearing his black barber smock, an unopened *Vibe* magazine in his lap.

"How things today?" Beasly asked.

"Just like they were yesterday, the day before that, and all the damn days before them."

"I see you put a nice cut on one head today."

71

"One head ain't enough, Beasly," Lewis said, sitting up, tossing the magazine from his lap toward a chair where more of them were sloppily stacked. "I got situations, man. Pressing shit that got to be taken care of, like, now. I'm thinking about quitting and finding something else to do."

"You ain't no quitter, boy."

"I ain't no fool, either," Lewis said.

"Then what you gonna do? Go out there and slang drugs, rob some store?"

"I don't know," Lewis said, under his breath. "Maybe."

Beasly went into his pocket again, pulled out some more money, and held it out for Lewis.

"Naw, Beasly. I don't want no more of your money. You already gave me enough."

"Who said I was giving you money? I want you to go down to the sub shop, and buy me a supercombo with everything and extra hot peppers. Get you one too if you want. There's enough."

Lewis looked up at Beasly as though the man had gone senile.

"I appreciate the money you gave me yesterday, but that don't make me your errand boy all of a sudden."

"Go and get the food, boy," Beasly said, grabbing one of Lewis's hands and slapping the money in his palm, closing his fingers over it. "It'll take your mind off of all your worrying. And you might be surprised. Things might look a lot better when you get back."

"Beasly," Lewis said, standing up from the chair. "I can't afford to miss any clients that come because I'm out fetching you some sandwich."

"Not to be mean or anything, boy. But you had one client in four hours. How many you think you gonna miss in twenty-five minutes?"

❦

Fat old man, Lewis thought as he walked back from the sub shop, with the grease-stained paper bag hanging from his hand. What the hell did he know anyway?

He wasn't in the situation that Lewis was in. He didn't have a nine-month-old daughter, born from a drug-addicted mother. A daughter that he thought about and feared for every day, and there were so many things to be afraid of.

Lewis was sure that Selena loved Layla. The woman was the child's mother. But Lewis also knew that Selena wouldn't have had their baby if she had had any other option.

He often worried that Selena would start using again, and Lewis feared that, having no money, she would do something like trade their baby for a hit. He knew it sounded ridiculous, but he knew the grip that shit had on people in his community, knew the craziness it had them walking around doing.

And then where they lived was a concern. Folks shooting, kids playing in the park, on their doorsteps, getting taken out by stray bullets whizzing by. Selena's place had been broken into twice since Lewis lived there. Thankfully, nobody was home both times, but what would've happened if they had been home? If those fools came in with a gun, started shooting or something?

Naw, Lewis couldn't allow anything like that to happen, and that's why he had to get his baby away from there. That's why he couldn't listen to an old fool like Beasly, who was probably gonna retire in a year, when Lewis hadn't even been working for a full one.

Lewis pulled the door of the barbershop open, a bell ringing, announcing his entrance.

The place was full, so full that a number of old men were sitting in the chairs in front of Lewis's station, because there were no other chairs to sit in.

Beasly was cutting some old guy's head as usual.

"I got your sub," Lewis said with attitude, walking past Beasly's chair.

"Put it in the back."

Yessa, massa, Lewis said to himself.

When he pushed back through the curtain hanging from the doorway, Beasly called him over.

"Got my change, boy?"

Lewis dug in his pocket, fished out Beasly's change, and set it on his work station.

"I don't have to count that, do I?" Beasly said, eyeing the money.

"Beasly, if I wanted your money, I wouldn't have come back."

"Just jokin', boy. Don't be so damn mean."

But there was nothing else for Lewis to be. It was after 1 P.M., a good chunk of the day gone, and still his chair sat empty. He didn't know why he even bothered. He looked back over his shoulder at all the men waiting, and thought of asking them one by one if they'd like a cut, but thought, What the hell, what's the use? Instead, Lewis headed for the door.

"Where you goin', boy?" Beasly said.

"Out. For a walk. Don't make no sense in me staying here."

"What you mean? All those men sitting in front of your chair need cuts."

Lewis turned around, looked back over at the six old men, their hair in various stages of needing attention. A couple were balding, some bearded, some with full heads of salt-and-pepper Afros, but they all definitely needed cuts.

"I thought those were your clients," Lewis said, practically astonished.

"I know those old fools. But they say they want a younger barber, say I don't know the new styles, so I told them about you," Beasly said, then winked at Lewis.

Lewis didn't know what to say, didn't know what to do. So he just told Beasly, "Thanks a lot," then rushed over, threw on his smock, and took his first client.

❦

When Lewis pulled his car in front of Selena's apartment, he had a hundred dollars in his pocket and a huge grin on his face. He had cut so many heads today that he was able to give Beasly back his $60, and have $100 left.

After he had finished with the last of Beasly's friends, it was only 5:30 P.M. Lewis walked over to Beasly and thanked him again.

"That's a mighty big grin on your face."

"Yeah," Lewis said, trying to shrink the smile, but he just couldn't. "I'm a happy man."

"Then why don't you knock off early? Ain't nobody probably gonna come in for you tonight, and I know you want to go home and tell your lady about how you got paid today."

"Yeah, I do."

"Then get out of here. I'll see you tomorrow."

Lewis climbed out of his car and knew that Selena would be surprised to see him this early in the day. She would wonder if he got fired or something, and then try to start yelling, but he would instantly shut her up with the money that he would show her, and then he would tell her that he was taking her and the baby out to dinner tonight.

Lewis slid his key in the lock, opened the door quietly, stepped in, and when he saw that Selena wasn't in the front room, he closed the door carefully behind him.

He was so excited, because now she wouldn't have to go out there and do that nonsense she was talking, and he knew that she would be so grateful to him for saving her from that.

Lewis took a step farther into the apartment when he heard something coming from the bedroom.

He stopped dead, his head whipping in that direction, knowing that he did not hear what he thought he had—a scream.

Lewis rushed toward the bedroom door, all the while with an image of some man that had climbed through the window, holding a gun to Selena's head. Or maybe he had used the gun already. Maybe . . .

Lewis shook the thought out of his head as he burst through the bedroom door—not to find a man with a gun to Selena's head, but to find some man stretched out naked across the mattress, Selena's naked body gyrating on top of his.

Lewis was taken aback, could not make his mind believe what his eyes were seeing at first. Then it all quickly came to him, the conversation last night, the need for money, for the bills, the medicine for Layla.

Lewis's eyes darted over to his daughter's crib, still in disbelief; he was relieved that at least she was sleeping.

Selena had whirled around on top of the man to see that it was Lewis who had rushed through the door, and not some intruder as she looked to have more than expected, because of how early in the day it was.

Selena looked to be trying to pull herself off the man, but couldn't quite dislodge herself, when Lewis grabbed hold of her by her shoulders and tossed her aside to the floor.

Lewis was now lunging for the man, who had for some reason spun onto his stomach, reaching frantically toward the top of the mattress.

"Lewis, no!" he heard Selena scream. He looked in her direction, then quickly looked back to deal with the man before him, when he heard a loud click and felt the barrel tip of a gun pressed to his head.

"Now what, nigga?" Lewis heard the man say, his voice low, heavy.

Lewis slowly raised his hands to shoulder level. "This my woman you in here with," Lewis said, trying to do everything within him to control his anger.

"I'm sorry to hear that, but we made a little business deal, and it looked like you was trying to mess that, and me, up."

"My little girl right there," Lewis said, cutting his eyes to see Layla, feeling his anger starting to get away from him. "You fucking my woman, and my little girl right there!"

"All right, nigga. Calm down," the man said, pressing the gun harder against Lewis's head. "I know that too. I said something about

76

the little girl, but yo' woman said leave her be. So I did. Didn't make me none."

Lewis now was staring at Selena with a look that could kill. A look that said she would pay for everything that was happening, once it was all over.

"So, looks like we got a situation," the man said. "What you want us to do about it?"

"I just want you out my fucking house," Lewis said, breathing hard, his chest heaving.

"I can do that. But I don't want you making no crazy moves while I put my shit on. You hear me?" the man said.

"No!" Selena yelled from the corner of the room.

Both the man and Lewis looked over at her.

"Do I still get my money?" Selena asked the man.

He chuckled some, shaking his head. "The deal wasn't completed, baby."

"Then I want you to stay."

"What!" Lewis said, shocked.

"I said, I want him to stay. I need this money, Lewis. I can't be waiting—"

"I got money!" Lewis said, reaching for his pocket.

"Whoa!" the man said, pressing the gun again against Lewis's head, as if he was worried that Lewis was going for a weapon.

"I got money. A hundred dollars in pocket. I been working all day. I told you I was going to do it, and you go out and fuck this nigga!"

Selena looked a little surprised at first, then sadly shook her head. "It took you eight hours, what I'm gonna make in one. It ain't gonna work, Lewis. Just leave."

"No!" Lewis said. "No! What about Layla? I'm not leaving!"

"You can come back and see her, but right now, you gotta go. I got work to do."

"No!" Lewis said, starting to get up, trying to have at her. But he was stopped again by the gun to his head.

"You heard what the lady said. You gotta go, motherfucker."

Lewis stood up, the man standing behind him, the gun still on him.

Lewis gave a last look to Layla, then to Selena. "I ain't leaving my baby with you, Selena. I ain't leaving her like this."

"Whatever," Selena said, looking as though she didn't care about a word Lewis had said, as the man escorted Lewis out of the room.

16

Nate rode the elevator up to the floor his office was located on. It was packed tight with the usual wall of suited men and women, but he paid them no mind, for his thoughts were on last night.

His wife had apologized to him about lying, about the comments she made about suing him, and Nate let her believe that that was enough to erase the threat she had made, a threat he could never really forget, or forgive her for.

After she had read the card he had given her, after he said his little bit about how he had made a huge mistake for mistreating her the way he had, he took his wife by the hand, led her upstairs, and made love to her.

As always, she felt wonderful, and he could still feel the love he felt for her, but he couldn't allow that to get in his way. He wasn't having sex with her to profess his love, or to gain pleasure from it, but to distract her from the fact that he might be seeking a divorce. He wanted Monica to believe that everything between them was back to normal, that the incident with the baby had never happened. Their argument, and her question about whether he wanted a divorce or not, he wanted wiped from her mind. And when she started panting hard under his efforts to bring her to orgasm—when she started screaming, "Do you love me? Do you still love me?"— Nate replied with, "Yes, I do! I always will!"

Nate felt her body tighten, her nails digging into his back, her thighs clamp around his hips, the characteristic cry she emitted when she came.

Afterward, they lay face-to-face, Nate holding his wife very close, their lips barely touching.

"Are we going to be okay?" Nate asked Monica, one of his arms thrown over her side, gently stroking her back with his fingertips.

"If you ask me, we're already okay," Monica said, her eyelids very low, the corners of her mouth turning slightly upward into a content smile.

That was all Nate wanted to hear. He had done what he had to do.

About the matter of divorcing her, Monica receiving half of everything he earned, that would just have to be placed on the back burner until he found a better way to proceed.

Stepping off the elevator, Nate walked into his office space, nodded to the two receptionists after they gave him their greeting, then he headed to his office, toward the back of the floor.

When he got to his secretary's desk, he noticed that Tori had not come in yet. He glanced down at his watch and saw that it was still early, only 8:30 A.M., and Tori didn't normally come in until about quarter to.

Nate opened his office door, stepped in, and was startled by the big brooding man sitting behind his desk, his head dropped into both his hands.

Nate closed the door. The man didn't look up.

Nate walked closer to him, gently placed his briefcase down on the corner of his desk, and stood there in front of him.

The man's name was Barry Atkins. He owned the financial investment company upstairs. Nate had met this man the day he opened his business here, and Barry had been nothing but a friend from that moment on.

"If you need to know anything, just give me a ring. I know how it is being the new guy on the block," the chubby, balding man said upon first meeting Nate.

The two men played racquetball three times a week, golf occasionally, and did the routine business trip together every now and then.

He was a good guy, always upbeat, always a smile on his face, so Nate felt there had to be something terribly wrong to walk into his office and find Barry like this.

"Barry, what's going on?" Nate asked.

Barry looked up, appeared as though he had been crying, shook his head pathetically.

"That bitch," he said under his breath, raising himself out of Nate's chair and walking around the front of his desk.

"Who are you talking about?"

Barry was pacing back and forth now, mumbling something Nate could not make out.

"That bitch is having an affair."

"Who?"

"My wife!"

"No. No way. Lisa loves you like crazy. There's no way she'd cheat on you."

"Really," Barry said, standing, digging into his inside breast pocket, and throwing at least a dozen black-and-white photos down upon Nate's desk. The pictures spilled out, giving Nate a look at practically all of them. What he saw was a naked woman bent over a bedroom nightstand, a half-naked man grabbing her from behind, his head thrown back, mouth wrenched open, as if yelling in pleasure. Another photo was of the woman embracing this man, kissing him. There were more, the sexually explicit ones all seeming to be taken with a long-range lens, from outside the window of a hotel room or something. There were other shots, and clearly, on those, Nate could see that it was indeed Barry's wife.

"Damn," Nate sighed, standing over the photos. There was nothing else he could say.

"This motherfucker," Barry said, stabbing a chubby finger into the forehead of the man in the photo. "Look at him, will you? He's half my age, twice the man I am, and he's fucking my wife!"

"Why did she do it?" Nate asked. "She never—"

"I don't know. I don't know!" Barry said, shutting his eyes tightly, whipping his head back and forth, waving his hands in the air as if he was trying to rid his mind of the images on the photos.

"Well, something had to have led her there."

"I don't know. Maybe all the working I've been doing, the traveling, never being home. She was always complaining that we don't do anything anymore, that I'm never there. And when I am, it's like my mind is somewhere else, she says. But to fucking do this. She could've just told me. She could've told me first!" Barry yelled.

Nate wanted to tell him that it sounded like that's what she'd been trying to do, but that would've only been fueling Barry's fire.

"What do you want me to do, Barry? You need anything?"

Barry turned to Nate, wiped his face with a handkerchief he pulled from his back pocket, exhaled, and said in a relatively calm voice, "I want you to go with me."

They went to breakfast, where Barry didn't say or eat anything, just dabbed at his food with the tip of his fork. After that, Nate found himself parked before the elementary school where Barry's wife was the principal. After receiving the photos from the private investigator last night, Barry said, he couldn't bring himself to go home and face her. He rented a room in a motel, trying to find the courage to do what he had to do, which was end it.

Barry sat there in the running car beside Nate, just staring out at the building, like a fearful child on his first day of school.

"You all right, Barry?"

"Yeah, yeah," Barry said, sounding a little better, but still a bit shaken up. "I just never thought I'd be doing something like this."

"You want me to go with you in there?"

"No." Barry turned to Nate, smiling as best he could to show his appreciation. "I'm glad you brought me this far."

Barry reached out and hugged Nate. He could feel the big man trembling around him. Nate leaned back after he was released and watched Barry get out of the car, start walking toward the school, his head lowered.

For the rest of the day, Nate was worthless. He couldn't get his mind off what had happened to Barry, how torn up the man was about it. Nate tried to mentally place himself in that position. He wondered, even though he was trying to divorce her, if he could find out that his wife was cheating on him, see photos of her engaged in the act, and then not throw himself off a building, or hunt the man down with a shotgun.

The ironic thing, Nate knew, was that he needed exactly that to happen to him in order to divorce his wife without handing over a fortune.

When Nate got home from work, Monica was there as she always seemed to be. She was happy to see him, especially since their reconciliation last night, and she jumped from the sofa when he walked in the door, was in his arms only moments after he had set down his briefcase.

She kissed him on the lips, smiled as she excitedly spoke to him about something, but her words went unheard by Nate.

His mind was elsewhere, stuck on how life would be without his wife there at home for him when he walked in the door, without her smiling in his face, jumping in his arms, like she had just done.

Nate sat and ate dinner with Monica, doing his best to listen to whatever she was saying, to pretend as though he was in the conversation, when he really wasn't.

That night he made love to her as passionately as he ever had, as though nothing at all was wrong.

After Monica had fallen off to sleep, Nate lay there beside her, his arms behind his head, staring up into the darkness, listening to his wife breathe.

"Monica," he whispered lightly, checking to see if she was still awake. When she didn't answer, he pulled the blankets back off himself, and quietly got out of bed.

Nate ended up on their balcony, his bathrobe pulled tight around his waist, the cool night air blowing past him as he looked down the sixty-five stories onto the brilliant night lights of the city.

Nate placed both his hands on the balcony railing, stepped very close to it, and looked out over the edge.

It was a decision that Nate didn't want to make, but he would have to decide. What was most important to him—having his wife, or having a family? Because he could not have them both.

Nate pulled the cordless phone from one of the big pockets in his robe. He stared down at it, trying to decide if he should make the call he was considering making.

He shouldn't, he concluded, but found himself punching in the numbers anyway.

The phone rang, then a slightly groggy voice answered.

Nate looked back over his shoulder, through the balcony doors, making sure that Monica had not awakened and come downstairs.

"Hello," Nate said, seeing that he was alone. "I woke you, didn't I?"

"I was just nodding off," a female voice said. "Is everything all right, Nate? You don't sound good."

"It's just everything that's going on. I need to talk to you tomorrow."

"I don't think we can avoid that, Mr. Kenny."

"No. Not like that. Lunch, dinner maybe. I mean, I really need to talk."

There was a moment before a reply was made, and Nate felt himself becoming uneasy.

"Okay," the woman finally agreed. "Just let me know."

17

Lewis had stood outside Selena's apartment the other night, just after he had had a gun pressed to his head.

The man that Selena was having sex with walked Lewis through the apartment wearing nothing at all, making sure that the tip of the gun barrel stayed flush against the back of Lewis's skull.

"Open it," the man said, once they got to the front door.

Lewis did as he was told. He stood in front of the screen door, looking out on the street, kids playing in front of him as they always did, this naked man behind him, threatening his life.

"It's fucked up how this is going down, and on the real, brotha," the man said, Lewis hearing some actual sympathy in his voice, "I feel for you. But shit is how shit is. Now get the fuck out, and I wouldn't come back until I'm gone, 'cause I wouldn't want to use this on you."

Lewis slowly stepped out of the screen door, looked back to see the man eyeing him. All the kids on the street were looking at the naked man holding the gun as well.

The man closed the door, and there Lewis stood, fuming, an anger raging in him so intense that he considered bursting back in and taking his chances at getting shot, just to get his hands on Selena, then grab his baby out of there.

After a few more minutes of standing by the door, he walked around the back of the apartment, to the bedroom window. He

85

cupped his hands, pressed his face up against the glass, trying to see through the pink bedsheet that hung there.

He couldn't see a thing, but he didn't have to, for he heard enough to know what was going on. He didn't know if it was an act or for real, but Selena was moaning and carrying on like she had never had sex before.

Lewis heard his daughter start crying, and that's when he had to force himself away from that window. He jumped in his car, sped away as fast as he could before he did something stupid.

Lewis ended up at a childhood friend's house. His name was Freddy, and actually the house was his mother's. Freddy lived in the basement.

It was after ten o'clock, for Lewis had driven around for as far as his tank of gas would take him, trying to figure out what to do, when he landed there.

He tapped on the basement window where Freddy lived, and when his bony friend finally came and pulled back the curtain, Lewis motioned for him to go to the basement door.

"I need a place to crash tonight, Freddy," Lewis said. Freddy stood in the doorway, jeans sagging off his narrow hips, and no shirt covering his skeletonlike torso.

"Can't do it, man. You know my moms ain't like you since we got caught stealin' in third grade."

"Selena just kicked me out, and I ain't got no place to go. Just this one night, Freddy," Lewis pleaded. "I can sleep on the couch, and I'll be out of here in the morning before anyone even wake up."

Freddy looked at Lewis long and hard, as if trying to determine if he was trying to run a game of some sort, then he stepped back from the door, saying, "All right, but if she find out, I'm gonna say that you broke in, and I didn't even know you was here."

That night, Lewis slept on Freddy's lumpy old love seat, which smelled of mildew and was so short that he had to hang his legs over one of the arms.

Freddy was nice enough to give him one of the blankets off his bed, which might as well have been made of paper towel, considering how thin the thing was.

Lewis lay there in the dark most of the night, shivering against the drafts that blew over him, thinking about his daughter and wondering just how he had gotten to where he was.

Bad decisions, he told himself, not wanting to think in detail about every single mistake he made, knowing it would only make him feel worse. Lewis knew he had to concentrate on how to better his situation. And he knew the first thing he had to do was get his daughter.

The next morning, Lewis was up, folded the bedspread, and set it neatly across the love seat. He was out of Freddy's basement before he or his mother had gotten up.

Lewis had gotten only about two hours of sleep, but regardless of how tired he was, he knew he still had to go to work. He needed the money now more than ever, since he would possibly have to pay for some place to stay, if Selena wouldn't let him back in.

After spending half a day at the barbershop, Lewis discovered that work had just that quickly gone back to the way it always had been. None of Beasly's old friends were lined up in Lewis's chairs waiting for haircuts, and by the time six o'clock inched around, Lewis had a whopping forty-five bucks in his jeans.

He stood outside, leaning against the building, pulling in smoke from a cigarette he had bummed off another barber. Beasly was beside him, doing the same, only half smoking and half chomping on the butt of a fat cigar. Lewis had pulled him out of the shop for the express purpose of telling him all that had recently gone on, and asking him just what he should do.

"Well, that ain't no place for no nine-month-old little girl to be," Beasly said, after taking the cigar from his lips.

"I know that. But I ain't got no place to stay myself, let alone a place to keep Layla."

"Then you got to smooth things over with your girl till you can get a place."

Lewis looked at Beasly, thinking about all that would take, and he shook his head.

"I know what you thinkin', boy. Your woman layin' up with another man, and you having to look past that, but you just gotta tell yourself you doing it for the sake of your daughter. You hear that," Beasly said, nudging Lewis with the hand he held the cigar with, then sticking it back in his teeth. "Do it for the sake of your daughter."

After work, Lewis went straight to Selena's. She opened the door for him, after Lewis had knocked.

"I came to see Layla," Lewis said, hoping that she did not slam the door in his face.

"I know why you here. She's in the bedroom," Selena said, stepping aside. "But don't take all night, I got something I got to do."

Lewis hurried toward the bedroom, but slowed just before he walked in, half expecting to see the naked man with the gun, hanging out, watching TV, or something.

When Lewis stepped through the doorway, he saw Layla on the mattress, playing with a plastic doll he had given her. Lewis immediately lowered himself, scooped his daughter up, and rolled on his back, placing her on his stomach.

He had missed her so much. He didn't even think it was possible in such a short period of time.

Layla smiled and giggled as Lewis raised her high over him, then brought her back down and kissed her face.

Lewis stopped his play with his daughter when he saw Selena leaning against the door frame.

"Thanks for letting me see her."

"You still her father."

"Yeah, I guess so," Lewis said, kissing his baby, then setting her aside on the mattress and sitting up so he could better look at Selena.

"About the other night. Why did you have to go and—"

"No," Selena said, waving her hand before her. "I ain't talking about that."

"I told you I was going to try harder to make some money, and you didn't have to—"

"Lewis! I said, I ain't talkin' about that. I did what I felt I had to do, and that's all that's to it, all right?"

"All right. But I want to come back."

Selena didn't say anything, just pressed her palms to her forehead and slowly dragged them down her face, while she shook her head.

"What?" Lewis said.

"You can't come back."

"Why not? I'll forget about what happened the other night. I won't ask you no more about it. It's over."

"But it ain't over, Lewis. I still need money, and I'm gonna continue to make money. And as a matter of fact," Selena said, glancing over at the alarm clock, "you got to be going. I got some stuff I gotta do."

"What stuff?"

"Stuff, Lewis. Now you gotta go."

Lewis quickly stood up from the mattress, placed himself right in front of Selena. "You ain't telling me that you throwing me out, cutting my time short for seeing Layla, because you got some nigga coming back through here. I know you aren't telling me that."

Selena looked squarely into Lewis's eyes, not a hint of intimidation there. "Okay, then I'm not tellin' you that. But you still gotta go." Selena walked around Lewis, threw open a dresser drawer, and plucked some clothes from it.

He was right behind her, grabbed her by one of her arms, spun her around. "You ain't gonna keep on doing this! Not while my daughter is here!"

"And who's gonna stop me! This is my place, and I can do whatever the hell I want to in it!" Selena said, yanking her arm away from Lewis, going back to the drawer.

"Then I'll tell the police. I tell them that you're prostituting in here."

Selena turned back to Lewis, chuckling pathetically at him. "Yeah, you go right ahead and do that, especially since you care so much for your daughter. But when they come up in here, and take me away for prostitution, what you think they gonna do with Layla?"

He knew exactly what they would do with her. She would go in a home, Lewis told himself.

"Then give her to me."

Selena laughed even harder. "You talk about this ain't no place to raise her. Where you living, Lewis? How you think you gonna care for her?"

"I'd find a way," Lewis said, angry at how she was mocking him.

"Thank God that that ain't the only choice that Layla got. Now if you don't mind, can you leave so I can get ready . . . unless you want another gun pressed to your head."

18

Earlier that day Nate felt distraught as he prepared for work. He stood in his closet, looking over the long line of tailored suits hanging before him, trying to decide which one of the expensive outfits he would wear.

He reached out and grabbed the first thing his hand landed on; because of the way he was feeling at that moment, it really didn't matter to him what he wore.

Sitting at the dining room table, the paper to his side, unopened, he ate his breakfast of ham and eggs that Monica prepared for him, only because he did not want to alert her to how it was he was feeling.

She sat across the table, staring at him, sensing that something was wrong, anyway.

"What's on your mind, Nate?"

"Nothing," Nate said, but he was lying. Last night after he had come from the balcony, after he had made his phone call, he crawled back into bed, but took forever to fall asleep. When he did, he was troubled by guilty thoughts again, regarding his decision to seek a divorce from her.

"Are you sure?" Monica said.

"Yeah," Nate said, working hard to display a smile. "Everything is fine."

"Then I want to know if I can take you out to dinner tonight."

"Why? What's the occasion?"

Monica couldn't help smiling, and said, "I'm just happy that things are back on track for us, that's all. And . . . well, there is something I wanted to talk to you about."

Nate was curious as to what that was, but didn't feel like going into it at that moment. "Yeah, dinner will be fine," he said, less than enthused.

On his way to work, Nate stared out emotionlessly at the stoplight before him. He sat still and quiet in his Bentley, no music playing, the hum of the smooth-running engine almost inaudible.

The downtown Chicago morning traffic was thick as it always had been, but Nate wasn't concerned, didn't care if he was late, for he knew his morning and early-afternoon schedules were both light.

The traffic light above him flashed from red to green, and Nate slowly accelerated, when his cell phone started ringing. He was startled by the abrupt break in the silence around him, and blindly reached over, grabbing the phone from the passenger seat and placing it to his ear.

"This is Nate Kenny."

"Nate. You busy?"

It was Barry Atkins calling, the poor sap whose wife cheated on him.

"No, Barry. I'm not busy. Was just heading to work. What's up?"

"Just wanted to call and thank you for yesterday, is all," Barry said, his voice still sounding kind of shaky. "I really appreciated all that."

"You okay, Barry? Did everything work out?"

There was silence for a long moment. Nate thought he heard Barry trying to gather himself on the other end of that phone.

"We're getting a divorce, Nate," Barry finally said, and now Nate could hear just how shaken up his friend was.

"Barry, look, I'll be in the office in fifteen minutes or so. I'll come up and—"

"I'm not at the office today. I needed to take some time."

"Then I'll come to your place. Where are you at, again?"

"No, no, Nate. You don't have to do that. Everything—"

"Barry, I'm coming over," Nate said. "It's not a problem. Besides, I don't really feel like going to work this morning either."

Barry lived in a downtown town home, only three blocks from the lakefront. Nate had been there only once, pulled up in the driveway to pick Barry up for a racquetball workout, but he had never been inside.

Nate pulled into the driveway now; the iron fence automatically rolled back on its track, allowing Nate entrance to the grounds.

When Barry opened the door, he stood before Nate in suit pants, a shirt, and tie. Nate didn't know if Barry had plans to work today, and at the last minute changed his mind, or if he dressed like this all the time, sporting slacks and ties on weekends and holidays like any other workday.

"Thanks for coming by, Nate," Barry said, closing the door behind him. He held a short glass in his hand, a single ice cube swimming around in a brown liquid, obviously alcohol.

Barry must've seen Nate take note of that, and said, "I know it's early, but I needed a shot of something. You want a drink?"

"Just orange juice if you have it," Nate said.

Barry disappeared into the kitchen, leaving Nate standing in the center of his living room.

The place was beautiful, majestic, Nate thought as he gazed up at the high vaulted wooden ceilings. All the walls were a dark wood as well. Three ancient-looking chandeliers hung from above, and beautiful, intricately woven area rugs lay across the brilliantly shiny hardwood floors.

All of this should've given anyone who walked into this home a very warm feeling, but for some reason Nate felt more of a chill than warmth, and he didn't know just why that was.

Barry appeared before Nate with a glass of orange juice.

Nate took it.

"Have a seat," Barry said, then took a seat opposite the leather chair Nate lowered himself onto.

"So, yeah, we're getting a divorce."

"You're doing the right thing, Barry."

"Is wasn't me that asked for it," Barry said, shaking his head. "It's funny. She's the one that gets caught cheating, but I'm the one begging her to stay."

"She wants to leave?"

"She's . . . in love," Barry said, standing from his chair. "I'm forty-five years old. I've been married to this woman for twenty-five years of my life, gave her everything, and now she tells me that she's in love with another man, and she wants to leave me."

As Barry paced past Nate, the glass of liquor still in his hand, Nate wanted to say something, anything. He just did not have any words.

Barry stopped in front of the huge fireplace at the front of the room, facing the mantel that hung above it, and the larger-than-life painting of some royal-looking bearded man.

"And what do I have now?" Barry said to himself, his back still to Nate. "Yeah, I have my company, and all the money that it generates. I have this house, and cars, and boats, and whatever the hell else money can buy. But my wife is gone."

Barry turned around, took a drink from the glass, then gestured at Nate with it. "I remember when she kept on talking about having kids. She had said she always wanted a family, but I told her no. I wanted to devote as much time as I could to the business, and then, once things slowed down, there would be time for children. That time never came, Nate," Barry said, a sad smile appearing on his face.

And Nate realized just then why he felt that chill. Yes, the house was beautiful, and it was meticulously kept—looked as though it had not been lived in at all, but that was the problem.

On that mantelpiece there were no photos of children, or any other family for that matter.

Nate figured that if Barry had had kids when he was twenty-five or thirty, he would still have them running around at that moment. Maybe a fifteen-year-old son or a twelve-year-old daughter to help him get through this, an accomplishment he could value more than just the earning of dollars.

"But I guess it's a good thing that I never did get the woman pregnant," Barry said, walking back toward Nate. "She would've still probably up and left, and taken me for alimony and child support as well. At least now I don't have to worry about that."

☙

When Nate finally made it to work, sometime after 3 P.M, he walked briskly past his secretary and said, "Cancel whatever is left for today."

"But Mr. Kenny," the secretary said.

Nate stopped beside her desk, frustration clear on his face.

"Two of the clients had been rescheduled from last week," she said.

"Then reschedule them again for next week, Tori!" Nate said, angrily. "Can you do that?"

"Yes sir," Tori said, lowering her eyes.

Nate walked into his office, slammed the door behind him, dropped his briefcase to the floor, and fell into his executive chair.

If it wasn't bad enough he felt like crap when he woke up this morning; he had to have that depressing meeting with Barry, which only pitched Nate into a deeper pit of despair.

Nate sat in his office for better than three hours thinking, and watching as the clear squares on his phone flashed to life, then remained lit for a moment, then darkened again.

They were calls to him, calls that he didn't feel like answering today, but Tori handled whatever matters they presented as she had been doing since he hired her.

A soft knock came at the door. Nate pulled his head from his hands, and looked up at the clock on the wall. It read quarter past six.

"Come in," he said, just loud enough for his voice to be heard.

The door opened, and it was Nate's secretary. Tori stood just outside the doorway, as if afraid to step in. "Everyone is gone for the evening," she said. "Is there anything else?"

"Come in, Tori," Nate said, standing behind his desk, and then he started to move around it.

Tori did as she was told.

"Close the door."

Again Tori did as she was instructed, and stood there as Nate continued to near her.

It was wrong what he was about to do, Nate told himself. It was wrong, and maybe he should've thought about it first, given it even a fraction of the time he devoted to thinking about all his other problems, but he did not. It was something that had to be done, and not deliberated over, or else he would back down. Given his circumstances, that was no longer an option.

Nate closed the distance between himself and his secretary. She did not back away when he walked right up on her, did not look oddly at him when he stared deep into her eyes; and when he grabbed her around the waist, pulled her firmly into him, covering her lips with his, sinking his tongue into her mouth, she did not fight him.

Nate felt her body relax, almost go limp in his arms, as if giving him permission to do whatever he chose with her.

19

Monica sat on the living room sofa, dressed in a new outfit she had bought today especially for the occasion of going out tonight and telling her husband about the adoption information she had gotten.

The folder was sitting there in front of her, for she had taken the literature and the photo of little Nathaniel out almost half a dozen times, skimmed over them, wanting to make sure her presentation to her husband was flawless.

But Monica was starting to believe the dinner wouldn't happen, for her husband said that he would be home at his regular time, which was around 6:30 P.M., and now it was already a few hours past that.

Maybe he had been held up by some business matter, Monica tried to convince herself, but she had phoned both his office and his cell phone more times than she wanted to remember, and all she had gotten was voice mail.

The adoption information was spread out across the coffee table, and now Monica gathered it together and slid it back into its folder, finally deciding that, no, Nate would not make dinner.

She grabbed the cordless phone and called Nate's brother, Tim, this time.

"Have you spoken to him at all today?" Monica asked, moments into their conversation.

"No. Not today. Maybe he's just out with a client."

"I thought of that, but he still usually answers his cell phone," Monica said, sounding worried.

"I wouldn't worry about it. I'm sure there's a good reason, and he'll come in eventually."

Monica was hoping that Tim was right.

She told herself not to worry, took off her new dress, and slipped into some nightclothes. She went down to the kitchen, was preparing to make herself something to eat, when she realized she had no appetite for food.

Monica glanced at the clock on the microwave, and it read 11:13 P.M.

Upstairs in bed, while David Letterman displayed his gap-toothed grin across a muted television, a silly thought crossed Monica's mind.

What if Nate's never coming back? What if her being unable to have children was all of a sudden just too much to deal with, and he decided to leave all his things behind, and never return?

Or maybe it was Monica's attempt to adopt. He did say that he didn't want to do it when she asked him before. Now, maybe he had somehow stumbled across the adoption packet, saw what Monica's plans were, and when she asked about dinner tonight, he decided he would be done with it all.

No, there was no way, Monica thought. He hadn't found the packet, because she was careful to keep it hidden, and he wouldn't just leave her like that. Nate loved her. He said it, and more important, she knew that to be true in her heart.

Monica grabbed the TV remote, pointed it, and clicked off the television.

She slid under the blankets, reached over, clicked off the bedside lamp, and told herself that everything would be fine. She would go to sleep now, stop herself from foolishly worrying about all the nonsense her mind was conjuring up, and in the morning, when she awoke, her husband would be at her side.

20

Nate lay naked on his back, in bed, beside his secretary, his eyes wide open.

He didn't know just what time it was. There was an alarm clock on her nightstand, but he would have to lift the arm that was under her to get a look, and he didn't want to wake her. Five, maybe six in the morning, he guessed, as he looked toward the window. The shade was drawn, so there was no telling whether or not the sun was rising.

Yesterday, after he pulled away from his kiss with Tori, she looked into his eyes and said, "So when you called me last night, I thought you said you wanted to talk to me about something over dinner."

"I do."

"What?"

"I'm not certain just yet, but I'll know once we sit down to eat."

Nate had decided he didn't want to be out, so he asked if they could go to her apartment instead. She gave him a strange look, as if to ask why all of a sudden he wanted to go to her place, then Tori simply said, "Sure. That'll be fine."

Her apartment was a modest one-bedroom, located on the South Side of town. Her furniture was cheap, but well maintained; the decor looked more like something that belonged to a college student than a twenty-nine-year-old woman. None of that surprised Nate, for he had seen her place quite a few times before.

Tori had made herself and Nate fettuccine noodles, with chicken and Alfredo sauce.

They had eaten at her small dining room table with all the lights off, her portable stereo playing soft music and a single candle flickering between them.

They had drunk a wine that had a screw-off cap and tasted like spiked Kool-Aid, but it did what it was supposed to after enough glasses, and that was to soothe Nate's nerves some.

After the plates had been cleared and stacked in the kitchen sink, the candle, the glasses, and the bottle of cheap wine were taken into the living room. Nate and Tori sat facing very close to each other on the love seat.

"So, why are you here? Why, after four years, are you sitting on my sofa again?" Tori had asked.

Nate had known the question would come. "Because I had a conversation with Barry Atkins from upstairs."

"I don't understand."

"Barry's wife cheated on him, and he doesn't know why that is. He thinks it may be because he was at work so often, that he hadn't paid her enough attention. But regardless of the reason, she cheated, and now they're getting a divorce. I went to his house today to talk to him, and he was pathetic. He talked about how he had nothing, talked about how he was lucky that he never brought any children into this world so his wife couldn't use them against him, but I know, could tell by looking at him, that he regretted that." Nate paused to take a drink from his glass. "I told myself that moment that I never wanted to be like him, but something told me that if I continued to allow what's been going on, that's exactly who I'd be like."

Tori looked confused. "What does that have to do with me?"

"Tori, how do you feel about me?"

A look of even greater confusion covered Tori's face now. She inched back from him some. "You don't have the right to ask me that question now."

"Why not, when I want to know?"

"Because you just don't!" Tori said, abruptly rising from the sofa.

She was angry, and Nate knew it was because of what had happened those years ago, before he met his wife.

He had hired Tori one week, and the next they were sleeping with each other.

She was beautiful, and intelligent, and catered to his every desire, far beyond what she was paid for, but Nate knew their relationship could go only so far.

They saw each other a couple of times a week, having dinner or seeing a show or a movie out, and then afterward, always back to his place or hers for sex.

This lasted for three months, Nate telling himself he would let it continue until she started expecting things, until she started developing those feelings that women get for a man, that have them seeing themselves in that man's future. He would continue seeing Tori until that point, and then he would end it with her.

At about the three-and-a-half month mark, Tori started asking where they were going, how he truly felt about her, and where he saw them in the future.

Nate tried his best to simply ignore or avoid the questions, because he was truly fond of Tori. He had looked forward to those nights when they spent time together, but the more she pushed, the more he felt pressured to tell her the truth.

The night of Tori's birthday, after they had spent the full day of activities Nate had planned for her, after he had given her the tennis bracelet he had bought for her, they had made love. Afterward, the two of them lay together on a bare mattress, their heads at the foot of the bed, the sheets and blankets somehow thrown to the floor during their wild lovemaking.

Nate was laughing about something, he couldn't really remember what, a joke he had told her or something, when Tori asked the question again.

"Where are we going with this?"

"Tori," Nate sighed. "Do we really have to—"

"Yes, Nate." She rolled up on an elbow to look down onto his face. "We have to do this, because I want to know. I need and deserve to know. We've been seeing each other for almost four months now. I love spending time with you, love seeing you every morning when you walk into your office. I just keep asking myself, why can't we see each other when you go home too?"

And there it was, Nate thought. She was talking about marriage, or at the very least, moving in together, neither of which he had planned for her.

"That can't happen," Nate said, softly, but loud enough for Tori to hear.

"Why not?"

"Because it just can't."

"Nate, I love you," Tori said, after rolling over on top of him.

"Don't say that."

"And why not? I do. Don't you feel the same way about me?"

Nate pushed Tori off him and was out of bed, picking up his clothes from the floor.

Tori followed behind him as Nate stepped into his slacks and walked out of the bedroom.

"Just tell me why. You always tell me that you want to get married one day, that you want to have a family. Why can't it be me?"

Having arrived at the front door, his pants on, and now pushing his arms through his shirt and buttoning it, Nate spun around to Tori, and said, "Because it just can't! Okay. It can't. Period."

Tori stood naked before him. How sad she appeared. All Nate wanted to do was grab and hold her, tell her that he was sorry, but it would only have her believing that there was still a chance for her, when he knew there wasn't. Knew there would never be . . .

Until last night when, faced with never having a family, Nate was certain that this woman, who loved him so in the past, could rescue him from that fate.

"So I want to know how you feel about me. I want to know if there is still something there," Nate said.

"Why do you want to know this now, all of a sudden? I loved you then, begged to be with you, but you wouldn't allow it, and now you're asking me how I feel. What happened then?"

"I wasn't ready," Nate lied.

Tori must've known that, for she said, "You can get out of my house. You dump me, and six months later, I hear you are engaged. If you don't want to tell me the real reason, then you don't have to. But then don't go asking me about my feelings."

Tori stood by the sofa and turned her back to Nate, as though waiting for him to consider what she had just said, and finally tell her the truth. He had no other choice, even though he knew it might hurt her.

"When we first lay down together and had sex, I told myself that that was as far as it could ever go," Nate confessed.

Tori turned around. "Why?"

Nate hesitated only for a moment. "Because you worked for me. I was your employer, and regardless of how you felt for me, how we felt about each other, I couldn't be seriously involved with my secretary. I had just started my business, and it just wasn't professional, wasn't right."

Tori lowered her head. "I see," she said, saddened by the news.

"But things are different now," Nate said, jumping up from the couch and grabbing Tori by the shoulders. "And they can work if you just tell me how you feel about me."

"I don't feel anything," Tori said, bitterly.

"You're lying. Why have I never heard you mention another man's name since me, seen anyone come by, heard of anyone calling? I've seen how you look at me sometimes. The same way you looked at me when we were seeing each other. I know when a woman feels something for me, Tori, especially you, so why don't you just tell me?"

"Why? So you can leave me again?" Tori said, struggling, trying to free herself from Nate's grip.

"No. That's not why."

"Then it's because your wife can't have your children, and you don't want to be like Barry from upstairs. So you want to fuck me, so I can have your kids. Is that it?"

"Not quite, but something like that," Nate said. "And if you still feel something for me, we can do that, because I still care for you, Tori," Nate said, pulling her closer to him, kissing her on her neck and behind her ear.

"No! Stop!" Tori said.

"You don't mean that," Nate said, and he knew he was right, for he felt the level of her struggle, knew she was strong enough to tear away from him if she truly wanted to.

"I loved you, but you left anyway."

"I know, but that won't happen again," Nate said, continuing to kiss her as he quickly undid the buttons on her blouse, then reached behind her and unclasped her bra.

"Don't do this, Nate. Please don't do this," Tori begged, but Nate didn't hear her. He felt her body go weak again, and now he knew she wanted him to do this as much as he wanted it to happen, even though she said differently.

He bent down and scooped her body up, carried her into the bedroom, and laid her across the bed. Nate straddled her, kissing her again on the neck, working his way down, cupping one of her breasts in his hands and taking it into his mouth, sucking it gently at first, then harder, the way she liked it. Nate felt her body respond, heard her moan, noticed her back arching up toward him.

He worked his way farther down still, undoing her belt, looping his fingers under the waist of her skirt, stockings, and panties, preparing to pull them all down.

"Don't do it," Nate heard Tori say. Her voice sounded weak, in between her quick breathing. "I almost couldn't let you go last time. Please don't start this if you won't be able to finish it. Please."

Nate ignored what she said, quickly pulling her clothing down to expose her bare thighs.

He peeled his clothes off as fast as he could, then stood there naked at Tori's feet, his hands grabbing her ankles as she looked dizzily up at him. Nate climbed on top of Tori's trembling body, the tip of his penis hard and heavy, gently grazing her most sensitive parts.

Tori looked up at him, her eyes half closed. She reached up, grabbed his face in her hands. "Don't do this if you aren't sure."

"I've never been more sure of anything in my life," Nate said, then he slid inside.

❦

Now it was the next morning, and Nate lay naked in bed beside Tori. He had been drinking, but his recollection of last night was not difficult.

He remembered last night, feeling his body nearing orgasm, remembered crying out to Tori that he was going to come.

He felt her hands push into his chest, trying to force him off of her.

"Pull out! I'm not on the pill. Pull out!"

But Nate just grabbed her tighter, pushed farther into her, exploding in a painful pleasure.

She was not mad at him, told him that she probably wouldn't get pregnant, because she had just finished her period, but she told him she would not be some woman on the side, some baby's mama.

"I don't want you to be," Nate said. "If you're my children's mother, then you'll be my wife."

Even though it seemed that she tried very hard to suppress her happiness, Tori was unable. She joyfully screamed out, threw her arms around Nate's neck, and kissed him all over his face.

"So how are you going to work all this out with your wife?" she asked him later.

That Nate didn't know, actually had no clue about. But as he gently slid his arm from under Tori's head, trying not to wake her, and finally getting a peek at the clock, which read 6:08 A.M., he realized the first thing he needed to do was get home.

105

21

Lewis woke up with a start, sitting bolt upright in the reclined seat of his car to see a police officer standing just outside it. The cop tapped a knuckle against the window, as if Lewis was still asleep, and not staring right at the uniformed man.

"Move it along, or get a ticket," Lewis heard the cop's muffled voice say.

Lewis was still not quite awake and looked at the cop as if he could've been part of a dream.

The officer pointed up to a sign, standing on the other side of the car. "No parking zone. Move it, or get a ticket," he said louder.

Lewis understood, nodded his head, as he wiped sleep out of his eyes. He raised the driver's seat back up, pulled the car keys out of his pocket, and tried the old car's engine. Thankfully, it turned over on the first try, because Lewis didn't have the money for a ticket. Lewis didn't have the money for much of anything now.

Last night after Selena forced him out for a second time in a row, she told him to give her his house key. He reluctantly pulled it from his key ring and handed it over to her. Now he knew she never wanted him back there.

He had thought about going back to Freddy's house, but knew the man wouldn't let him in.

He had no other friends' places he could crash at, and the thought of going to Beasly, asking if he could sleep in the barbershop's break room, seemed like too much of a burden to the man, after he had already loaned Lewis money.

So last night, Lewis pulled his car to the curb and parked for the night. He reached over the passenger-side seat, grabbed the bag of White Castle hamburgers he had bought moments earlier, and started eating.

When the cop woke Lewis up this morning, he thought that he had been dreaming. Not just about tossing and turning, trying to sleep in his car with nothing but his jacket to use as a blanket, but about everything that had been happening to him. Everything concerning Selena and Layla, he just knew was a dream, until he was rudely awakened, and it all came back to him.

So what was there to do now, Lewis asked himself as he drove slowly east along Eighty-seventh Street. He had asked himself this question a million times since last night, and it pained him deeply trying to come up with an answer but never finding one.

It was because there simply wasn't one, Lewis thought, feeling a depression start to come over him. He had a job, but it made him no money. His woman no longer wanted him with her, and that wasn't the end of the world, because, honestly, Lewis could live without her. But she held his baby, and Layla was someone he would not live without. Unfortunately, he had no way of getting her away from Selena. He had nothing that he could use to bargain, especially a huge sum of money, which he was almost certain Selena would maybe consider.

Something would come to him. Something had to, Lewis told himself, looking up and, just in time, noticing the pickup truck that was stopped at the red light in front of him. He slammed on his brakes, and to his amazement, his incredibly worn brakes caught and held the car immediately, the tires squealing, the back end of the automobile hiking up.

Lewis saw the eyes of the driver in front of him staring angrily back at him through his rearview mirror, and Lewis mouthed the word "Sorry."

He would have to keep his mind on what he was doing, and not

worry too much about his problems, he knew, as he slowly accelerated through the now green light, making a left onto Stony Island
Avenue.

He picked up speed to move with the brisk flow of early traffic,
and again his thoughts receded back to his problems.

Of all the places he could've seen himself being, of all the problems he could've imagined himself dealing with, Lewis never
thought that he would find himself in the hell he lived in. He never
thought things could be as bad as they were.

The traffic light a hundred or so yards in front of him blinked
from green to yellow, and this time Lewis was paying attention, so
he covered the brake with his shoe and applied pressure, but this
time nothing happened.

It had to have been the wrong pedal, Lewis told himself, trying to
quickly steal a peek down at the floor; then, realizing it was the right
one, he pressed harder onto it.

Still nothing.

The car continued to sail forward, past the slowing and stopped
cars on either side of him, even though Lewis was now digging his
foot as deep into the car's floor as possible.

He grabbed tight to the steering wheel, yelling prayers to be
stopped, seeing the halted car's brake lights in front of him bleed a
bright red as he moved quickly closer and closer toward them.

After the brakes refused to catch, Lewis knew he would crash. All
he could do was brace himself for the impact.

22

Nate didn't go straight home. When he pulled himself from Tori's bed, he had awakened her, despite his efforts not to.

"You want me to make you some breakfast?" she asked.

"No. I really need to be going."

"Home to your wife, right?"

Nate, putting on his shirt, stopped in midmotion and stared oddly at her.

"I'm sorry," she said, walking over, wrapping her arms around him. "You know how I get about you. I loved you then, and just like you suspected, I never stopped. I guess I'm just anxious for that part of your life to end, so ours can start."

"Don't worry," Nate said. "It will. But I have to go."

When he got out to his car, he checked his cell phone, and as he had imagined, there were eleven missed calls. Ten of them were from his wife, and one from his brother, Tim.

Tim lived not far from Tori, so that was the direction Nate pointed his car in.

When Tim came to open the door, he was wearing a bathrobe, a T-shirt, and jeans underneath.

"Nate!" Tim said, surprised. "Your wife has been—"

"Were you busy, Tim?" Nate said, walking past him into the house.

"No," Tim said, closing the door and then walking into the living room. "But Monica has called already three or four times asking me where you were at. After a while, I started to wonder myself."

Nate took a seat on the arm of Tim's sofa. He still had on the suit from yesterday, the tie stuffed into one of his pockets, the shirt unbuttoned at his neck.

"I've been here, Tim," Nate said, coolly.

Tim looked bewildered. "What do you mean?"

"I mean last night, I was here with you. I came by around ten, and we started drinking, and we both passed out here."

"But Monica called last at around eleven."

"Well then, I came at eleven-thirty."

"Nate, I don't want to lie to your wife."

"But you're going to, right?" Nate said, confidently.

"What's going on? Where were you really, last night?"

"You don't need to know that," Nate said, getting up from the sofa, walking to Tim, and slapping a palm on his shoulder. "But just in case Monica brings this up again, you know what to tell her. Now I really got to be going." Nate pulled open the door and was about to step out, but stopped when he heard his brother say, "I told you, I don't think I want to lie to her."

"Really," Nate said, turning back to face his brother. "And why is that?"

"Because I just don't think it's right."

"Not even for me?"

"I don't know."

"Try your best. This one last time. This means more to me than you know. Will you help me out?"

Tim shook his head, as though he knew he was doing the wrong thing, but said, "All right. This one last time, Nate. But not again."

"That's my boy," Nate said, then walked out.

Now that Nate covered that end of his story, he would stop and get some roses for his wife. She would most likely be at home, eyes bloodshot, looking a wreck, because she had been up all night, worried sick about him.

He would tell her that it was the business with the baby messing with him again. He needed to talk to family, sort some things out in his head. They had a drink that turned into a few more, then one for the road, which took away Nate's ability to make it to the road, so he crashed out on Tim's couch. Simple as that.

There was the issue of Monica saying something about taking Nate to dinner, something she had to talk to him about, but they could just do those things tonight.

Nate turned his Bentley onto Stony Island Avenue and headed north to get onto Lake Shore Drive, and into downtown. What Nate really needed to concern himself with now was what he was going to do about Tori.

If it wasn't a certainty before, it definitely was now: he would have to divorce Monica. But still there was the issue of the money she would be entitled to if he did just divorce her with no reason.

He thought for a moment, tried to search his mind, as he slowed his car to a stop for the red light just in front of him. Was there any way that he could free himself from his marriage without incurring such a penalty? No. Nothing came to him right away. He would have to devote much more time to it.

Nate thought about the possibility of just coming clean with Monica. Telling her the truth, that her inability to have his children made it impossible for him to have his family, so he wanted a divorce. But that would surely make her furious, resentful of him, and want to take him for every red cent he had. No, he would definitely not do that.

And honestly, he decided not to worry anymore for a little while, because he was actually feeling somewhat giddy, almost happy.

A smile appeared on Nate's face as he thought about what he did last night and what would ultimately come of his actions if he continued to do the same with Tori.

Like Tori said, she probably wouldn't get pregnant this time, but Nate had a feeling that she eventually would, and she would bear him some beautiful children. He couldn't believe it, but he started to get that feeling again. That same feeling when Monica said it was okay for them to start trying, that feeling of excitement that came with knowing that one day soon he would be a father.

No. Nate really couldn't believe it, but considering all that had gone on over the last few weeks, he actually felt happy. So happy that he threw his head back in laughter; but all of a sudden, without a moment's notice, there came what sounded like an explosion from behind him.

His entire car shook, and Nate's body was violently thrown forward, then was painfully yanked back by the safety belt, his forehead coming dangerously close to impacting with the windshield and shattering it.

The wrenching sound of twisted metal, the popping of bulbs exploding filled Nate's ears almost simultaneously with the heavy, heart-stopping thud of the impact from behind.

Shards of glass came flying into the car's cabin, pelting the back of Nate's seat and falling to the floor behind him.

His car was pushed out into the intersection, Nate's foot still on the brake, his eyes ballooning in his head, as he saw blurred cars on both sides of him swerving to miss his.

His car spun to a halt. A dead silence surrounded him.

After a moment, Nate opened his eyes, checked his body for injuries, and felt there were none. He slowly turned his head, and was thankful there was no pain, or stiffness. To his right and left, cars were bunching up on either side of him.

He was rear-ended, he knew. Nate also knew that his car was in pretty bad shape, even though he himself seemed okay. He didn't have to see the damage that had been done for him to know the extent of it.

He reached for his seat belt buckle, and started to unclasp it.

"No, don't get out!" shouted an aging redheaded woman, wearing a worried expression, standing at his window.

"I'm okay," Nate said, reaching for the door handle and trying to push it open.

"We've called an ambulance. Maybe you should just—"

"I'm okay!" Nate said again, his irritation obvious in his voice. The woman stepped away, and Nate got out.

The damage was as Nate had suspected; quite bad. The entire back end of his Bentley had been compressed, and shoved toward the backseat of his car. The back windshield had shattered; bits and pieces of red brake-light glass were scattered across the pavement. The car looked like an accordion with wheels. It was totaled.

Nate was lucky and thankful to be alive, he told himself, but he was still mad as hell that some fool, who obviously didn't watch where he was going, wrecked his beautiful car.

Nate turned his head to see just who had done this to him.

Cars were starting to honk their horns, drivers sticking their heads out of their windows to see what had happened, as Nate walked the ten feet between the two cars, and stopped just in front of the car that had wrecked his. It was amazing, considering all the destruction that had been done to Nate's car; the other car seemed to have nothing more than a couple of dents and chipped paint, which made Nate even more insane with anger.

He hurried around to the passenger-side window and yelled at the driver.

"Do you see what you did to my car! Do you see what you did to it!"

The driver, a man, just sat there, looking straight ahead, not seeming to want to look at Nate.

"Do you hear me! Do you see! Say something!"

"I'm sorry," the man finally said.

"You're sorry! You plowed into my car with this"—Nate was unable to immediately identify the make and model, so he quickly stomped to the back of the car, read the badge, and stomped back—"this fucking AMC Gremlin, and you say you're sorry. Get out of the damn car!" Nate said, yanking at the door handle, planning on knocking the man to the ground as soon as he stepped out. "I said, get out!"

"All right, all right," the man said.

And when he stepped out of the car, Nate figured he probably wouldn't go knocking him to the ground just yet, because the man was the same height as Nate, a little heavier, and more muscular. But still Nate was very angry.

"Give me your insurance information," Nate said, digging into his wallet to retrieve his own. He held them out to the man, waiting for his in return. When the man failed to produce his, Nate said again, "We need to exchange insurance information."

"Sir, I don't have any insurance."

"What!" And that was the last straw for Nate. That was it. He dug into his pants pocket, pulled out his cell phone, dialed three numbers, pressed send, then placed the phone to his ear.

"Sir, sir!" the man said, stepping closer to Nate. "What are you doing?"

"I'm calling the police. Having your ass taken off to jail. No insurance is illegal."

"But sir, you can't do that."

"I can, and I will."

"Please, sir, please," the man begged. "I don't have nothing. No home, no money. That's why I couldn't get my brakes fixed."

"Nine-one-one emergency," Nate heard a nasally woman's voice answer.

"Yes, I'd like to report an accident."

"Sir, sir," the man said, this time grabbing Nate by the sleeve, tugging him like a child trying to gets its mother's attention. "Please, just hang up the phone."

Nate looked down at him. How pathetic he thought this man was. How in the world did this man mess up in life to leave him homeless and penniless? He could've done more, Nate figured. He looked able-bodied, was young, a good-looking fellow—

"Where did the accident take place, sir?" the woman on the phone asked.

"Please don't do this," the man said again. "I don't have no money, or no insurance, but I'm sure we can work something out. Anything. Just hang up the phone."

Nate looked at the man again with even more pity now. We can work something out, Nate heard him say, and he had to laugh at that. What in the world could this loser do to help Nate out? Of what value could this fool be to him, other than to wash his and his wife's cars for life? But since Nate's car was totaled, that just left—

"Sir, where did the accident take place?" the voice insisted.

—Monica's car. And then something all of a sudden came to Nate. A brainstorm. No, bigger. A mental monsoon!

"Sir—"

Nate didn't answer the woman, but disconnected the call, and then said to the man in front of him, "Okay. Maybe we can work something out."

23

Monica slammed the phone down to the table and sprung from the sofa when she heard someone at the front door.

When it opened and Nate walked in, she raced over to him, threw her arms around him, and squeezed him hard. "Where have you been?" she said.

When she heard a faint groan escape her husband, she loosened her embrace and stepped back from him. "Are you all right?"

"I've been in a car accident," Nate said, wincing just a little.

"What! Did it happen last night? Is that what happened to you? Why didn't you call me?" Monica said, sounding hysterical.

"Calm down, calm down," Nate said, walking into the living room. "It happened this morning."

"Well, are you all right?" Monica said, following closely behind him. "Did you go to the hospital?"

"No. I didn't go to the hospital, because I'm fine."

"Then how do you know that, if you didn't go?"

Nate stopped walking toward the kitchen and turned around. Monica was right there behind him.

He grabbed her by the shoulders. "Monica," he said. "I'm fine. I was a little shaken up, but other than that, I am just fine. Okay?"

It took Monica a moment to respond, but finally she said, "Okay. What happened to the car?"

Nate shook his head. "I had it towed, but it was pretty bad, and I'm sure they'll total it out."

"I'm sorry, baby," Monica said, hugging him again, taking care not to squeeze him too hard. "The most important thing is that you're all right. I was so worried about you all last night. I thought you said we'd be able to do dinner. Where were you?"

"I was over at Tim's," Nate quickly answered.

"But when I called over there, he said he hadn't spoken to you."

"I didn't get there until sometime after eleven."

"Then where were you before then?"

Nate sighed, reached around his back, grabbed Monica's hands, unclasped them, and stepped out of her embrace. He turned away from her. "Just out walking around."

"Why?"

"I had things on my mind."

"What things?"

"Things, Monica!" Nate said, turning, raising his voice.

Monica was startled, and jumped just a little bit. "Then why didn't you call me? At least I would've known that you were all right."

"I don't know why I didn't call you. There were just things that I had to work out in my mind, and I guess I lost track of time, or something. I ended up at Tim's because I needed someone to talk to about all this."

"You could've talked to me."

"It needed to be Tim."

"And that stuff that you talked to him about," Monica asked. "It had to do with us?"

"Yes," Nate said. "Is there anything in there to eat? I'm starving." He sat himself down on the sofa.

"Yes," Monica said, feeling as though she and the discussion had been dismissed. "I'll make you some breakfast. Have a seat at the table."

Everything was supposed to have been better now, Monica

thought as she pulled open the fridge. But things weren't. He was still thinking about Monica's condition, still resenting her for it. She could tell just by the way he looked at her, by the way he answered her when she asked him, was it them he had to speak to his brother about?

Monica pulled the carton of eggs and package of bacon from the fridge, and set them on the counter.

If she had any doubts about checking into adoption, they weren't there any longer. And once again, she was certain that it was the only thing that would get them back on track.

The presentation she had for Nate last night over dinner was all planned out. She had rehearsed it over and over again, and was confident that he would've agreed with everything she had discussed, and would've been willing to go ahead and take the next step toward adopting little Nathaniel, if he had heard it. But she would just have to save it for another time, because considering all he had just gone through, and the little argument they just had, now would be the worst time to bring that up.

Monica grabbed a skillet from under the sink, and was just about to set it on the stove when she froze, remembering that she hadn't put away the adoption materials after she had taken them out again this morning.

She set the skillet aside and hurried into the dining room, hoping to catch her husband before he decided to take his seat at the table.

When Monica made it out of the kitchen and was approaching the table, Nate was doing the same, was pulling out his chair, and was ready to sit down. Monica practically stepped in front of him and said, "Let me clear these things from out of your way."

She started to gather them when Nate said, "Hold it." He grabbed some of the pages out of her hand and said, "What is this?"

"It's nothing," Monica said, trying to take the pages back.

"No. It's something." He read the letterhead on one of the pages. "The True Home Adoption Agency."

"We don't have to talk about this right now." Monica took the pages from him. "I'll make you breakfast, and we can talk about it

another time." She moved away from the table with all the literature bunched up in both hands.

"No, we can't talk about it another time, because I thought we already had this conversation, and decided against it."

Monica stopped and turned around. "No. We didn't decide
against it. I mentioned it to you, and you rejected the idea. But *we*
didn't decide anything."

"Well, there's nothing else to talk about."

"Yes there is, Nate," Monica said, feeling as though he was trying
to dismiss her yet again. "You wanted a family, still want one, but I
can't give you that."

"It's not important anymore."

"Bullshit! If it wasn't important anymore, what was last night
about? Something that's not important anymore was so much on
your mind that you couldn't come home, but had to walk around
just to sort it out, and then couldn't talk to me, your wife, about it,
but had to go to your brother. And you tell me it's not important."

"Monica, I just don't think it's a good idea."

"Why?" Monica said, taking steps toward him. "I've been trying
to ignore it, but it feels as though our marriage is falling apart because of this. I know you see it too, Nate. Don't try to deny it."

Nate said nothing.

Monica walked very close to him, the adoption papers still in her
hands. There before him, she shuffled quickly through the pages and
pulled out the photo of the little infant boy.

"Here."

Nate turned away from it. "I don't want to see that."

"Look at it!" Monica demanded.

Nate took the photograph.

"That's a little boy named Nathaniel. He has the same name as
you, and we can adopt him if we want. That could be the son you always wanted, our son. All you have to do is say yes."

"Monica, I don't know."

Monica threw the other papers to the sofa and stomped a couple
of steps away from him. "Will you at least think about it?" she said,

turning back to face him. "I really feel that this will make the difference in whether or not you and I will stay together. Will you think about it?"

Nate looked down at the photo one last time. "I can't promise you anything, but I'll think about it."

"Fine," Monica said.

24

Lewis walked into a motel room and closed the door behind him. He stood there a moment, looking around, wondering why he was even standing there, why he had taken the money from that man only hours ago, and agreed to do what the man had told him.

The man—Mr. Kenny, he said his name was—asked for Lewis's driver's license after he had put his cell phone away and agreed not to call the police.

Lewis pulled the license from his wallet and gave it to the man, as Mr. Kenny went about taking out his own wallet.

He took Lewis's license, didn't even look at it, but slipped it into his own billfold.

"Hold it. What are you doing?"

"You said you wanted to work something out," Mr. Kenny said. "And in order for us to do that, I have to know where you are." Mr. Kenny pulled out a number of twenty-dollar bills and held them out to Lewis. Lewis looked at the money oddly.

"Go on, take it."

Lewis did as he was told. "What am I supposed to do with this?"

"You said you're homeless, right? Get yourself a room. And once you get there," Mr. Kenny said, pulling out one of his business cards and handing it to Lewis, "call my cell phone number, and leave the address and phone number of the motel you're staying in. Do you understand that?"

Lewis answered with hesitation. "Yes. But why are you having me do all this?"

"I don't know yet."

"And what if I said I don't want to do it?"

"Then I'd take my money, give you your license back, call the police, and press charges against you."

That was the last thing Lewis needed, so he took the money, found the nearest motel, and checked in.

He walked across the small room, over to the nightstand, and sat on the edge of the bed. He had pulled out the business card Mr. Kenny had given him, and was staring at the number.

He picked up the phone and was about to dial the number when he punched in another number.

The phone rang several times, and then to his disappointment, the call was transferred to voice mail. He heard the recording of Selena's voice telling him that she was not home, and to leave a message.

Lewis slammed the phone into the cradle, wondering just where in the hell she could be at a little after nine in the morning.

He would've gone over there if that man hadn't had his car towed, bad brakes or not.

All he could do now was call the number this man gave him, then sit and wait for however long it took for him to call Lewis back.

25

While sitting in his home office later that same day, Nate had received the voice mail from Lewis, giving him the name, address, and phone number of the motel he was staying in.

Immediately, Nate called the number of the motel.

"Red Roof Inn, may I help you?" a woman asked.

"Yes," Nate said. "Do you have a Lewis Waters staying there?"

There was a moment's pause, then the woman said, "Yes, I'll connect you."

"No," Nate quickly interrupted. "I just want to pay up his room for a week." This would allow Nate to keep the boy close to him, until he decided what the next move would be. But just what in the hell was that? Nate asked himself, racking his brain. That was the reason he was in his office at that moment to begin with, trying to decide what use there would be for the boy, if any.

Just then, his phone rang.

It was Barry. He called to tell Nate what was going on with him and his wife.

"She wants half of my shit, Nate!" Barry said, an incredulous tone in his voice. "She cheats on me, and she wants half my shit!"

"You didn't have a prenuptial agreement, Barry?"

"I loved that woman. I didn't think I'd need one. I never thought she'd do this to me."

"Did she ever confess to you just why she did it?"

"It's what I expected. She said I wasn't there, I wasn't paying her any attention, acted as though I didn't find her attractive or beautiful anymore. That shouldn't be enough to go out and cheat on your husband."

"I'm sorry, Barry, but I guess it was, for her."

Just that moment, the wheels in Nate's head started spinning; an idea came to him that he thought just might work.

Immediately Nate reached into his desk drawer, pulled out paper, and started jotting figures on it. After he got off the phone with Barry, he made a number of calls, the most important one to the manager of his real estate properties.

When he got the manager on the phone, Nate said, "The town home, west of downtown, have you rented that out yet?"

"I showed it today," the man said, "but no, I haven't rented it yet."

"Good. Don't show it anymore. It's taken. I'll call you back tomorrow with the particulars."

Next Nate called Lewis back at the motel.

"I've paid up your room for a week. I want you to stay there."

"But why, Mr. Kenny?"

"I'll tell you when I have everything worked out."

"But why do you want me to stay here?" Lewis asked.

"Do you have anywhere else to go?"

The boy didn't answer.

"Good. Stay put, and like I said, I'll call you back when I have things in better order."

For the rest of the night, Nate sat in his office, the lights low around him, as he meticulously devised a plan that he hoped would solve all his problems.

26

Nate spent a week putting his plan into effect, and after running all the errands, placing the phone calls, spending the money, and adopting the behavior his plan called for, he felt as though everything was in order.

On the last night of that week, Nate stood shirtless in front of the bathroom mirror, wearing pajama bottoms while brushing his teeth. He was preparing for bed much later than he usually did, because over the last five days, he had been coming home much later than usual.

Tonight he walked in the house at ten-fifteen. The night before that it was after ten-thirty, and the night before that, it was even later.

Monica was not surprised or upset by his late arrivals, because he had told her to expect just that.

"We just took on a new client, so I'll be getting in late," he told her the evening after creating his plan. He barely stood there long enough to get those words out, then turned and headed upstairs to his home office, not saying another thing to her.

Since that moment, that was how Nate had been treating his wife—as though she was practically a stranger. The affection he used to show her all the time, before all of this happened, like hugging and kissing her when he walked in the door, now stopped. The way he would suggestively brush against her while they were both standing in the bathroom, kissing her neck—that no longer took place. Now, he avoided stepping in there or any other close quarters whenever she was occupying them. Every sign of intimacy, affection, or romance that Monica was accustomed to him showing her had now halted.

He could tell that Monica felt as though there was something wrong with him, but she seemed reluctant to approach him with it, probably because he told her that he would be considering the possibility of adopting the child, when she had brought that issue to him. For the moment, he assumed that was enough to keep her satisfied.

"You coming to bed soon?" Nate heard Monica call through the bathroom door. Nate spat the toothpaste out of his mouth and into the face bowl, rinsed, but did not answer.

It was rude, and that made him feel bad. It was not like him to ignore her like that, but he forced himself to remain mute, convincing himself that it was for the greater good.

Nate placed his toothbrush in the medicine cabinet, then closed the mirrored door, his face all of a sudden staring back at him.

He had to turn away, because he knew he would ask himself why he was doing what he was, why he had done all that he had up to that point. But Nate didn't want to confront those questions. It was best that he just proceed with the plan that he had set in motion, because he knew what he wanted the outcome to be. He could no longer worry about who got hurt, and what was right or wrong. What had to be, had to be.

Nate placed himself in front of the toilet, lifted the seat, pulled the front of his pajama pants down, not to take a leak, but to check to see if he could get an erection.

He tugged on his penis a few times, thought about his wife lying in the next room practically naked, thought about every other woman in his past that had aroused him, but when Nate looked down, he had not grown at all.

"Good," he said to himself, washed his hands, then walked into the bedroom.

Monica threw back the blankets, welcoming her husband in, and under those blankets, she was wearing nothing but a tiny satin nightie.

Nate crawled into bed, climbed on top of his wife without as much as even looking in her eyes, then kissed her on the mouth.

Monica looked oddly up at him. "Are you all right?"

"I'm fine," Nate said, showing little expression, then kissed Monica again, this time longer, slipping his tongue in between her lips.

"Nate, what are you doing?" Monica asked after their kiss.

"I want to make love."

"But we tried every night this week, and nothing happened. Why don't we just give it some time, and let it happen naturally?"

Nate gave his wife a look that let her know he was hurt and offended by what she had just said. He started to slide off her, but she grabbed him and held him there.

"Nate, you haven't been yourself lately. I know you said it was stress from work. So, you aren't feeling that anymore?"

"I don't know what you're talking about, but if you don't want to make love, then just say so." Again he tried to slide off her, but again she caught hold of him.

"Don't be silly. You know I love you. I just don't know what's going on," Monica said, looking truly puzzled. "But if you want to make love, you know we can."

Nate didn't respond to a word Monica said, but lowered his face into the crook of his wife's neck and started kissing her there. He did everything that he knew worked to turn her on, and as always, his efforts did just that. He heard his wife panting under him, felt her body squirming. She was reaching down, groping blindly for what was in between his legs.

She would be terribly disappointed that there was nothing there, at least nothing that would be of any use to her. Nate was about as hard as an overcooked egg noodle, and when she reached for it, felt how flaccid he was, Nate said without sympathy, "I'm sorry."

"Sorry about what?" Monica said, pushing him off her, rolling him over onto his back, and straddling his knees. "You just haven't had the proper motivation."

She yanked his pajama bottoms farther down his thighs, took his shriveled penis in her hands, and started slowly massaging it, kneading it in between her palms like dough. Nothing happened. She quickened her movements, her hands pulling at him at an almost blurring speed, but still there was nothing.

Nate knew nothing would happen, was sure of it, but Monica continued on, as though she had to prove to herself that she could somehow force an erection out of her husband.

After almost five minutes of trying, Nate reached down and grabbed both his wife's hands.

"You should stop. It's not going to work." He pulled Monica off him, and instead of hugging her, as he would've if this was really an issue, he turned away from her, onto his side, without saying a word, and pretended to go to sleep.

It was an evil thing he was doing, and he could feel his wife sitting up, just behind him, probably looking down on him, wondering how he could be so thoughtless as to not say a word to her when he knew that she was probably asking herself if it was her fault. Was his inability to get an erection due to the fact that he was no longer attracted to her?

If Nate had actually turned around, and honestly answered that question, he would have to tell his wife that it had nothing to do with her, or stress, or anything. It was all part of the plan that Nate had come up with.

As well as every other aging man, Nate knew there was a pill that helped men gain an erection. But what he didn't know was if there was one that would help him guarantee against attaining one.

Nate visited his old doctor friend from undergrad, and found out there indeed was. It wasn't the drug's purpose, although it was a side effect that occurred when this pill was taken.

Nate's friend seemed hesitant when Nate asked for a prescription for the drug he could not even pronounce. But Nate reminded him of when Dr. David was struggling through chemistry, how he not only helped him get through that course, but helped him study, and pass two other exams.

"C'mon, David. If it wasn't for me, you wouldn't even be a doctor."

David looked up at Nate skeptically. He pulled his prescription pad from his lab coat pocket, along with a pen.

"Fine," he said, scribbling something across the pad. "But if you can't ever get it up again, just remember, you asked for it."

Nate stopped at the soda machine just outside the doctor's office after getting the prescription filled next door. He grabbed a Coke, and downed a handful of the pills. Two days later, he had gotten what he wanted. Nate was impotent.

Every night since that day, he had tried and failed to have sex with his wife, knowing both the terrible physical and psychological effect it would have on her.

27

The next day after work, there was something very important Nate had to take care of, so he left work early, considering there was really no new client he had to stay late for, as he had told his wife.

Nate drove south in the new Mercedes S500 he had bought only three days ago, while dialing Lewis's motel room on his cell phone.

"Don't go anywhere. I'm going to be picking you up in half an hour. I have something to show you."

When Nate pulled up in front of the Red Roof Inn, Lewis was standing outside his door.

Nate pulled in front of Lewis and allowed him to climb into the car.

"How have you been, Lewis?" Nate said, not liking the look of the boy. "Looks like you haven't been getting much sleep. Is everything okay?"

"Everything is fine, Mr. Kenny," Lewis said, giving him a quick glance, then looking out his own window. "Just been sitting in that room for the last week, waiting for everything to happen."

"So, you okay with what we've been talking about?"

"Yeah," Lewis said, not turning his face away from the glass.

"I didn't hear that."

Lewis looked around at Nate, then said, "Yes, Mr. Kenny. I'm all right with it."

It didn't seem that way, Nate thought.

Two days ago, while Nate was enacting his plan, he called Lewis, told him he was picking him up, because there was something very important they had to discuss.

Nate drove them to the first bar he came across. It was a small place called Taylor's, and as they walked from the car toward the front door, Nate said, "I hope you don't mind, Lewis, but I did a background check on you."

Lewis looked surprised, looked as though his head had just filled with a million questions.

"You're probably thinking how I did that, I know. But I have your license, remember. And there were some things that I just had to know about you."

Lewis continued to look at him, unable to speak, as though in shock.

"But I'm glad to see that you've never been to prison, aren't a violent person, and haven't committed any crimes—that is, other than not having insurance, then ramming me from behind." Nate pulled the door open, a kindly expression on his face. "But we'll talk about all that after we grab a drink. After you," Nate said, waving Lewis in.

After Nate had ordered a scotch on the rocks, and offered to get Lewis something several times, which the boy refused, Nate decided to discuss the matter at hand.

"I've been thinking hard about this over the last couple of days, and I've found a way for you to pay me back for my car."

Nate noticed a grave look in Lewis's eyes. "Don't worry, I'm not asking you to kill anyone, or anything like that."

"What is it?"

"There's a job I want you to do for me."

"What kind of job?"

"I want you to get to know someone. A woman."

"That's all?"

"I want you to really get to know her. I want you to get to know her so well that eventually you will have sex with her."

"Mr. Kenny, who is this woman?"

131

Nate thought about keeping this information from him, but he would eventually have to know, so it might as well be then.

"My wife," Nate said, grabbing his glass and quickly kicking back the last of its contents. He set the glass down on the table hard, then looked up at Lewis, who had an unbelievable look on his face.

"Do you have a problem with that?"

"I . . . I . . ."

"Spit it out, Lewis. Is there a problem?"

"I don't think that's a good idea, Mr. Kenny."

"I didn't ask your opinion, Lewis. You wrecked my car, you begged me to work something out with you, and I'm doing that. This is the offer. Either you accept it, or you know what the consequences will be."

Lewis pushed a nervous hand through his long hair, shook his head.

"Why you want me to do this?"

"I'm seeking a divorce from her, and this is the way it has to happen," Nate quickly answered.

"But why?"

"That's nothing that you need to concern yourself with."

"You want me to get to know your wife, and sleep with her. I got to know why," Lewis said, not backing down.

Nate grabbed his glass as though he was preparing to drink from it, realized again that it was empty, then dropped it hard back onto the table. He motioned impatiently for the waitress to get him another.

"I want children, and she can't have them. There," he said. "Now you know."

"Don't you think—"

"I said, I'm not asking for your opinion on the matter," Nate said, knowing that he was about to give just that. "You asked me why, and I told you. So do we have a deal?"

"I don't think I can, Mr. Kenny. I'm sorry, but—"

"I'll pay you."

Lewis looked up at Nate, his attention arrested. "How much?"

"I don't know. How much will you be requiring?"

Lewis looked at Nate as though he was joking, and when Nate didn't say anything, Lewis continued looking at him, although differently, as though he was assessing just how much money Nate could've had, how much he could've afforded considering the car Lewis wrecked was a Bentley, and the one Nate was now driving was a giant Mercedes.

"Ten thousand dollars a week," Lewis threw out, knowing that it would be rejected.

"I can't do that."

"Then maybe we shouldn't—"

"But I'll do half," Nate quickly finished.

Lewis stopped what he was saying in midsentence, his mouth hanging slightly agape.

"What do you say to that, Lewis? Can you do it now?"

Lewis mouthed a word, but no sound came from his lips. He swallowed hard, shock still in his eyes, then said very slowly, "Yes, Mr. Kenny. I think I can do it now."

Now Nate was eyeing Lewis sitting beside him in the Mercedes, wondering if he for some reason had lost heart, was planning on going back on the deal they made a few days ago. After all the work Nate had done, it would be a huge mistake if that was what the boy had in mind.

But then again, Nate was quite confident that after Lewis saw what Nate had to show him, whatever fear the boy was feeling would quickly disappear.

When Nate finally parked his Mercedes, they had stopped in front of a beautiful brick brownstone, sitting on a quaint, tree-lined street, just west of downtown.

"Get out," Nate said, stepping out of the car himself.

Nate walked down the path leading to the house, Lewis following behind him.

"My wife has been married to me for four years, and although she doesn't come from money, and does not have much of her own, I don't believe she would go for any man who was not ridiculously paid, like myself."

Nate stepped up to the door, pushed his key in, unlocked it, and opened it to reveal a huge, open living room, spilling into a dining area. The floors were hardwood, the ceiling stretching overhead some twenty feet, where there was a loft.

The place was brand-new, still smelled of paint and floor wax.

Nate and Lewis walked in; the sound of their heels against the floor echoed throughout the space.

"This will be your home. It's one of many buildings I own. Can never have too much investment property," Nate said, giving the key to Lewis, then closing the door behind both of them. "I would take you for a tour, but there's plenty of time for you to do the exploring yourself. All the utilities are on, as well as the cable. Furniture will be delivered later. I'll call and let you know when to expect it. Understand?"

"Yes," Lewis said, obediently.

"There's something else. Follow me."

Lewis followed Nate through the dining room, through the kitchen, and out the back door. They walked out onto a wooden deck, just built, down some stairs, and through a small backyard, out to the garage.

From his inside breast jacket pocket Nate pulled a remote, clicked it, and the garage door started rolling up.

There inside the garage was a brand-new black Cadillac Escalade, equipped with all the options, and even aftermarket chrome wheels.

"How does your generation say it? This truck is sittin' on dubs." Nate smiled at his use of slang. "I'm not a fan of these things myself," he said, opening the driver's side door, where keys hung in the ignition, "but I know it's what guys your age drive. It's on loan to me from a dealership I've sent a lot of business to, but if you do what you're supposed to, then it's yours."

Nate pulled the keys from the ignition and tossed them to Lewis.

Lewis caught them, looking as though he didn't know just what to say or think about this entire situation.

"So, how do you feel so far?"

"I don't know how to feel, Mr. Kenny."

"Well, in the matter of a week, you went from being homeless, penniless, and potentially facing a lawsuit that would land you in prison, to making five grand a week, living in one of the most up-scale neighborhoods in the city. You should feel overjoyed."

Nate walked Lewis back into the brownstone, and into the kitchen. There on one of the counters was a shoe box. Nate lifted the top, and pulled out its contents, one at a time.

"These are your business cards," Nate said, lifting a small rubber-banded block of cards and handing it to Lewis. "You're a real estate developer, and your investments are only worth a couple of million, but that's better than I was doing at your age, so it's acceptable.

"Here's your bankbook, and information on an account I started for you. There's also a gold credit card linked to it, along with a check card. Use it when you're out with my wife, as though you're accustomed to having good credit. Paying cash for everything is how these thugs who make their money unlawfully do it. We don't want her getting ideas that that is who you are."

Nate grabbed a cell phone out of the box. "This is yours. It's turned on, powered up, ready to use. The business number on your card will ring at my office. There someone will answer the phone, claiming to be your secretary. At that point, if it's business hours, the call will be directed to this phone, and you'll answer it, as the president of your real estate company, 'Waters Real Estate.' Not 'Wass-up? This Lewis,' but 'Waters Real Estate.' Understand?"

"Yes," Lewis nodded.

"Also, here is a two-way pager, just in case I need to contact you that way. Finally, here are some photos of my wife."

Nate handed four shots of his wife to Lewis. Two were close-ups, the others were from when they vacationed in Brazil. Monica was suntanned, and clad in the skimpiest white thong bikini.

"Wow," Lewis said slowly, almost breathless. "She's beautiful."

"The last two shots I threw in for your benefit. Added motivation."

"What's her name?" Lewis said, still speaking softly, not taking his eyes away from the pictures he scanned in turn.

"Monica," Nate said, snatching the photos away from him, uncomfortable with the way Lewis was salivating over them. "You'll have time to further acquaint yourself with these later. Now comes the important part. In your bank account, I've deposited another five thousand dollars, a clothing allowance, if you will. My wife works at a clothing store downtown. You'll walk in there, wanting to buy some suits; that's how you'll meet her."

Nate passed Lewis a card, which he examined. "The address and phone number are there. She works days. Nine to five. She is the manager. Buy something suitable to wear when you walk in the store for the first time, but from then on, I want you to buy everything from my wife. But not all at once. If there are four suits you like, buy them over the course of four days. This will give you more opportunity to get to know her, endear yourself to her. Understand?"

"Yeah. I think so, Mr. Kenny. When do I go there?"

Nate took a moment to think about it. "I don't see anything wrong with tomorrow."

"Tomorrow! I haven't had time to—"

"You don't need time to do anything. For the past week, I've been treating my wife as though I barely know her. She's used to me being a very affectionate person, so right now she's probably starved for any attention at all from a man. All you have to do is go in there, be the player that I know you can be, buy a suit, and come on to her in the process."

"But, Mr. Kenny—"

"Lewis," Nate said, grabbing him by one of the shoulders. "You're putting way too much thought into this. Forget about me, about the money, about the fact that this is my wife. Act as though you're walking along and you just happen to see a beautiful woman. What would you normally do?"

"What?" Lewis said, as though he didn't understand the question.

"If you see a fine woman on the street, what would you do!"

"I'd talk to her."

"Exactly! That's what I want you to do in this case. Talk to my wife. But she's there every day, so you don't have to rush in, trying to win her over the first time you see her. It'll take some time. You want to grow on her, so making ground a little bit every day will be what works."

Lewis nodded his head at what was told to him.

"So, tonight and tomorrow, I want you to get used to living like this is your life. Go out, spend some money. Buy yourself some stuff, a little something to wear as well. The first five thousand for the job is already in your account, along with the additional five for clothes, so there shouldn't be any problems. But if something does come up, don't hesitate to call, no matter what time. Do you understand all of this?"

"Yes, Mr. Kenny," Lewis said.

"And get a haircut. A successful businessman would not walk around with that bird's nest atop his head. Okay?"

"I'll do that."

"Good. Everything is in play," Nate said. "Now we do what needs to be done, and just see what happens."

28

Monica sat with Tabatha at the bar of a popular downtown restaurant. It was after work, happy hour, so the place started to fill with men and women in business attire. They crowded in, leaning over the bar, raising hands with dollar bills clasped in them, wanting to order drinks.

Tabatha and Monica had already gotten theirs, were working on their second, because they had left straight from work, and got here in time to get good bar seats.

It was Tabatha's idea. She had approached Monica toward the end of the day.

"You got plans after work?" she asked.

"No."

"Then you need to go with me to get a drink."

"What are you talking about?" Monica said.

"You've been funky all day. I don't know what's going on with you, but you can tell me once we get out of here. First round is on me, okay?"

After they had sat down at the almost empty bar, Tabatha ordered both of their drinks, then turned her stool toward Monica, a polite smile on her face.

"Now tell me what's wrong."

Monica took a moment to think. "I don't know what's wrong. My husband, he—" Monica stopped what she was saying when the bar-tender placed the drinks in front of them.

Tabatha passed him her credit card. "Start a tab, please." She pushed Monica's glass in front of her, grabbed her own, and took a drink. "Go on."

"It's like he's not my husband anymore. Over the past week, he's been coming in late, he barely talks to me, he shows me no sign of affection, and we haven't had sex in I don't know how long."

"What!" Tabatha said. "Why is that?"

"Because he can't. He says it's stress from this new client that's keeping him out late, but . . ."

"But what?"

"I don't know what to make of it. I try to ask him, but he says there's nothing wrong. What do you think?"

"Do you really want to know what I think?"

"Of course."

"He's cheatin', girl," Tabatha said without hesitation.

"No, he's not. How could he be having sex with someone else, when he can't even have it with me?"

"Maybe he can't have it with you *because* he's having it with someone else."

"I don't believe that, because I don't have proof, and that's what I would need to just all of a sudden distrust my husband."

"But why—," Tabatha tried to say, but was cut off when Monica turned to her, and firmly said, "He's not cheating, all right!"

"Oh, okay," Tabatha said, backing off some, grabbing her drink and turning on her stool to face the bartender.

The room started to fill—standing room only—professional men and women standing in small circles, drinking, talking, and laugh-ing.

"It's getting pretty tight in here," Monica finally said, after her few moments of silence.

"Uh, yeah," Tabatha said, turning to meet eyes with a man across the room that she noticed had been checking out Monica for some time. "And I think this guy that's been checking you out is coming over here to talk to you."

Monica turned in the direction Tabatha was looking, and saw the guy approaching.

"Shit," Monica said, under her breath, then turned away. A moment later, a handsome brotha in a blue suit, holding a drink, was standing beside her.

"How you ladies doing today?" he said, directing the question more to Monica.

"Fine," Monica said, not even looking into the man's face.

"You are really looking nice. I love your hair," he said, but again Monica didn't look up, just said, "Thank you."

The man looked around Monica over at Tabatha, as if for direction. Tabatha hunched her shoulders, as if to tell him he was on his own.

After a few more moments, the man said, "If I'm being a bother, I can just leave you alone. I didn't mean to interrupt you."

"I'm sorry," Monica said, finally looking into the man's eyes. "It's not you. I just have some things on my mind, okay."

The man smiled, dimples appearing in both cheeks. "I understand," he said, then extended a hand. "Well, my name is Terrance. It was nice meeting you."

Monica shook his hand. It was soft. He turned and walked away, and she watched him for a few moments, then swiveled back around to face Tabatha.

"He was beautiful," Tabatha said. "I wonder what Nate would think if he found out you were cheating with him."

"I wouldn't cheat on Nate."

"Oh, yeah. Wouldn't want to get caught, and forfeit all that money that would be due you."

"If I were to cheat, Tabatha, I wouldn't get caught. It's not about the money. I just wouldn't cheat on my husband," Monica said, very seriously.

"Yeah, but if you were to cheat," Tabatha said, looking out into the crowd to locate the man again, "that would be the one to cheat with, because he was fine."

Monica looked at Tabatha, the stoic expression still on her face.

"All right, girl. I know you won't cheat. But c'mon, give it to me, the man was fine, right?"

Monica all of sudden smiled, and said, "Oh, yeah. He was fine as hell." She held up a palm and received an energetic high five from Tabatha. Then almost immediately, Monica become melancholy, introspective, grabbed her drink, took a sip, then said, "Like I said, I wouldn't ever do it, but I can understand why some women do. With that one compliment that man gave me, and the touch of his hand, I feel closer to a complete stranger right now than I do to my own husband."

29

Nate sat comfortably on Tori's sofa, his stocking feet kicked up on the coffee table, the television remote in his hand, as he watched a rerun of a popular nineties sitcom.

His belt was unbuckled, the clasp on his trousers undone, for he had just finished enjoying a huge dinner that Tori had made them.

"Hey, baby," Tori said, stepping into the living room. She must've finished putting the food away and washing the dishes. She was smoothing lotion into her hands as she walked to him, and sat down beside him.

"It's so good to have you here like this. You'd think after seeing you all day at work, and then you coming back to my place for a week straight, I'd get sick of your butt," Tori said, smiling. "Who would've thought I could've tolerated you like I have?"

"Tolerate?" Nate said. "You know you love it."

The smile left Tori's face, something more serious appearing there, as she looked deeper into Nate's eyes. She moved closer to him, kissing him on the lips. "Yes I do, Nate. I do love it."

"Then why do you look like that?" Nate said, caressing her face.

Tori pulled away from him. "Because I don't want to get my hopes up. I'm getting used to you being here, but what if it doesn't really happen? You've been coming over here after work, but what if your wife gets suspicious, all of a sudden?"

"I told you she won't. I told her there's a client that I'm working

142

with that's requiring me to stay at work late for the next couple of weeks." Nate reached out for Tori, grabbed her, pulled her back next to him, wrapping his arm around her shoulder.

"And the two weeks—why do you need that? Because you're still unsure if you really want to get the divorce?"

"If I was unsure, I wouldn't be here. If I was unsure, I wouldn't have done what I did with you that night last week when we had sex. You never told me what became of that."

"I took a test. I'm not pregnant."

Nate felt relieved to hear that, but also felt the slightest bit of disappointment. "I see," he said.

"And why haven't we made love since then?"

"It's all part of this plan I have going."

"Plan? What plan?"

Nate told Tori everything. How, if he just asked his wife for a divorce, she would be entitled to millions of dollars, which Nate still could not see himself parting with. He told her the reason why they hadn't made love was that he couldn't. He had been taking a heavy dose of the prescription pills he had gotten from his doctor friend, and they had definitely rendered him impotent. Nate told Tori that staying away from Monica would make her more vulnerable to the advances of this character Lewis he had literally bumped into, put up in a house, and was paying to seduce his wife.

"Is it worth all that?" Tori asked, concern in her eyes. "Maybe you should just tell her you don't want to be married to her anymore. Maybe she wouldn't want any of your money."

Nate gave Tori an unconvinced look. "If things were turned around, and it was you I came to, saying I wanted a divorce because you couldn't give me children, you wouldn't want any of the money your attorney said you would be entitled to?"

"Well, if you put it like that. But what happens after she cheats? If she cheats?"

"I hire a private investigator, document it, then file for the divorce."

"Will it work out?" Tori said, Nate hearing what sounded like desperation in her voice.

"Yes."

"Are you sure?"

"I hope so."

❧

While Nate was driving home, he realized how dependent Tori was on him. He wasn't sure how he felt about that, but knew that it was partly his fault. He was the one that told her he wanted her to have his children, tried to get her pregnant to prove it. He was the one that told her she'd one day be his wife.

Since he'd been seeing her, he'd brought her home flowers practically every day he'd come over there, filled her fridge with groceries, and before leaving every night, asked how she was doing with money.

"I don't need anything. You pay me enough at work, Mr. Kenny," Tori said, kissing him on the cheek at the door before he walked out.

But those weren't the only reasons why Tori seemed to be heavily relying on the success of Nate's plan. While they were lying on Tori's sofa the other night, candles lit around them, she confessed something.

"I need to be honest with you," she said. "When you said you knew that there was no one in my life, you were wrong. There was a man that I've been seeing."

Nate sat up some on the sofa, intrigued. "And . . ."

"I had been seeing him for the last two years, but he thought there was more to it than I knew there was. He wanted to marry me."

"And what did you tell him?"

"I never told him anything, because I knew I really didn't love him, but I didn't want to be by myself the rest of my life, so I made him wait."

"Until . . ."

"Until last week, when you came to me. The very next day, I told him it was over."

"Are you sure about that?"

"Yes."

"But it was two years," Nate said.

"Nate," Tori said, adjusting herself so she could look into his eyes. "My mother left me when I was a child, and my father died, leaving my grandparents to raise me. After that, I had abandonment issues. After you left, I told myself I'd never trust another man again. But if you tell me that I can, I will."

"You can," Nate said. "You can."

When Nate opened the door and stepped into his house, Monica was on the living room sofa, her legs stretched out onto the coffee table, watching TV as she sipped from a glass of wine.

Nate closed the door behind him, and Monica stood. "Hey, baby," she said, a cheery smile on her face.

Nate took another step in, then felt that something seemed not quite right. Monica was wearing some bright red lace bra-and-panty getup, covered by a long, sheer nightgown. She walked seductively toward him, and through the garment's material, Nate could see the dark circles around his wife's nipples, the dark patch of hair between her legs. Her face was completely made up, and her hair was done, as though she had just spent the last half hour at a cosmetics counter, and some time before that at a hair salon. She stopped in front of him, wearing matching red heels that had to have been three inches high.

With the wineglass still in one hand, she extended her arms. "Well, aren't you going to give me a hug?"

Nate set his briefcase down and stepped into his wife's embrace.

"I missed you," Monica whispered into his ear.

"I missed you as well," Nate whispered back, with not nearly as much passion.

She grabbed his hand, pulled him into the living room, and sat him down on the sofa. "This is a good movie," she said, sitting down on the coffee table in front of him. "It just started."

She lifted his feet, one at a time, into her lap, untied and pulled off each of his shoes.

"You comfortable?" Monica asked, standing before him now.

"Yeah, sure," Nate said, having not the slightest idea of what was going on.

"Are you hungry?"

"Uh, no. I ate out with my client."

"Then do you want some wine? I opened a fresh bottle."

"No."

"Mixed drink?"

"No."

"Beer?"

"No."

"You have to want something. Let me get you something," Monica practically pleaded.

"Okay. A glass of water, please," Nate said, and watched as Monica took the long way around the coffee table, as though she were modeling her new nightwear for him.

When she returned, she handed Nate the glass of water, a paper towel wrapped around it.

She sat down beside him quietly, but still Nate felt on guard. He took a sip from his water to appease his wife. She smiled at him, as though happy he was enjoying it, then he set the glass down, and told himself he would watch a little of the movie since it was on, and his wife gave it a good endorsement.

Five minutes later, he felt his wife occasionally taking a glance at him, but Nate simply ignored her.

Monica must've sensed that, and was offended by it, for five minutes later, she stood up from the sofa. "So, you aren't even going to compliment me, are you?" she said, her hands on her hips.

"Monica, what are you talking about?"

"I'm talking about me! This!" she said, gesturing with a hand at her hair and outfit. She walked in front of the TV, blocking it, at what happened to be a very good part in the movie, then said, "I did all this. Bought a new night set, did my hair, my makeup, just so you would have something nice to look at when you got home from a hard day's work, and you don't acknowledge it, act like you don't even care."

"I care," Nate said.

"Then why didn't you say anything about it?"

"I noticed you the moment I walked in the door."

"Then why didn't you *say* something? Would it have been too much for you to do that?"

Nate didn't answer.

"Are you even attracted to me anymore?"

"Of course I am," Nate said.

"You don't act like it. You don't look at me anymore. Don't touch me, kiss me. Nothing. You act like you're sharing this house with your brother or something. So I'm asking you again, are you still attracted to me?"

"And like I said before, yes."

"Than prove it," Monica said, slipping the sheer gown off her shoulders, and letting it fall to the floor. She slid her panties down from her hips, and let them fall as well, stepping out of them. "Prove it to me. Make love to me, right now," she said, then unclasped her bra, letting her breasts fall naturally in front of her.

"Come over here and make love to me."

"Monica, you've been drinking."

"I know I've been drinking. That's one of the reasons I'm so damn horny. But the other is that you haven't given me dick in a week. Now come over here and do it to me!"

"I can't."

"You can. You say you're still attracted to me. What is the problem?"

"There's a lot on my mind. Still stuff with the baby, the adoption you asked me about."

"Forget about that!" Monica insisted. "The baby is over with, and don't even worry about the adoption. Right now I don't care if we ever do that. All I'm thinking about is you and me, you inside me. I want to feel you, know that I still do it for you. Now come over here and fuck me!" Monica demanded, practically yelling.

Nate shot up from he sofa. "I can't!" he yelled himself.

Then there was silence, as he and his wife stood across from each other, the coffee table between them, Nate fully clothed, Monica stark naked.

"Then what is it, are you gay?"

If his reason for doing this weren't so serious, Nate would've probably laughed at what was just said to him.

"No."

"Then what, Nate? What? Make me understand, so I know how to behave, know what to expect."

Nate paused a moment before answering, then simply said, "It's stress." He grabbed his glass of water from the table, took a sip, set it back, then turned and headed for the stairs. "Don't forget to turn the TV off before you come up."

30

Before going to bed, Lewis looked over the photos of Mr. Kenny's wife several times. The pictures were propped up against his clock radio.

The first time he looked over them, he told himself it was preparation. He was studying the woman because he wanted to be able to pick her out in a crowded room. The next time when he grabbed the photos, he knew it was more than him familiarizing himself with the woman's appearance. That time, he was gazing at the woman in the photos, almost admiring her. As he looked closer at the images, the photos only inches from his face, Lewis wondered what she was thinking at the time each one of the pictures was taken.

In three of them, she was smiling, looking genuinely happy. In the other, she appeared simply content. She wasn't smiling, but Lewis thought that the look on her face said that there was nothing more that she wanted than what she had at that moment.

Happy and content summed up the four photos, but he wondered, wherever she was, was she feeling that way now? Considering all that her own husband was going through, all that he was paying Lewis, she couldn't have been feeling the same way. She had to have been feeling just the opposite.

Why would her husband be doing this to her? This woman was not only amazingly beautiful, she was probably the sweetest thing in the world, probably loved the hell out of that bastard husband of hers, and Lewis was about to help him do something that he knew was incredibly wrong.

That moment, Lewis told himself he couldn't do it. He reached for the phone that lay beside him, preparing to call Mr. Kenny and tell him the entire thing was off.

But then Lewis thought about everything that was going on in his life. He needed that money, because with it, he figured, he could get his own place. A place where he could take his daughter and raise her the right way.

Lewis set the phone back down, knowing that he had to go through with it. His sorry circumstances had tied his hands.

Still staring at the photos of Monica, he apologized to her for what he would soon do, leaned across the bed, clicked off the lamp, and called it a night.

Upon waking up this morning, grabbing the photos again was the first thing he did. He looked at them for only a moment, slid open the nightstand drawer, placed them in, and closed it.

There was no more time for questioning himself. He had to do it, whether he liked it or not.

Lewis took a hot shower, brushed his teeth, shaved, and combed his now short hair.

Yesterday evening, after Mr. Kenny left, Lewis did as he was told, going out and buying something he could wear when he met Mrs. Kenny today. He went to the bank first, stopped at the Gap, bought one pair of khakis and a shirt, then jumped in his truck to have his hair taken care of.

He pulled the big Cadillac up to the curb just in front of Classic Clippers' huge storefront window. All the barbers stopped what they were doing to check out the truck with its gleaming chrome wheels, and when Lewis stepped out of it, he saw them point and shake their heads.

Lewis activated the alarm on the truck, and walked into the shop. He nodded at a couple of the barbers, said, "What's up?" to two more, then headed directly over to Beasly's chair.

"Haven't seen you around in a couple of days, boy," Beasly said, clipping the stray ends from off the top of a graying man's head with a pair of shears.

"Yeah, a lot's been going on. Do you think you can give me a cut when you're done with him?"

Beasly looked over Lewis suspiciously, glanced out at the Cadillac sitting outside the store, then said, "Yeah. I don't see why not."

When Lewis finally did sit in Beasly's chair, the old man threw the cape around the front of Lewis, secured it around his neck, then asked, "How do you want it?"

"I don't know," Lewis said. "Short. Businesslike, whatever that is."

"Taper the back, close at the temples?"

"Yeah. Sounds good."

Beasly grabbed his clippers, was preparing to start on Lewis's hair, when Lewis said, "I'm here to get a cut, but I also wanted to tell you that I ain't gonna be working here no more, and I got the money to pay you my booth rent." Under the cape, Lewis pulled out a small wad of money, pealed off four hundred-dollar bills, folded them, and offered them to Beasly.

"Your rent is only half that."

"I know, but I just wanted to thank you for helping me out when you did."

"By that car you driving, and the money you trying to hand me, look like you don't need no help no more."

"No. I don't," Lewis said.

"I wonder why that is. If you out there doing what you ain't supposed to be doing, I don't want your money, not even what you owe me."

"I ain't doing nothing like that, Beasly. I'm just doing what I got to do, but it ain't nothing like that. Now just take the money," Lewis said, still holding it out for him.

"I said, I just want the two."

"Fine," Lewis said, keeping half the money back and handing the other two hundred over to Beasly.

Both men remained silent for the duration of the haircut. Beasly pulled the cape from around Lewis and gave him a mirror. Lewis gave his new haircut a quick glance, liked what he saw, then stood up from his chair.

He dug back in his pocket to pay Beasly, when the old man said, "Don't worry about it. That one's on the house."

"Thanks," Lewis said. "For everything." Then he turned and headed for the door."

"Lewis," Beasly called.

Lewis turned around, just after he pulled the front door open.

"If you doin' the wrong thing out there, it'll catch up to you," Beasly warned. "Trust me, it'll catch you, boy."

After that, Lewis walked out the door.

Now, this morning, Lewis stood in the living room of his brand-new temporary housing. He looked over himself in the full-length mirror. His khakis were neatly pressed, the button-down shirt made him look like an overgrown schoolboy, but his hair didn't look as bad as he thought it would.

He slapped some grease into it, took a brush and a wave cap, and when he was finished, he had a clean-cut style, with thick, shiny waves running over the top of his scalp.

He smiled wide into the mirror, and his teeth appeared straight and white behind his lips.

"Well," Lewis said to his reflection, then sighed. "This is it." He walked to the front door, pulled it open, then walked out.

✿

The store where Monica worked was not hard to find, but he had to park his truck in a garage and walk the two blocks over. He stood across the street from the store on Michigan Avenue, practically on the curb, just staring at it, as cars whipped back and forth in front of him.

It was 9:30 A.M. Morning traffic was still heavy, but Lewis told himself he wanted to get to the store early, hoping that he would be the only customer there, and wouldn't have to share Mrs. Kenny's attention with anyone else. He knew he would need time to make his impression, and he didn't want either of them to be rushed.

The name of the store was AERO. Huge black letters hung over the plate glass windows announcing that he had the right place.

When the traffic signal displayed the illuminated walking figure, Lewis quickly crossed the street. He walked right up to the door, grabbed the handle, and was all of a sudden frozen with fear.

What if she sees right through me? Lewis thought. What if she somehow knows that I was sent by her husband, knows about everything we spoke about? What would I do then?

But there was no way, he tried to reason, tried to force himself to believe. It was just his nerves talking; and then, trying to find a way to calm down, he asked himself why was he tripping. Just a little while ago, he was standing around looking like a fool, begging people on the street to cut hair for $15, and now he's getting paid five grand a week to come on to a beautiful woman. He felt a slight surge of confidence flow through him, and then he pulled the door open and entered the store.

When Lewis walked in the store, it immediately reminded him of the town house he was living in. It felt like someone's home. He walked across the hardwood floors, trying to appear as though he was accustomed to walking into places like this, and headed for a rack of suits.

To his left was the store's checkout counter, and there was a slim sister standing back there, writing something with a pen. It wasn't Monica, he knew right away. She looked up from what she was doing, gave Lewis a smile, which he returned, and then he kept on walking.

A funky, jazz-soul-like music played at a low level throughout the store, which further helped to relax Lewis as he browsed through the countless suits on the rack before him, but he wondered if he had walked into the wrong store.

He started to feel a little anxiety build inside him, wondering what he should do next, when someone said, "May I help you with something?"

Lewis spun around, and was shocked to see Mr. Kenny's wife standing just before him.

It was her! He couldn't believe it. The two-dimensional woman from the photos was now standing just in front of him, and it was amazing how little justice those snapshots did to this woman's appearance.

What he saw before him was a tan-toned woman with jet black hair pulled back into a ponytail. Her skin was flawless, radiant. Her lips were full, and pink, a beauty mark lying just to the left corner of her mouth. She stood somewhere between five two and five four, just the height Lewis loved his women, and the shape that Lewis saw under that floral spring dress was that of a goddess.

All of that caused Lewis to stutter when he tried to answer Mrs. Kenny's question.

After tripping over his words a number of times, Lewis finally said, "I'm looking for a nice suit."

"Well, then you came to the right place," Mrs. Kenny said, smiling. "Follow me."

Lewis watched her walk away, slightly transfixed by the smile she had given him.

When Mrs. Kenny turned around and found Lewis not behind her, she called, "Uh, sir. Follow me, please."

"Oh, yeah," Lewis said, quickly following behind her.

Fifteen minutes later, Monica opened up one of the dressing rooms, and hung three suits on a hook for Lewis.

Lewis stepped in, and before closing the door, Monica said, "Okay, Lewis, let me know if you need another size, and I'll grab it for you, okay?"

"Okay," he said. She had asked Lewis's name, after she had pulled the first suit she wanted him to try on. "And my name is Monica," she told him, extending her hand for him to shake. Lewis did, and almost tripped up and told her he already knew her name was Monica.

But since then, he barely said two words to her, afraid that he would say the wrong thing, or that she wouldn't be receptive to what he did say to her.

Lewis looked at himself in the mirror as he started to undress, already starting to accept the fact that he was failing at the task that was given to him. He pulled off his shirt, stepped out of his pants.

He couldn't fail, he told himself. He was getting paid a ridiculous amount for this, and besides that, if he was successful, he would end up one day making love to that beautiful woman walking around out there.

Just the thought of that started to make Lewis grow just a little bit within his boxer shorts. Yeah, he had to do something that would tilt things his way, he told himself.

He looked at himself again in the mirror, saw that his muscles all still looked pretty tight from his intense workout a week ago, and without giving it any more thought, he opened the dressing room door and walked out into the store.

He called Monica's name, but the person whose attention he had gotten was the woman who was standing behind the counter when he first walked in.

She was draping clothes across a sofa when she turned and caught sight of Lewis half naked, his muscles bulging and rippling under his dark brown skin.

Tabatha stood up straight, her mouth falling open, her eyes ballooning.

"Have you seen Monica?" Lewis said, naively. "I need another size."

Tabatha didn't answer right away; it didn't even seem to Lewis that she had heard a word he said, because all of her attention seemed to be directed toward his crotch.

"Excuse me," Lewis said again. "You see the woman that was helping me?"

Just then, Monica came from around a corner. "Oh! Lewis, I'm sorry," she said, hurrying toward him, trying to turn her head away at the same time. "You can go back into the dressing room. What size do you need?" she asked, sounding slightly flustered, after he walked back in.

"Forty-eight."

"Okay. Be right back."

Lewis pressed up very close to the door when he heard the women's voices.

"Girl! Did you see all that brotha had going on!"

"Shhhhh! Come over here," he heard Monica say. "He might hear you."

"I don't care. He knows what he has. And if he doesn't, I'd like to point it out to him."

Lewis laughed, shaking his head, and waited till Monica brought back his correct size.

Fifteen minutes later, Lewis wore the suit he had chosen, facing a three-way mirror as Monica placed the last straight pin in the hem of his trousers. She stood up and walked behind him, and checked the waist of his jacket to make sure she marked that right, along with his shoulders and arms.

"Okay. That's perfect. The tailor will have this ready for you tomorrow," Monica said.

"You really like it?" Lewis said.

"Yeah. It looks good on you. It accents your broad shoulders."

"Thank you," Lewis said, smiling. "How about that tie over there?"

Monica pulled the tie Lewis was referring to from the shelf, and draped it over one of his shoulders. "Yeah, this look good. You want it?"

"I want to see how it looks on first."

Monica held out the tie to him.

"Can you do it for me?"

Monica looked at Lewis oddly for a moment, then said, "Sure."

She slipped the tie under Lewis's collar, then stood just in front of him measuring the two sides.

"You know, I'm kinda embarrassed to say this, because I know you get it all the time," Lewis said, "but I think you are very beautiful."

"Well, thank you," Monica said, avoiding eye contact with him.

"I would really like to get to know you better."

"I'm sorry, but I'm married," Monica said, halfway through with the tie.

"You're husband's a very, very lucky man. I hope he's treating you right."

Monica's motions stopped for a moment, as if a thought entered her head, then she continued.

"Does that mean he's not?"

"That doesn't mean anything," Monica said, looking up at Lewis. "If it means anything, it's that it's none of your business how my husband treats me."

"Then how about we be friends? Who doesn't need a friend to talk to every now and then?"

"You know, that's the lamest line in the book," Monica said, pulling on his tie, tightening the knot. "You get an F for originality for that one. There. The tie looks good. See."

Lewis turned around to face the mirror.

"Now go back in the dressing room, take off everything, and I'll make sure the tailor gets it."

"You sure you don't want to help me?"

"Oh, I see you're a clown. Bring the stuff up front when you're done, please, sir," Monica said, chuckling, waving him off.

Lewis closed the door of the dressing room and started to disrobe, actually feeling pretty confident about himself. Yes, he was blown off, but she wasn't angry or offended by his come-on. She laughed him off, and even though it seemed like forever since he really made an effort to get with a new woman, back in the day, his game was pretty tight.

Joking as though he really wasn't interested in them, but making women sure that they always had the option to accept his advances if they eventually became interested, was how he found himself between the thighs of many women.

He would just continue to play it that way, and if Mr. Kenny continued to hold up his end, then everything should work out just as they planned.

31

Lewis Waters was the name on the card he had given Monica, after he had paid for his suit.

Monica looked down at it as she was waiting for his receipt to print out.

"Oh, real estate developer, hunh?"

"Yes." Lewis nodded.

"Well, I won't be needing any real estate anytime soon, so I guess I won't be needing your card." She handed it back to him.

"Keep it anyway. My office number is on there, as well as my cell phone, and I've written my home on the back, just in case," he said, playfully winking.

"You are a trip," Monica said, handing the man his receipt. "You can pick that up anytime tomorrow."

"What time will you be here?"

"You can pick it up whenever. I don't have to be here."

"I know. I just want to see your smiling face again."

"Good-bye, sir," Monica said, waving him off, walking away from the counter.

Tabatha still stood there, eyeing Lewis, a sly smile on her face.

"See you tomorrow." Lewis waved.

"Byyyyye," Tabatha said, dreamy-eyed, waving good-bye.

When the store door closed, Tabatha rushed from around the

counter and into the storeroom, where Monica was pulling some garments out of plastic.

"Did you see that brotha!"

"Yes, I saw him," Monica said, not turning around, and not equaling Tabatha's excitement.

"Did you see his body!"

"Yeah. Saw that too."

"Well, what did you think?" Tabatha said.

"Why does it matter what I think?"

"Because he obviously has a thing for you."

Monica turned around, garments stacked in her arms.

"Not to sound high on myself or anything, but practically every guy that comes in here is hitting on me or you. Why should he be any different?" she said, walking past Tabatha and out of the store-room.

"Because he was, like . . . wow!" Tabatha said. "You see his abs? You see that smile?"

"Naw, I didn't notice all that."

"And that's why you were like, Aw, you so crazy, sir. Laughing at all his jokes, batting your eyes at him," Tabatha said, making fun of Monica.

"I was not."

"And you were blushing, smiling all up in his face."

"I don't know what you're talking about, girl," Monica said in denial.

"I'm sure you'll have a better idea of what I'm talking about tomorrow, then."

❧

When Monica walked in the store that next morning, she hoped Tabatha wouldn't notice, but the woman immediately busted her out upon seeing her.

"Oh! Did a little something different with your hair. I wonder why that is?"

"Maybe because I got tired of the old style I was wearing," Monica said.

"And it has nothing to do with Mr. Real Estate Developer, who you know is coming to pick up his suit today?"

"Get back to work, Tabatha."

When Lewis did return, he greeted Monica with that wide, white grin of his, giving her a compliment the moment he set eyes on her. "Hey, I love the new hairstyle," he said. And it happened to be the right compliment at that.

"Thank you," Monica said, unable to stop herself from smiling.

From the corner of the store, she felt Tabatha give her a look, which Monica did not acknowledge.

"So, I believe your suit is ready, sir," Monica said, walking from behind the counter and toward the tailor's suite.

"Would you stop calling me 'sir'? My name is Lewis," he said, before agreeing to follow her.

Monica stopped, turned back to face him, then said, "Okay, then. Your suit is this way. You can follow me, Lewis."

"Okay, but first, I think I saw another one I might be interested in."

He tried on the suit, liked it, and Monica went about the task of measuring him, marking and pinning the suit while he wore it. All the while, he complimented her on every little thing he could think of. He commented on how nice her hands were, how pretty her nails were.

"You must work out," he said. "You have such a slim figure . . . I love your voice . . . it's too sexy . . . Don't ever change your hair. It's perfect just like that."

Monica really tried to keep herself from blushing, from smiling, but all the while she was working on his suit, she could not help herself. Maybe because his flirting wasn't offensive. It wasn't like he was some construction worker on a corner, a jackhammer in his grip, flicking his tongue out at her, yelling, "Hey, pussycat. I'd love to stroke your fur."

No, this was a successful, handsome, polite man, who was buying his second suit in excess of $700. And then there was the fact that he was funny, interesting, and she enjoyed his company. Monica figured if she wasn't helping Lewis out, she would be doing the same for some other guy, so why not let it be him?

Then Monica realized that the true reason she was so receptive to this man's flirting was simply that she was not getting it at home, when she had grown so accustomed to it.

This morning, when she was walking into the kitchen, her husband had seen the new hairstyle but said nothing of it. Barely lifted his head out of the paper long enough to verify that it was his wife walking about, and not some stranger.

But this Lewis guy picked up on it the moment he stepped in the store.

At the register, Lewis had the suit he bought yesterday thrown over his shoulder, and Monica had given him back his credit card.

Lewis took the card, slipped it into his wallet, then said, "So, I'll be back tomorrow to pick it up."

"Sure," Monica said. "And thank you." She was still smiling as she watched him turn and walk toward the door. He stopped just before reaching it, looked down at his watch, then turned back and approached the counter again.

"You know," Lewis said, "I feel hungry all of a sudden, and after checking my watch, I see it's lunchtime. You want to grab something with me?"

Right before he finished the question, Tabatha was walking out of the storeroom. She stopped in her tracks and stared up at Monica, as if waiting to see what her answer would be.

She didn't decline right away, but finally said, "I don't think that's such a good idea."

Lewis looked over at Tabatha, then back at Monica. "Are you sure? Just a little harmless lunch. I swear I won't try to cop a feel under the table."

Monica let out an uncomfortable laugh. "No. I brought some stuff in Tupperware anyway, but thanks."

"Okay," Lewis said. "Guess I'll see you two tomorrow."

After he left the store, Tabatha said, "It was just lunch."

"Yeah, right," Monica said.

The next day Lewis came, he bought yet another suit, Monica marked it, and they spoke some more. This time, deeper things, like where she went to school, what did she want to be when she grew up, and not quite so many compliments, although there were enough to have her smiling and blushing again. And after their ritual was over, it was lunchtime again.

"So how about today? Lunch?"

"No. I don't think so," Monica said, feeling just the slightest bit guilty about turning him down, because he was so nice, had bought three suits from her, and she figured, if they could have a good time while she stood around and hemmed his pants, lunch would probably be a blast.

So the next day, the fourth day in a row that Lewis appeared at the store, he did not sway from the routine. Again he bought another suit, and again he proposed they go for lunch.

Tabatha was standing beside Monica at the counter, and she said, "Yeah, you should go. It's slow around here."

Monica cut her eyes at Tabatha, then said to Lewis, "I had a big breakfast, so I'm okay."

Lewis smiled. "Okay, I'm going to do something different, then. I'm telling you today that I want you to eat lunch with me tomorrow. That way you'll know not to have a big breakfast."

"Lewis, I really—" Monica tried to say, but was stopped.

"Nope. I just lost my hearing. I'll be back tomorrow to pick up my suit, and to have lunch with you. See you then, and bye, Tabatha."

Lewis left the store, and left Monica looking evilly at Tabatha.

"I like him" Tabatha said, "because he never forgets to say goodbye to me. He makes me feel included."

"To hell with your inclusion," Monica said. "Why are you trying to convince me to go to lunch with that man? Have you forgotten, I'm married?"

"Excuse me. I'm not the one you need to be reminding of that. That seems to have slipped your husband's mind."

"Nate hasn't forgotten anything."

"So you guys are all lovey-dovey again? Everything back to normal, is it?"

"Not quite."

"He kisses you every morning before leaving for work, tells you how much he loves you, and makes passionate love to you every night before going to bed?"

"I can't remember the last time he told me he loved me. Can't remember when he paid me my last compliment, and I almost forget how sex feels, it's been so long, but—"

"But what?" Tabatha said. "No one's telling you to sleep with this Lewis guy. You obviously have fun with him. I hear you guys laughing like crazy while you're marking his suit. Hell, go to lunch with the man. He's crazy about you, and he lets you know it. If your husband don't want to stroke your ego, let another man do it. You don't have to spread your legs to say thank you. Just say, 'Thank you,' and walk your ass back here to work afterward."

Monica took in everything that Tabatha said. And in many ways she was right, but still Monica shook her head, and said, "Naw. If I'm going to lunch with a man, it should be my husband."

"Okay. Okay," Tabatha said, picking up the phone and handing the receiver to Monica. "Dial up old Nate, and tell him that you want to have lunch with him today."

Monica looked hesitantly at the phone. "I don't know. Maybe—"

"No," Tabatha said, forcing the phone into her hand. "If you're going to lunch with a man, then it should be your husband. Dial the numbers, Monica."

Monica dialed Nate's number, got his secretary, and surprisingly, a moment later was speaking to Nate. Tabatha stood beside her, intently listening.

"Yeah, baby. I was wondering if you wanted to go to lunch today . . .Well, I can go whenever . . . Then I can just come over there," Monica said, turning away from Tabatha, who was staring right into her mouth. "No, it's really not a problem. I could just pick up something, and we can eat in your office, like we used to do sometimes . . . Well, are you sure, because . . . Yeah . . . yeah . . . I understand . . . Okay, I won't wait up. Good-bye."

Monica slowly handed the phone over to Tabatha, who placed it back onto its base.

"So?" Tabatha asked.

"So, what? You heard what happened."

"So you'll be going to lunch with Lewis tomorrow. It's just lunch, like I said."

"No," Monica said. "I'll be going to lunch with my husband tomorrow."

"Is that what he said."

"No. But he'll be taking me. Trust me."

32

Nate hung up his office phone, picked it back up, and quickly dialed another number.

When the phone was picked up, Nate said, "Lewis. Are you somewhere you can talk?"

"Yes."

"I just got off the phone with my wife. She seemed adamant about me taking her to lunch. Exactly what's going on?" He had just spoken to Lewis yesterday, as he had been doing every day to keep abreast of Lewis's progress. The boy told him everything he was doing, and Nate approved his steps, but the phone call from Monica today made Nate feel he needed to check in.

"Nothing's going on, Mr. Kenny. I just been asking her out to lunch like I told you. But today, I told her I was taking her whether she liked it or not. That's all."

Nate didn't like the idea that Lewis felt he could demand anything of his wife, but he was paying the boy to get results, and if that's what he had to do to achieve them, then so be it.

"And that was it?" Nate said. "You aren't moving too fast?"

"No, Mr. Kenny. I'm only doing what I told you I was."

"Okay. And that's the way it's going to continue. I don't need you messing all of this is up, by trying to make decisions on your own. Understand?"

"Yes, Mr. Kenny."

Nate hung up the phone without as much as saying good-bye.

Just then, a soft knock came at the door. Tori entered the office. She set a file on his desk, then said, "Mr. Hiller wants to know if he can push back his appointment with you half an hour. He said he believes he'll be late."

"That's fine," Nate said, barely looking up from his work.

Tori was about to turn and leave, but she halted, looking at Nate oddly for a moment.

After feeling her standing there, just feet from his desk, Nate looked up.

"What is it, Tori?"

"Is everything okay? You look angry."

Nate paused to think about what Tori had said, and sure enough, he felt that his eyebrows were furrowed, his facial muscles tight. He made an effort to smile.

Tori walked back over to Nate's desk, a smile on her face. "That's better," she said. "And I had a wonderful time last night." She turned, walked out of his office, Nate watching as she closed his door.

Nothing out of the ordinary happened last night. Tori made dinner as she always did. They ate, watched a little TV, drank a little wine, and then lay around in the dark, him holding her, while Tori dreamed aloud how life would be once Nate divorced his wife. She mentioned repeatedly her excitement about having his children, and Nate didn't know if she did that on his account, or if she really looked forward to it that much.

"It is still going to happen, isn't it?" Tori said, looking into his face to see his response. She made a point of continually checking the status of what was going on between him and his wife.

"Yes, it is still going to happen," Nate said. He would guarantee that, and that's why he had quickly called Lewis after he had received the call from Monica.

When Nate had gotten home that night, after spending the evening with Tori again, he walked into his bedroom to see Monica sitting up, waiting for him, even though he specifically told her that she didn't have to.

Nate glanced at the clock on the nightstand, seeing that it was just minutes to 11 P.M.

He pulled off his jacket and tie, and draped them across a chair that sat in the corner.

"You're still up," Nate said, heading toward the bathroom.

"Yeah, I need to talk to you."

"All right, I just have to—"

"I need to do it now. It'll be quick."

Nate stopped just feet from the bathroom door, and said, "Okay. What is it?"

"Lunch tomorrow. We need to go."

"I can't," he answered right away.

Monica appeared thrown by the abruptness of his answer, then asked, "Why not?"

"Because I have work."

"You don't get a lunch break? C'mon, Nate, you're the president. It's not as though you have to ask permission."

"And you don't think I know that?"

There was an awkward silence, then Monica said, "Considering how things have been between us, I don't think I'm asking too much to want my husband to take a break from his busy fourteen-hour day and take me to lunch."

"Monica, I can't get out tomorrow, okay," Nate insisted.

"Then I'll come to you."

"That won't work, either."

"It *won't* work, or you don't *want* it to work?" Monica said.

"And what do you mean by that?"

"Nothing. I just really need for you to take me to lunch tomorrow," Monica said, almost desperate.

"What's the big deal about tomorrow?" Nate said.

"There is no big deal," Monica said. "I just need you to take me."

"Well, it's not going to happen."

Monica dropped her head in defeat. "Are you sure?" she said, looking sadly now at him.

This was the moment, Nate thought. This was his wife giving

him his last chance before she ventured down a path that could lead to their marriage changing, and he knew their future more or less lay in his hands. He could tell her that, as a matter of fact, he could make room. He would take her to lunch, call Lewis tonight, cancel everything, and then Nate could do whatever it took to put things right back with his wife.

Or he could let the course of events continue as they had been, by simply saying, "I'm sure. I won't be able to go to lunch with you tomorrow." Which is exactly what he said.

Monica looked even more disappointed, and said, "Okay. Thanks for trying."

Nate turned, stepped into the bathroom, and closed the door.

33

The next morning, when Lewis knocked on Selena's door, he was surprised that she answered, considering he had been missing her every time he tried to stop by there.

What surprised him more was the huge smile on her face, once she saw that it was him standing in front of her.

"Hey, Lewis. C'mon in," she said.

Lewis stepped in, feeling weird for some reason, unable to remember the last time he had gotten this sort of reception.

He looked around, noticed that the place wasn't nearly as dirty as the last time he had seen it, but it still could've used a little attention.

"So, you lookin' good," Selena said, eyeing him from head to toe. "Got a new haircut. I like it." And now she was slowly walking around him. "And got some new clothes."

He was wearing jeans, a jersey, and a pair of T-MACs, all stuff that he had bought the other day. But judging by the way that Selena was checking him out, he could've been wearing one of the expensive suits he had bought from Monica.

"Where's Layla?" Lewis said, not responding to Selena's compliments.

"She's in the room."

"Can I see her?"

"What's the rush?" Selena said, grabbing Lewis's hand, walking him to the sofa, and sitting him down there. "I haven't seen you in more than a week."

"Whose fault is that? I've been coming by here like crazy."

"I know. And I got what you left me last time you was here."

Last time Lewis came by the house, and didn't find Selena there, he slipped $300 in an envelope and slid it into the locked mailbox.

"I ain't just left it for you, but for you and Layla. Did you pay the bills?"

"I did what I could with it, but it was only three hundred," Selena said, looking sadly toward the floor. "I would need some more to take care of everything." She looked back up at Lewis. "You think you got any more?"

Lewis shook his head, wishing that there was someone else he could give his money to, so he would know that it would benefit his baby, but he would just have to trust Selena.

"Where you getting all this money from, anyway? I know you ain't cutting heads like that at the barbershop."

"It ain't important where I get it, as long as I have it," Lewis said.

"Can you let me hold some more . . . to pay the bills with?"

"Get Layla. Let me see her first, and then I'll see what I can do."

Selena sprung from the sofa and hurried into the bedroom. When she came back out, Layla was in her arms, the child sleeping. She gingerly handed over the baby to Lewis, who thankfully took her.

"She ain't get to bed till early this morning, that's why she still sleep."

Lewis thought of asking her, just why in the hell was that?—what was she doing up until early in the morning?—but figured, what good would it do?

"You can wake her up if you want. She'd be happy to see her daddy."

"Naw. She needs her sleep," Lewis said, lowering his face to kiss her softly on the cheek.

He held her for a little while longer, then passed her back to her mother.

Selena took her back into the bedroom, then returned and sat back on the sofa.

Lewis pulled another $300 from his pocket, money he knew he would be giving Selena when he planned to come over here.

Before he handed the money to her, he said, "I want to take her with me next time I come by."

"What do you mean, take her with you?"

"I mean, spend time with my daughter away from here, at my place."

"I don't even know where you live."

"You didn't seem worried about that when you threw me out," Lewis said, still resenting that action.

"I still don't know. I have to think about that," Selena said, as if this was causing some huge dilemma.

Lewis reached into his pocket, pulled out his wallet, and with Selena watching closely, fingered out another hundred-dollar bill, and placed the four hundred in her hand.

"Can I take her next time, or what?" Lewis asked again.

Selena smiled, folded the bills, and slid them under the sofa cushion she was sitting on.

"Yeah. You're her father. You can take her."

Lewis gave Selena a long look, hating how he was considered Layla's father only when he paid to be.

He stood up. "Then I'll call to let you know when. I hope you have the phone on by then."

Lewis walked around the table to the front door.

"Hold it," Selena said, quickly following up behind him. "You leaving already, and you ain't even giving me no hug."

Lewis didn't say anything, just stood there, allowing Selena to throw her arms around him. She pressed hard up against his body. "I missed you," she said.

"Okay," Lewis said, not caring a bit.

Selena leaned away some to look into his eyes. "You know I do, right?"

"Okay," Lewis said again.

Then Selena all of sudden pressed her lips into Lewis's, trying to stick her tongue into his mouth, before he pulled away.

"What are you doing?"

"I told you, I missed you, and it feels like you missed me too," she said, her hand grabbing him in between the legs.

Lewis stepped back from her. "You don't know what you talking about."

"Then let me show you what I'm talking about. Let me thank you for the money you been giving me." She was at his pants again, this time trying to undo his belt buckle.

Lewis grabbed both of her busy hands, held them firmly up to her chest.

"Selena, I ain't give you that money so I can have sex with you again. I gave it to you so you can take care of our daughter, so you can take care of the things you need to get done around here. You got that?"

Selena looked into Lewis's face as though she hadn't comprehended a word of it, then said, "You don't want to stay just a little while?"

"I ain't those men that you been fuckin', okay? Yeah, I gave you money, but you don't owe me nothing but to take care of Layla."

"Oh," Selena said angrily, yanking her hands away from Lewis's hold. "So you lookin' down on me for doing what I had to do."

"Selena, I'm not gonna get into this with you."

"So you better than me now, because you got a little money?"

"Selena, I told you—"

"Fuck you, then! I was just trying to show you a little appreciation, but since you don't want it, fuck you!"

Lewis stood in front of her, not saying a word, sorry that it had to be the way it was between them.

"So I'll call you when I want to come and pick Layla up."

"I might be home," Selena said.

Lewis turned and walked out.

When he walked in the door of AERO later that day, the episode with Selena was still on his mind. He was disappointed with how it went down, but he was hopeful that she would keep her promise, and let him take his daughter like she said.

It was five minutes past noon when Lewis stepped up to the counter, to see just Tabatha standing there. He felt that there was probably more disappointment on the way, thinking that she would tell him that Monica wasn't there, that she had stepped out to lunch only moments ago.

But when Lewis asked, "Is Monica here?" he heard a voice answer from behind him. "Right here, and ready to go to lunch," she said, walking near him, looking very beautiful, wearing slacks and a waist-length denim jacket. Her hair was still the way he liked it, and she had her purse on her arm.

Lewis was shocked, wondered what changed her mind, but he wouldn't concern himself with that. Just be happy that she was willing to go.

They ended up at the Cheesecake Factory, just down the street from where she worked.

Surprisingly, they were seated, and had already been served drinks, and their food orders had been taken just fifteen minutes after they arrived. Lewis sipped on a raspberry iced tea, but he was surprised to see that Monica had ordered a glass of wine.

"So, you really look beautiful today," Lewis said, sincerely.

"Thank you." Monica smiled. "But you're the one looking like a million dollars. Could that be a new suit you're wearing?" Monica joked.

Lewis had specifically picked the best of the suits he had just bought from her store to wear today. "Naw, just some old getup I thrown on to hang out in."

They both laughed a little, then Lewis said, "I'm glad you decided to come to lunch with me. What finally changed your mind?"

Monica took another sip from her wine. "Stuff. Just stuff, is all. But what's your story? Why were you all bent on getting me out here, wouldn't take no for an answer?"

"Because over the week that we've been getting to know each

other, I found out that you're a sweet woman, with a great personality, ridiculous body, and as gorgeous as she want to be."

"And there's a zillion more just like me walking down Michigan Avenue. Only difference is, is that they're single. So why would a handsome, successful, kind brotha like yourself be pursuing me?"

"Who said I was pursuing you?" Lewis said. "We're having lunch. When did that become pursuit?"

Monica smiled, shaking her head. "Okay, so you want to play games. Lewis, you've been in my store every day this week."

"Buying suits."

"You couldn't buy all four suits in one day? No," Monica answered for him, "you had to stretch it out so you'd have a reason to come back and see me, right?"

"I like the store."

"Right."

"And like I said, we spent a lot of time together, and it's been fun. Don't you think?"

"Yeah," Monica hesitated to say. "It has been fun. But why me? You still haven't told me."

"I already gave you all the reasons, and then there's the fact that it's you. No one else is like you."

"Oh, you are so full of it. Lewis, you can tell me. It doesn't matter. Nothing's going to happen between us. I'm a happily married woman. See," Monica said, displaying her ring, as if he hadn't already seen it. "I just want to know, what's your deal?"

"Are you happily married?" Lewis questioned.

"What difference does it make?"

"I don't know. None, I guess. I was just wondering, because that time I asked you, it looked like you got sad all of a sudden."

"Then I'll say that yes, I'm happily married, but a marriage isn't always going to be happy."

"I'm guessing that this is one of those times when it's not."

Monica looked in Lewis's eyes, as if almost ashamed to give her answer. "Then you're guessing right."

Lewis felt sorry for her. "If there's anything you need, anything I can do for you, you know you can always ask."

"And just what could you do for me, Lewis?"

"I don't know. Anything. I just don't want to see you sad. It just makes me feel like giving you a hug. Yeah, that's what I can do," Lewis said, pushing back in his chair.

"Lewis, don't you get out of that chair. I'm fine."

"A hug has never hurt anyone," Lewis said, standing and walking around the table, wrapping his arms around Monica, rocking her back and forth, giving her an exaggerated hug.

"Lewis," Monica said, laughing, smothered under all his affection, "get off me, boy!"

"There," he said, giving her a fat kiss on her forehead as she continued to struggle. "That'll make it all better." He stepped back around the table and took a seat.

"How's that?" he said.

"Gee, Lewis, thanks. I feel so much better."

After Lewis had walked Monica back to the store from lunch, and picked up his suit, they stood outside the doors, talking.

"So, same time tomorrow?" Lewis asked, hopeful.

"No. This is not going to become a habit."

"Okay. Well, did you have a good time? Enjoy yourself?"

"Yes. I had a very good time, and I'm glad I changed my mind," Monica said.

"Good, I'll see you whenever, then."

"Okay," Monica said, seeming uncertain of how she was feeling about that.

They stood facing each other for another moment of silence, then Lewis spread the one arm that he wasn't holding the suit with, and said, "Well, do you think I can get a hug good-bye?"

Monica didn't answer right away, then after a moment said, "Sure. Why not?"

She moved into Lewis, gave him a hug. Lewis pressed her body gently but firmly into his, and he was thankful that she didn't give him the old "just friends" pat on the back. He hated that.

They pulled away from each other, and Lewis had to stop himself from leaning in and kissing those full, pink lips of her.

"Okay then, whenever," Lewis said.

"Whenever," Monica said in return.

She turned, about to go in the store, as Lewis walked away, but then he stopped.

"Monica."

She turned back around, and Lewis hurried up to her. "You know, I wasn't going to ask you this," Lewis said, digging into his pants pocket and pulling out something. "But I figure, I can't get anybody else to go with me, I might as well ask my new friend."

"Ask your new friend to go where?"

Lewis held up two tickets. "*The Lion King*. I've been wanting to check it out, and I got tickets for tomorrow night, but I have nobody to go with me. I was wondering—"

"No, Lewis," Monica said, shaking her head. "I can't."

"Are you sure?"

"Positive."

Lewis sighed and looked at the ticket in his hand. "Here, take it."

"I said, I can't—"

"Just take it," he insisted.

Monica took the ticket from him.

"I'm not asking anyone else to go, so just hold on to it. I know you can't go, but if you happen to, at the last minute, be able to make it, then I'll just see you there. How does that sound?"

"It sounds just like it sounded before, Lewis, because I can't go."

"Then what are you doing tonight?"

"Definitely no. I have big plans for tonight."

34

Much later that evening, Monica looked down at her watch. It read fifteen minutes after eleven, and she still didn't want to do it, but she reached down, undid the tiny buckle on her pumps, and slid one of the shoes off.

The shoe was a beautiful black-and-silver one that Monica had bought three months ago and had never worn, because she wanted them to be brand-new for this occasion.

They matched a beautiful evening gown she had worn only once before, and that was to celebrate her first wedding anniversary with her husband. She was hoping that it would create some kind of magic, him seeing it on their fourth wedding anniversary, which was tonight. But that didn't happen, because Nate never came home. He didn't even call.

Monica pulled off the other shoe, threw the shawl from her shoulders, and kicked her feet up, then stretched out across the sofa in the evening gown.

Maybe she should've reminded him, she thought now, but she had never had to do that in the past. For the three previous years, there was never any mention made of it; she would just be ready on that night. Nate would come home from work, take her out, and they would have the most wonderful time.

Monica figured she didn't call Nate because she was just being hopeful. Hopeful that, regardless of all that they had been going through, he wouldn't let some things change. The fact that he still loved her, the fact that he still honored their marriage and wanted to show her that, especially now, should've been enough to keep him from forgetting. But obviously it wasn't.

As Monica sank deeper and deeper into the cushions of the sofa, she had to stop herself from thinking that maybe Nate didn't forget at all. Maybe he knew it was their anniversary, and just decided to remain with his client anyway, or do whatever it was he was doing at that moment.

If that was the case—if he really stopped caring that much about Monica—then she'd . . . she'd . . . An image of Lewis invaded her mind.

Off and on she'd think about him, think about lunch. It was the only thing that brought a smile to her face while sitting there practically four hours waiting on Nate to show.

❦

"So," Tabatha had said, standing in the center of the store when Monica walked back in after lunch. "How did it go? What did he say?"

"I don't know what you're talking about," Monica said, walking right past Tabatha.

"Oh, no you don't," Tabatha said, catching her. "What happened?"

Monica didn't know why, but she felt giddy, giggly, like a teen with a crush.

"It was nice," she said, trying to suppress her smile.

"Nice? That's all there is?" Tabatha said, unsatisfied.

"What more do you want? We had hot sex in the men's room of the restaurant."

"Oh, girl! Did you!"

"No, fool. We had lunch, and that's it." Monica started to walk away.

179

"That's it?"

"Well," Monica said, stopping and turning around slowly. "He did give me a ticket. He had the nerve to ask me out to see *The Lion King* with him tomorrow."

"So what did you tell him?"

"What do you think I told him? No."

"Really." Tabatha sounded disappointed.

"Really. Everybody seems to keep forgetting I'm married."

"But that's a hard ticket to get, and I heard it's really good."

"So I should cheat on my husband, because *The Lion King* is good?"

"Well, he's cheating on you," Tabatha said.

"My husband is not cheating on me!"

"Might as well be, considering how he's treating you."

"Well, he'll have his chance to make all that up to me tonight," Monica said.

"You think he's going to actually remember your anniversary?"

"Of course," Monica said. "He's never forgotten in the past. And I sure as hell didn't forget. I've had his gift wrapped and sitting on my shelf for a month now."

"And what if he does forget?"

"He won't."

"But what if he does?" Tabatha insisted.

"Then I'll . . . ," Monica said, giving it some thought.

"You'll what?"

"I'll be mad as hell."

"And what else?"

"I'll . . . I'll . . . I'll . . . sleep with Lewis!"

"Ohhhhhh," Tabatha said, her eyes bulging as she threw her hand over her mouth. "You would not!"

"He is really nice, and you saw how good he looks in his drawers."

"You wouldn't!" Tabatha said, slapping Monica across the shoulder.

"Naw, I wouldn't," Monica said, slyly.

"Would you?"

Monica got up off the sofa, walked across the living room floor in her stockings, and grabbed the purse she had carried to work all week. She dug through it and pulled out the ticket Lewis had given her. She went back in the purse, found his business card, and pulled that out as well.

She walked back over to the sofa and placed both cards on her knees. The phone was sitting beside her, from when she had been considering calling Nate to ask him if he had forgotten about their night. But she had decided against it.

Monica flipped the business card over, saw Lewis's home number there, and thought for a moment about calling him, but then told herself no.

Just what in the hell was she doing—was she thinking? Everybody had forgotten that she was married, including herself.

Monica lifted the cards from her lap and set them down on the coffee table, telling herself she wouldn't think any more about it.

But again, an image of the man popped into her mind. She thought of when he came from around the table at lunch, gave her the big bear hug, and kissed her on the forehead. That made her laugh, and a bit of a chuckle escaped her lips that moment.

She was thankful for that, for that brief respite from her sadness, and as the smile slowly faded from her lips now, her attention was drawn again to the cards.

Monica looked at the time. It was almost quarter to twelve. She looked at the door—no one was coming through it, and that made up her mind.

She knew it was late, knew the man was probably sleeping, but Monica grabbed the phone from beside her and dialed his number anyway.

35

When Monica woke up the following morning, Nate lay beside her. She did not wake him, didn't nudge him even a little. She simply slid out of bed, showered, got dressed, and headed downstairs to make herself something for breakfast before she went to work.

She made herself some oatmeal with fresh fruit, along with a glass of orange juice and a cup of yogurt. When she brought it out to the dining room table, Nate was sitting there wearing his bathrobe.

Monica paused in the entrance to the room, the food in her hands, then proceeded to sit down as if he wasn't there.

She dug her spoon into her oatmeal, was about to lift it to her mouth, when she heard her husband say, "You could've made me something."

Monica's movement halted, the spoon floating an inch from her lips. She wanted to say something, wanted to explode, but what was the point, she reasoned, and just stuck the spoon full of food into her mouth, ignoring him.

Nate opened up yesterday's *Wall Street Journal*, which was sitting on the table beside him, and created a barrier between them.

Monica glanced up at him hiding behind the paper, wondering why he still hadn't given her an explanation for last night. Again, she considered confronting him about it, but didn't.

She finished most of the food, but after a while, just didn't want to sit there at the same table with her husband anymore. She gathered her bowl, cup, and glass, quickly washed the dishes, and headed out of the kitchen to grab her purse and coat for work.

As she approached the door, she still couldn't believe her husband continued to sit in that chair, reading that paper as though there was nothing that had to be talked about.

Monica grabbed the front door handle, opened it, and was about to walk out when she heard, "Monica."

She looked over at her husband.

Nate lowered the paper. "I'm going to be home late again tonight, so don't wait up. I just thought you should know that," he said, then raised the paper back in front of him.

And that was what made it impossible for Monica to hold her tongue any longer. "Just thought I should know that!" Monica said, angrily slamming the door. "Did you ever think I should've known that you were going to stand me up on our anniversary?"

Nate lowered the paper again.

"I had a lot of things on my mind. It wouldn't have been a good night for that."

"You could've come home anyway. We didn't have to go out," Monica said, furious. "We could've just been together."

"I felt like being alone."

Monica was immediately silenced by his selfish response. "Oh," she said. "You felt like being alone."

"That's right."

"So if I felt like being alone, stayed out all night, and didn't call you to let you know whether I was dead or alive, that would be just fine with you?"

"You're a grown woman."

"Oh!" Monica said, not just shocked now, but terribly saddened. Because it no longer sounded like he was just being selfish, but as though he just didn't care.

"I see," Monica said, trying to hold back tears she knew would fall. "I see now. I see perfectly." She stared at her husband a long

183

time, letting him see just how hurt she was, while hoping that he would say something to, in some way, try to make up for all that he'd done. But he did not.

Monica opened the door and walked out.

❧

"I called him last night and told him I would go with him to see the show," Monica told Tabatha later that day at work.

"Nate forgot about your anniversary, didn't he?"

"He didn't forget," Monica said, lowering her head. "He said he felt like being alone."

"Aw, sweetheart," Tabatha said, hugging Monica.

Monica hugged her back, feeding off just the touch of another person. "I hate him so much right now," she said.

"Then you're going out with Lewis just to spite your husband?"

Monica leaned away from their hug and said, "I don't know."

"You aren't going to sleep with him, are you?"

Monica looked Tabatha seriously in the eyes and said, "I don't know that either."

When Monica finished work, on the walk home, she called Lewis from her cell phone.

"Are we still on?" she asked him. He enthusiastically said yes.

Monica gave Lewis her address, and told her to meet him around the corner from her building. "Call me when you're a block away, and I'll meet you down there."

Lewis told her what type of car he drove, and Monica continued on her way home.

She picked out one of her more seductive dresses, one that fit just right all over, showed a little cleavage, but not too much, and just the right amount of leg. Her shoes were sexy, opened-toed to show off her recent pedicure, and the bra and panty set she would wear tonight were Nate's favorite. Or at least they used to be.

Monica styled her hair just the way Lewis liked it, but let a single long curl hang over her eye and into her face. After she was completely dressed, she sprayed herself with her favorite perfume, grabbed her purse and coat, and headed for the door.

Just then her phone rang. It was Lewis letting her know he was waiting outside, around the corner.

When she approached his truck, he was waiting by the passenger door, looking as handsome as she could've imagined him, in one of the new suits he had just bought. He was smiling widely, and when she was just a few feet from him, he opened his arms and took Monica into a huge hug. Monica hugged him back.

"You look incredible," he said, his lips pressed very close to her ear. "And you smell too good!"

On the ride to the theater, Lewis kept looking over at Monica, almost gazing at her at red lights, down at her legs, at her hair. He complimented her the entire trip, so much that if she hadn't been so neglected recently, she would've gotten sick of the constant doting. But she didn't. Monica loved every minute of it.

The seats Lewis had for them were fourth row, center. They could see everything.

They arrived twenty minutes before the opening curtain, so they sat, talked, and laughed until the lights above them dimmed.

They shared an armrest, their arms touching the entire time during the play. But in the second act, Monica felt Lewis graze her hand with his. She thought nothing of it until moments later, when he had lightly covered her hand, and then he had taken it, wrapped his hand completely around hers, holding it as if they were a couple.

Monica thought of yanking out of his grasp, thought allowing him to touch her like that was wrong, was disrespectful. But sitting there beside this man was wrong and disrespectful. Giving him her phone number, allowing him to pick her up, to hug her the way he did, everything that she had done to this point, and what she still considered she might do, was equally wrong and disrespectful, so why should she object to something as innocent as him holding her hand?

Monica slowly turned to look at him. Lewis looked back at her, and they both smiled.

After the show, and after they had found their way back to Lewis's truck, they stood outside it. It was 9:30 P.M., and he said, "Did you like it?"

"It was wonderful, Lewis. Thank you so much for inviting me."

"I'm just glad you decided to come."

They stared at each other oddly for a moment, then awkwardly looked away.

Lewis looked down at his watch again. "So I guess this is it. I should be getting you back, hunh?"

"No. I don't have to go back now."

Lewis looked surprised. "Oh. You want to get something to eat or drink?"

"No," Monica said, thinking a moment to make sure she was certain about what she was about to say. "I want to go back to your place."

⁂

When they walked into Lewis's town home, he had Monica by the hand, pulling her along into the dark living room. He closed the door, pulled her over toward the sofa.

"Let me turn this on," Lewis said, reaching to click on the lamp there before they sat down, when Monica said, "Don't. I want to go to your room."

Again Lewis looked shocked, and Monica had seen that expression in various degrees over the course of the night.

He looked at her, both of them still standing in the dark. "Are you sure?" he said.

She thought about herself waiting all night for her husband to show, thought about his worthless explanation this morning, then said, "Yes, I'm sure."

He turned, grabbed Monica's hand again, and led her upstairs.

Behind him, Monica continued to tell herself she was certain of what she was about to do. She wanted to cause Nate pain.

It wasn't like he would ever find out about it, but whenever he said anything hateful or uncaring to her, whenever he acted as

186

though she just wasn't there, or deserving of his attention, respect, or love, then she would think back to what she did that one night with Lewis.

She would be able to say to herself, Yes, you're treating me horribly, but I've done something horrible to you as well, so we're even. That would make her feel better. At least she hoped it would.

Lewis's bedroom was dark, but not very. There were large glass sliding doors at the back of his room that let out onto a patio. Moonlight came in through there, haloing everything in the room with a silver glimmer of light.

They stood at the foot of his bed, Lewis looking down into Monica's eyes, and if she didn't know better, by his stare it appeared that he could have feelings for her. She was sure she misread that.

He continued to stare into her face, and then he slowly moved closer to her, as though he wanted to kiss her.

She wasn't there for that, Monica told herself. She was there to have sex, and nothing else, so she started unfastening his belt buckle.

"I want you," she said, trying to manufacture as much fake desire as possible.

Lewis stopped attempting to kiss her, and started undressing her as well.

Monica dropped his pants, felt him pressing hard through his underwear.

Lewis slid her dress off her shoulders, where it fell to the floor. He then helped her with the buttons of his shirt, pulling it off, together with his jacket, and throwing them to a corner. Then he undid her bra, looking down as her breasts fell from the cups.

She heard him gasp, and then he pushed himself into her, her bare breasts against his hard, broad chest.

His big hands held her back, slid down, following the contour of her waist, then down farther, cupping her soft bottom.

Again she heard him gasp, louder this time, and felt him pulsate against her thigh.

She was not turned on by that, Monica told herself, feeling the slightest twitch in the small of her back. This was sex, she reaffirmed, nothing more. She was not doing this for enjoyment, but to simply get back at her husband, for revenge.

Monica was caught off guard when he scooped her up by her behind, her legs inadvertently spreading, wrapping around his hips, and laid her on her back across the bed.

He stood just to the side of her, wearing nothing but his underwear now, the bulge in front looking as though it would tear through the fabric if it was not released.

Lewis stared down at her, savoring every inch of her body, and as he did that, he grabbed Monica's hand.

"I want you to feel something," he said, pressing her hand softly against his penis.

As he continuing gazing over her body, rubbing a hand gently over her soft skin, she felt his penis react, jump, pulsate, and grow even harder.

"Do you feel that?" he asked, his voice raspy now.

"Yes," Monica said, her voice equally low.

"I want you to feel more." He pulled down the front of his briefs, and let himself jump out at her. He placed her palm on it, wrapping her fingers around it, motioning for her to stroke it. He moaned, and Monica felt her nipples start to harden.

No, she told herself. That's not supposed to be happening.

He must've seen it too, for he reached down, grabbed one of them between his fingers, and gave it a slight pinch. It sent a jolt through her entire body.

"I want you," Lewis said, climbing on top of her.

"I want you too," Monica said, but did not know anymore if that was part of the act, or if her body truly desired him.

He clamped his lips around her left breast, sucked it so passionately that she felt those emotions that she knew he couldn't have felt for her. He sucked the other one, quicker, then slowing down as he pushed her legs apart with his knees, positioning himself to enter her.

Monica still had on her panties, but Lewis didn't seem to mind. He pressed himself into them as though they weren't there, and to her surprise, this excited Monica beyond her expectation. Her nipples were almost painfully erect, and she was now so wet that she felt there was a puddle growing between her spread thighs.

Lewis must've sensed this as his cue, and he pressed the tip of his dick into the thin fabric.

Monica's eyes widened, and she knew he couldn't have, but it felt as though the very tip, the soft, round flesh of him, entered her, and just at that moment, he lowered himself, pressing his lips onto her mouth.

Without thought, she eagerly accepted his tongue, pulled on it, as though it was him. She felt her arms, wrapped around his ass, trying to pull him down, tear through the damn panties she was too stupid to take off, and then, all of a sudden, she regained her senses.

"No," she said, turning her face away from his kiss.

"What!" Lewis said.

"I said, no!" And now Monica was pushing her palms into his chest, forcing him off her.

He moved, allowing her to quickly climb down from the bed and search the dark room's floor for her clothes.

"Monica, what's wrong?" Lewis said, standing out of her way.

"Nothing," she said as she continued filling her arms with her things. But there was something wrong. She was feeling that shit. *Really* feeling it. She was loving the taste of his sweet tongue in her mouth, wanting to feel the man's dick inside her, and it didn't matter if he had feelings for her at that moment, because something told Monica, if she had let him slide that thing up in her, she would've been on her way to falling in love her damn self, and she couldn't have that.

"Nothing's wrong," she said, again. "I just have to go."

"But—"

"Please, Lewis," Monica said, looking up at him. "Don't ask me. Just tell me where your bathroom is, so I can get changed and get out of here."

36

Twenty minutes later Monica was back home. She swung open the front door, called for her husband, peeling off her jacket, kicking off her heels, leaving them in her wake as she made her way farther into the penthouse.

"Nate, are you home?" she called again, not seeing him on the first floor.

Still flustered, her body warm all over, she took the stairs two at a time.

"In here," Monica heard Nate call. He was in their bedroom, was walking toward the door. Monica quickly closed the distance, threw herself into him, pushed him backward toward the bed. She landed on top of him, and immediately started at the buttons of his shirt, fumbling with them, unable to push them through the tiny slits. She resorted to tearing it open, the resistant buttons popping and flying from the garment, hitting the bedroom floor.

"What are you doing?" Nate said, sitting up, looking at her with wide eyes, shock in his voice.

"I want you," Monica said, her words barely understandable, for she was kissing, licking, suckling her husband's chest.

He made a weak attempt at pushing her away.

She wasn't having it. She locked her hands around his wrists, pressing them down on either side of his head, forcing her weight down on him more.

"I want you, and I need it, now!" she said, squeezing his wrists a little tighter, trying to convince him of that fact. When she felt him no longer struggling, she kissed lower, lower, to his belly button. She quickly undid his belt buckle, unzipped his trousers, dropped to her knees, and forced the pants to his ankles.

To her disappointment, he was not there, was not where he needed to be to satisfy her, where Lewis . . .

No! She wouldn't think about him, Monica scolded herself. This was not about him, about that. It was her wanting to have sex with her husband. She lifted his wilted member and told herself it was no problem. This time she would get him there if it was the last thing she did. But after endless pulling, rubbing, stroking, licking, and sucking, there was nothing.

She looked at him, frustration in her eyes, wondering why in the hell this was happening.

Nate looked back at her, only a blank expression on his face.

"It can't be forced. It won't happen like this," he said, again offering no apology. "We can try again tomorrow."

Monica stood, her hair, her clothes a mess. She looked down at him, wanted to tell him that she had been waiting for two weeks of tomorrows, and that considering the horny fit she was in right now—had been in for the last hour—even another minute was far too long to wait.

Monica turned, stormed out the door and down the stairs.

"Monica," Nate called, but that's all he did. He didn't follow, as she thought he would, as she was hoping he wouldn't.

She ended up on the main level in the bathroom—her bathroom. She slammed the toilet lid, flopped down on it, and dropped her elbows onto her knees, her face in the palms of her hands.

All this time she'd been going without, and now, when she needed him, really needed him, he still couldn't get it up. Betcha there wouldn't have been that problem with Lewis.

Stop it! Stop it! she told herself. But she could not. She didn't want to go back there, but something was calling her, demanding that her attention return, and it did. She was there again, in that man's bedroom, seeing what would've happened if she had stayed. The moonlight cast over them, his body on top of hers, her legs spread wide, and this time she would have her panties off. She would reach down just before insertion, wanting to feel again what she was getting, and then the thought became too much.

In the bathroom, Monica was down on her knees, swinging the doors of the vanity cabinet open, digging around there for the vibrator that she hadn't used in forever, and had been forcing herself not to use since Nate had been unable to make love to her.

She pulled out the V2000. "The ultimate vibrator for the new millennium," she remembered the box saying when it was new.

It wouldn't take long for her to satisfy herself, she thought, her panties around her ankles, her legs spread after turning it on, the thing going crazy, undulating and pulsating in her hand like something living, crazed, desperately trying to escape her grasp. But its cry was only a low hum, and she was thankful for that.

She spread her legs wider, kicking one bare foot up on the face bowl, and then lowered the machine, touching it to her clitoris. She immediately threw her head back, wanting to scream, it felt so good. Instead, she brought the device up, found the intensity control, and rolled its dial from six to level ten. The machine whined at a higher pitch, vibrated, and jumped about in her grip even more. She lowered it back between her legs, rested it on her spot, and let her mind be pulled back to the man's apartment, just after he would've entered her. The movements that she saw him making in her mind were mimicked by her with the vibrator, and each time his body swayed to the left, so did her hand—to the right, and the vibrator did the same—and when he hit her spot, concentrated on it, like she knew he was so capable of doing, she did the same with her toy. And now, in her mind, he was telling her that he wanted her to come.

"You gonna come for me? You gonna come?" he demanded in his sweet, raspy voice, his chiseled arms on either side of her head, his chest, ripped with muscles, just above her, as he continued sliding in and out.

Her answer was yes. "Yes, yes. Goddammit, yes!"

But just when she felt she would release, felt Lewis was ready to receive all she had to give him . . . a knock came at the door.

"Monica, what are you doing in there?"

Immediately she cut off the V2000, whipped her eyes toward the door, suppressing her heavy breathing, and questioning whether or not it was just her imagination, praying that it was.

"Monica, what's going on?" It was Nate.

"Dammit!" she said quietly to herself, then quickly dropped the machine out of sight, behind the toilet, as if he had the power to see through doors.

"Nothing. I was . . . uh . . . just shaving my legs," she said, hoping that would account for the humming noise he may have heard through the door.

"Why are you . . . ," he started, then seemed not to even want to pursue the question. "Can you come out here when you're done with that?"

She did after some time, and when she went upstairs, Nate said some things that she didn't pay any attention to, didn't care to hear, because all Monica could do was think about how she was going to get back in Lewis's bed.

37

Nate threw his Mercedes into park, pulled the key from the ignition, and slumped into the seat, hanging his head low. Outside his window, the faded sign reading "Taylor's Bar" hung high above him. He had a lot on his mind.

The other night, while at Tori's, the woman handed him an envelope.

"What's this?"

"Open it."

When Nate pulled the sheet of paper out, and unfolded it, he saw names and numbers printed on it. "And this is what?" he asked.

"The numbers of private investigators. You said you needed to hire one, but I haven't heard anything about it, so I thought I'd help you out."

"Did I say I needed your help?"

"You haven't been saying much about anything anymore, Nate," Tori said. "Do you still want this? Want me?"

"Yes," Nate said, becoming frustrated. "I keep telling you that, but this takes time. You can't speed this along, regardless how much you want to."

"You made me a promise, Nate," Tori said, looking depressed. "You're going to do what it takes to keep it, aren't you?"

"Yes, Tori. I told you I would, and I will," Nate said, feeling then that things were starting to get out of hand. With each day that passed, Tori was becoming more restless and demanding, and Nate would have to determine a way to settle her before she did something more than just compile a list of names and numbers.

But Nate had something else that was bothering him.

Of late, he didn't know what was happening to his plan. It seemed to be going perfectly, but if that was the case, he asked himself, why was he feeling the way he was?

He knew part of it was because his plan required that he treat Monica like he could no longer stand her.

Over the last week and a half, he'd noticed every attempt that she'd made to get them close again, but he had had to ignore her, or treat her even worse with each effort she did put forth.

All the times that she'd wanted to have sex with him, and when he was unable to perform, he knew she believed it was her fault, that he was no longer attracted to her, but that was not really the case. How much he wanted to tell her that, let her know that it was just the pills; but that would ruin all the work that he had put in. So Nate would just roll on his side, or right out of bed, as though it made no difference to him that he couldn't make love to her, or as though it truly was her fault.

He remembered the night he came home and she was all dressed up in her new nightgown. All she wanted to do was be next to him, and get a little affection in return, acknowledgment that he still cared for her, and he knew that. But no, he couldn't give it to her. Even though her eyes begged him for it, pleaded for him to show her a single sign that he still cared for her, Nate could not show it. And instead, he turned, left her standing there naked in the center of their living room, and climbed the stairs as though she wasn't important to him at all.

And then, of course, there was their anniversary. Nate agonized over that one for quite some time. Every year in the past, he always made sure that they had a wonderful time on their night, but he was conflicted about what to do regarding this year.

If he were to take her out, or even recognize the night by staying home and having dinner with his wife, treating her any better than he had been, he was afraid that she might take that as a sign that they were getting back on track, and when Nate finally had Lewis make his move, Monica might hold out, because of the hope that Nate instilled in her on the night of their anniversary.

For that reason, he could not acknowledge it, had to act as though he just didn't care about such things anymore.

Since he had enacted his plan, Nate had been spending many of his evenings with Tori. That night he didn't. It just seemed too damn disrespectful in Nate's eyes, so he ended up at his brother's door. It was around eight that evening.

"What are you doing here?" Tim said. "Isn't it your anniversary?"

"Can you hang out for a while?" Nate said.

Tim looked at him oddly. "Nate, what's going on?"

"Tim, can you hang out, yes or no?"

"All right."

They ended up at a bar in Hyde Park, a neighborhood between where Nate lived and his brother's house. Nate had told Tim everything that had been happening over the past couple of weeks, while he downed his second scotch and tonic, and was waiting on his third.

Tim shook his head. A mask of disgust hung on his face, as he was barely able to look at his brother.

"You need to leave here right now," Tim said. "You need to take me home, head back home yourself, and try to salvage this night."

"I can't," Nate said, accepting the new glass of liquor that was placed before him, slowly bringing it up to his lips and taking a sip. "It's all part of the plan."

"The plan!" Tim said, turning his entire body around to face his brother. "You're treating your wife like shit. Do you enjoy that?"

"No!" Nate said, slamming his glass down, spilling some of its contents. "I hate it. I still love her."

"You could've fooled me."

196

"I'm still angry as hell at her for lying to me, for not telling me that there was a chance that she wouldn't be able to have my children. And no, I don't think she should be rewarded with millions of dollars for doing that. But I do still love her."

"And what about the other girl, Tori?"

"What about her? I see her more than I see my wife. She bugs me every day about when I'm going to divorce Monica."

"Do you love her?"

Nate looked at his brother as though he thought the question was an unfair one.

"I'm going to marry her, she's going to have my family, and I'll love her then."

"But do you love her now?"

"That's not important," Nate said.

"You don't. And if that's the case, then forget all this nonsense," Tim said, pulling his wallet from his jacket pocket. "I'll pay the tab, and let's get out of here."

"Put your wallet away. We're not going anywhere," Nate said, sipping from his glass again. "I hate what's going on. It's killing me. But I'd rather go through this pain right now than the pain of never having a family, of never having the children I want. That would last me the rest of my life." Nate was looking dead into his brother's eyes when he spoke those last words, and something told Nate that moment that maybe his brother, for the first time, understood how he felt.

Now, Nate stepped out of his car, walked toward Taylor's Bar, pulled the door open, and stepped inside.

As he walked toward a table in the back, he called out to the bartender, "Scotch and tonic, please."

After last night, when at 10 P.M. Monica still had not made it home, Nate began to suspect that she was out with Lewis.

Nate had been speaking to Lewis once a day via cell phone, getting updates, but the boy never told Nate that he had planned on seeing his wife in the evening. But then again, it was only a suspicion of Nate's.

When Monica did finally come in, when he saw her wearing that dress, those shoes, her hair all done up in this new style that she was sporting, his suspicions were all but confirmed.

Monica practically tackled him upon coming into the bedroom. She tore off his clothes, and although she'd tried in the past to get him ready for sex, she had never seemed so determined about it. She seemed feverish, as though there was something else driving her to want sex from her husband than what normally did.

Nate spoke to her after that, but got nothing out of her that explained why she had behaved the way she did.

And when he asked her where she had been, she simply answered, "I've been out."

She slept with her back to him, as far away as the king size bed allowed.

When Nate got to work that morning, the first thing he did was call Lewis.

"I need you to meet me at Taylor's, one P.M.," Nate said, when Lewis answered the phone.

"Mr. Kenny, I—"

"I don't remember asking you to say a word," Nate said, feeling extreme anger toward the boy and not knowing why. "Just meet me at Taylor's, like I said, at one."

The bartender brought the drink to Nate's table, set it down on a napkin in front of him. Nate dropped a ten-dollar bill on the woman's tray.

"Keep it," he said.

Just then the door of the bar opened. Nate saw that it was Lewis. He raised his hand and waved the boy over.

"How you doing, Mr. Kenny?" the boy said, extending a hand, that Nate did not shake.

"Sit down."

He did, and Nate eyed him closely. He was wearing a suit, a nice suit. Obviously one that Nate's money had bought him.

"Do you want something to drink?"

"No sir."

Nate stirred the cubes around in his glass with a pink plastic stirrer, still eyeing Lewis intensely. He raised the glass to his lips and took a drink.

"You enjoying your new life, Lewis?"

"Sir?"

"Are you comfortable? Do the new house and car suit you?"

"Yes, Mr. Kenny."

The boy's hair was different, as well. He had taken Nate's advice, went out and got a haircut. He looked like a different man. If Nate hadn't known better, hadn't seen the boy for who he truly was, a loser, a homeless thug, he probably would've been deceived by this façade as well. This front that his wife was probably deceived by, this lie that Nate had created.

"Did you fuck my wife last night?" Nate said, blatantly.

"Sir?"

"Just answer the question. Did you fuck her!"

"No, Mr. Kenny. I wouldn't—"

"Did you try?"

"Mr. Kenny—"

"I said, did you try?"

The boy looked Nate in the eyes, lowered his head, then looked back up again. "No, Mr. Kenny. I didn't try. All we did was go out to see *The Lion King* last night."

"And why didn't you tell me this? We spoke yesterday afternoon. Why didn't you tell me?"

"Because I didn't think you'd want to know every little detail that was going on."

Nate tossed his head back, let out a fake chuckle and smile, then returned his hard stare back to Lewis. "I saved you from the streets. I gave you a new home, clothes, money, a job that pays five thousand dollars a week. I don't care if you don't think I want to hear every little detail, you tell me anyway. As a matter of fact," Nate said, leaning onto the table, "don't think at all. From now on, you tell me everything that you're planning, before you do it. And you definitely let me know before you try to sleep with my wife. Do you understand that?"

"Yes, Mr. Kenny," Lewis said.

"Because if you don't, I would hate to see you back on the streets, or even worse, in prison."

38

Lewis sat in his Cadillac. He watched as Mr. Kenny drove his car out of the Taylor's Bar parking lot. The man shot him an evil glance just before making a left out onto the street and driving away.

Either Lewis was crazy or Mr. Kenny didn't like him. And maybe dislike wasn't even the best way of putting it. It seemed to Lewis, by the way Mr. Kenny was looking at him in the bar, that the man seemed to hate Lewis.

Exactly what did he do? Lewis asked himself. The man was paying him to try to get in his wife's panties, and now he's all pissed off because he thinks he did just that.

No. He wasn't exactly telling Mr. Kenny the truth when he said he hadn't tried to sleep with Monica, but the bottom line was, he hadn't.

Lewis stayed up well into the night trying to figure that one out. He had the woman on his bed, damn near butt naked; the only thing stopping him sliding inside her was a thin, saturated piece of panty material.

He had her right where he wanted her, and she was wanting him too, he could feel it, then all of a sudden . . .

Lewis ran the scenario over and over again in his head, and could come up with nothing that made sense, other than that she was married, and her conscience started getting to her.

Lewis slipped his key into the car's ignition and turned the engine over.

If she only knew the type of man she was married to, Lewis thought, she wouldn't have been troubling herself so much with trying to remain faithful to him.

And then that man tried to threaten Lewis just moments ago in the bar, by taking away everything that he had given Lewis. He knew it wasn't his, but Lewis didn't like the way Mr. Kenny was hanging it over his head, trying to punk him with it, even suggesting that he would still try to have Lewis put in jail.

He was a nasty man. He didn't deserve the woman that he was plotting so hard to get rid of.

Lewis could make it much easier for him to shake Monica, he thought. He could just go to her, spill everything about what her husband had been planning, and then it would be over.

But then where would that leave Lewis? There would be no more house, no suits, no money, no more Mr. Real Estate Developer. And considering that's the man that Monica thought Lewis was, there wouldn't be any more Monica either. Lewis definitely didn't want that, because he hated to admit it to himself, but he was taking a liking to the woman.

It was foolish, he knew, because regardless of how this entire thing ended, once she found out who he was, she would lose whatever interest, if any, she had in him.

Lewis threw the truck in gear and was about to drive off when his cell phone rang.

"This is Lewis," he said.

"Hello," a small voice answered back.

"Yes."

There was a pause, then, "This is Monica."

"Oh, hi Monica," Lewis said. "I'm glad you called."

"I want to talk about last night."

"Okay."

"Not now. Not on the phone."

"Okay, then where do you want to meet?" Lewis asked.

"You're place will be fine, if that's all right with you. Will you be finished with work by then?"

"Uh, yeah. Work will be done by then."

"So after you get off. Around five-thirty P.M., six?"

"Yeah. I'll see you then."

When the bell rang some hours later, it was Monica standing outside Lewis's door. He opened it.

"Hey," he said, staring out at her.

"Hey."

Lewis just stood there, marveling at how beautiful she was, surprised that she had even called him back.

"Are you going to invite me in?" Monica said.

"Oh," Lewis said, practically jumping to one side. "I'm sorry. I was thinking about something," he said, as she walked past him into his living room.

"Probably about my behavior last night. I'm sorry about that."

"No need to be. I shouldn't have taken you up to my room."

"You didn't take me," Monica said, moving one step toward him. "I asked to go up there, just like I asked to come back here last night. Remember?"

Lewis nodded. "But I'm saying I'm sorry, anyway. If I didn't ever ask you out to that show, none of last night would've ever happened."

"There's no need for you to be sorry. I enjoyed *The Lion King*. I enjoyed last night too," Monica said, her voice much lower when she spoke those last words.

Lewis didn't know just what was happening. Last night, the woman freaked out, practically ran out of his house with her panties in her arms, and now he thought she just said she had a good time.

"Oh, okay," Lewis said.

"So . . . ," Monica said.

"So?" Lewis said back, swinging his arms at his sides a little, as if waiting for something to happen.

"Well, that's all I really came over here to say."

"Okay," Lewis said, but he asked himself, why would she do that, when she could've just told him that stuff over the phone?

Monica walked slowly toward the door, Lewis walking behind her.

Was he supposed to say something? Should he make a move? He really didn't know, especially after last night.

Then he wasn't sure if he wanted to risk his new job by making another move too soon. Besides, wasn't he supposed to alert Mr. Kenny if he even thought about trying something with her again?

"Well, I guess I'll be seeing you around," Monica said, turning to face Lewis. She was standing in front of the door, making it hard for him to open it. After he finally maneuvered himself around her, and had it open, she stood there just inside the house, just looking up at him oddly.

"Yeah, I guess I'll see you," Lewis said back.

"Okay," Monica said, finality in her voice. "I'll see you."

She turned, but Lewis knew he didn't want her to go.

"Monica."

"Hunh?" she said, turning around, standing just in front of him.

The hell with it, Lewis thought. "Would you mind if I—"

And before he could finish his sentence, Monica had thrown her arms around him, and had pushed her lips into his.

They kissed, long and passionately, Monica's hands rubbing all over Lewis's back as she continued to deeply kiss him.

Lewis thought he heard Monica trying to say something to him.

"What?" he said, still kissing her.

"I said, take me inside."

Lewis slowly pulled away from her, looking her seriously in the eyes. "We tried that last night, and look what happened."

"That was last night."

"What changed your mind?"

"I have my reasons," Monica said, offering nothing else.

"I don't think you're serious."

"Take me back upstairs, and you'll see how serious I am."

There was nothing else to say. Lewis grabbed her hand and headed for the stairs.

39

So Lewis had sex with Monica, and during that act, she didn't all of a sudden jump up in bed, dive to the floor for her panties, and start screaming about how she had to get out of there, as he had thought she would.

They had sex for almost an hour, Lewis wanting to take as much time as he could to enjoy her, and give her as much pleasure as possible. He believed he accomplished that by the serene look on her face as she lay on her back afterward.

He was surprised she hadn't gotten up, kissed him on the cheek, telling him she had to get back to her husband, but instead relaxed beside him, as if she had all the time in the world.

Lewis rolled up on his elbow, stroking her hair, gazing at her.

Monica turned her head slightly to catch him staring. "So, was that serious enough for you?"

"As a heart attack. And you know, you almost gave me one."

"Yeah, right." Monica laughed, then turned, gazed back up at the ceiling. "I really needed that. Thank you."

"Thank you," Lewis said back.

Monica turned again, looked at Lewis. "You're wondering why I did this, when I was always going on about how I'm married."

"No. I wasn't wondering that. It's your decision."

"My husband wasn't treating me right, was treating me badly. He acts as though he doesn't even love me anymore. He just stopped

205

acknowledging me. Made me feel as though I was worthless, as though I wasn't attractive. So I had to do this for me."

"Do you regret it?"

"No," Monica answered quickly. "It was my decision and I made it. I'll probably even tell him about it one day, if it ever comes up."

Lewis had to damn near bite his tongue to stop himself from saying something about the prenuptial she had with her husband, and why would she risk what was coming to her for the sake of honesty.

"So, does that mean I'll see you again?"

Monica looked to be giving it some thought, then said, "I don't know."

Lewis was disappointed, but the following day he received a phone call from Monica, wondering what he was doing later that day.

"Nothing," he said, a wide smile on his face.

"Can I see you?"

"Of course."

This went on for the next three evenings, making it five days in a row that he had seen her, and each day he made love to her. Each day they lay in bed afterward, laughing, kissing, and playing.

One of those days, Lewis held Monica in his arms and asked her, "Do you ever wonder?"

"Wonder what?"

"Wonder if the people that we're with now are the ones we're supposed to be with forever."

"I don't know," Monica said, thinking on the question for a moment. "I believe that everything happens for a reason, and we'll ultimately end up with who we're supposed to be with."

"Do you think that person could be me?"

Monica rolled off Lewis so she could look him in the eyes. "I'm married, Lewis."

"I know that. I mean, if you weren't married. If I met you before he did, could I have been the person for you?"

Monica smiled, leaned in, and gave him a quick kiss on the lips. "Yes, Lewis. You definitely could've been that person."

Each of those days he had spent with Monica, he had also spoken to Mr. Kenny, but hadn't once told him that he was having sex with his wife.

When Mr. Kenny asked Lewis if he was close—did any opportunities present themselves?—Lewis told him no, and to Lewis's surprise, Mr. Kenny didn't sound too disappointed by that, which was a good thing.

Lewis wanted this situation to last as long as it could, because he would've been a fool not to acknowledge the fact that he was enjoying himself. He had never lived like that, never enjoyed the material things he possessed now, but most of all, never spent time with a woman like Monica.

Yes, he had beautiful women before, but none so caring or intelligent as her. Just being around her made him feel smarter, like a better person, so unlike being around Selena, which made him feel less than he really was.

And then there wasn't the negativity that Selena always carried around her. There was always some dark cloud hovering over her head. The world was always coming to an end with her, and that weighed on Lewis. It exhausted him many times, when he didn't even want to have a conversation with her because he knew, afterward, he would feel depressed.

With Monica, every time he spoke to her, he felt uplifted. He definitely wanted this to last.

The day after the fifth time he saw Monica, Lewis was supposed to go to Selena's to pick up his daughter.

When Lewis arrived that Saturday afternoon the apartment was cleaner than he had ever seen it.

Selena had Layla all clothed, a baby bag packed and sitting beside her on the sofa, ready to go.

Lewis leaned in and gave Selena a kiss hello on the cheek, but he noticed something didn't seem right with her. She seemed agitated, unsettled.

"Is everything okay, Selena?"

"Everything is fine, but I think I'm going to need a little money. You think you got that?"

"Why?" Lewis said, shouldering the baby bag. "I just gave you four hundred last week. What the hell you doing with it?"

"Things cost. The baby was sick. I had to buy the pink stuff, and other expenses came up."

"You ain't *working* no more?" Lewis said, using the term very lightly.

Selena looked as though she didn't appreciate the comment. "I only did that 'cause I had to. It ain't like I enjoyed it."

"You could've fooled me."

"I don't want to argue with you, Lewis. I just really need some money."

She looked pathetic there standing in front of him, Lewis thought. She appeared beaten, worn, as though she had been up for hours, and he wondered why he had ever been with this woman to begin with.

He pulled out his wallet, pulled out a hundred dollars in twenty-dollar bills, and handed it to her.

"Thank you, baby," Selena said, leaning in with a kiss directed toward his lips.

Lewis turned his face and received the kiss on his cheek.

"I'll bring her back this evening, okay?"

"Okay, but don't be too long."

When Lewis got to his place, he gently lifted Layla out of the car seat he had bought for her a couple of days ago, when Selena said it would be all right to take her.

He walked her toward the house, excited.

"I got something to show you," Lewis said, unlocking the door and walking in.

He walked slowly through the house, giving his daughter a tour.

"Here's the fireplace," he said, walking through the living room. "We got a chandelier up there, see it," he said, once they were in the dining room. And when he walked her into the kitchen, Lewis said,

"We even have a dishwasher, so when the dishes get dirty, we don't have to let them all pile up in the sink, and sit for days like Mommy does." Lewis laughed at his remark, and his daughter laughed as well, as if she knew what he had said.

"But that's not what I really wanted to show you. I got something special for you." They headed upstairs.

He made a left in the hallway, instead of the right he normally made, leading to his room. He pushed open the door that led them into another bedroom, and there sitting in the middle of that room was a brand-new, top-of-the-line baby's crib, a huge red bow tied to it.

"Look at that!" Lewis said, standing in front of it with his child, admiring it like it was a brand-new car. "How do you like that?"

He carried Layla over to it, and set her down in it.

"What do you think? It has an extra comfort mattress. Can you feel that?" he said, reaching in and pressing down on it himself.

Layla responded with a number of "goo's" and "gah's," smiled, and rolled around on her back.

"You like that, don't you?" Lewis was smiling, watching his child, but then the smile disappeared from his face. "You shouldn't have to live the way you're living, baby. Your moms shouldn't be neglecting you like she's doing, exposing you to things you're seeing," Lewis said, picking her up out of the crib and taking her in his arms. "But I'm gonna make sure that don't last too much longer. And it won't be this one," Lewis said, walking Layla toward his bedroom. "But we're gonna get us a nice place, and I'm going to bring your crib, and we're gonna live the way we supposed to. I'm promising you that, baby," Lewis said, sitting on the edge of his bed, staring into his daughter's big round eyes. "I promise you."

When Lewis walked in Selena's door later that evening, Selena looked much calmer, more relaxed.

"Did she act okay?" Selena asked about Layla.

"Yeah, she was fine," Lewis said, holding his daughter out for Selena to take.

"Why don't you put her in her crib in the bedroom?"

Lewis did as he was asked, kissing Layla, then lowering her into the crib and giving her one of her toys.

"Daddy loves you, okay? And remember what I said."

When he walked back out into the living room, Selena was waiting for him.

"Well, thanks for letting me take Layla. I hope you'll let me do it again sometime."

"Okay," Selena agreed.

Lewis walked over to kiss her good-bye, but Selena leaned away from him. "Do you have to leave this minute? I want to talk to you."

"What's up?"

Selena walked around the coffee table, had a seat on the sofa, and placed her hand on the cushion next to her, gesturing for Lewis to take a seat.

He sat, feeling as though something strange was going on. "So . . ."

"I'm gonna come straight out with it. I miss you, Lewis."

Lewis shook his head, stood up from the couch, and was about to leave, but Selena grabbed his arm, pulled him back down.

"I miss you, and I still love you. I mean that."

"You weren't loving me when I was working at the barbershop. You weren't loving me when you had that man in here, fucking him in front of my baby. Where was all the damn love then, Selena!"

"I told you. I needed that money."

"But now that I got money to give you, then everything is cool, we can be one big happy family again."

"Yeah."

"It'll never happen. Do you hear me?" he said, leaning in closer so there was no room for misunderstanding. "That will never happen again, so just get it out of your head," Lewis said, standing and moving toward the door.

"So you want to take a chance on never seeing your daughter again?"

Lewis stopped, slowly turned around. "What are you saying? You threatening to not let me see Layla again?" He felt himself becoming infuriated.

"I ain't threatening nothing."

Lewis raced over to her, grabbed her by her shoulders, shaking her. "Is that what you doing!"

"Lewis, stop!" Selena said. "I ain't sayin' that!"

Lewis stopped, pulled his hands from Selena. "I'm just saying, if it gets too tough for me to afford this place, then I don't know where me and Layla going to go."

Lewis knew this was Selena making another attempt to get him to come back there. He thought about it, only briefly, imagining himself able to be with his daughter all the time; but knowing Selena, the moment things got rough again, she'd be trying to put him out.

No. He wouldn't fall for it, he thought, looking down at how pathetic Selena appeared to him now.

"I'm just gonna have to take that chance," Lewis said, turning toward the door again, knowing he would have to do something soon to get his daughter away from the woman.

40

In the storeroom at work, Monica was checking inventory when she heard Tabatha calling her.

When she came out, Tabatha was standing behind the store's counter, holding a bouquet of a dozen roses.

"Aw, for me? You shouldn't have," Monica said, taking them from Tabatha.

"I didn't and you know it. It's from Lewis, again," Tabatha said, flipping over the envelope and seeing his name on it. "It's the third time this week. What are you doing to that boy?"

Monica headed back to the break room with the roses, Tabatha following her.

"Nothing more than he's doing to me," Monica said, placing the flowers on a counter, tearing away the paper.

"And that's all right with you?" Tabatha asked, having a seat at the table.

"Tabatha, please don't start again with that."

"You've been bouncing around here all week like you just won the damn lottery, and—"

"And what?" Monica said, turning to face Tabatha. "Can't I be happy? Is there anything wrong with that? You know everything I've been going through, how Nate has been acting toward me. Now that I found something to take my mind off that, give me a little happiness, I gotta get speeches from you every day."

"You said you were going to sleep with him one time, get back at Nate, and that's it. Now it's practically an everyday thing."

"What, are you jealous?" Monica said.

"Of that?" Tabatha said, shaking her head, chuckling sarcastically. "You live in a penthouse. Your husband is worth millions of dollars. You work this job just because you want to, when I *have* to. If I'm not jealous of those things, why would I be jealous of you fucking some strange man just because he dropped a line on you? I could have that anytime I want."

Monica didn't respond at first, then finally said, "That wasn't nice."

"I know. I'm sorry," Tabatha apologized. "But neither is what you're doing to Nate."

"You're the one that suggested I go out with Lewis, because you kept saying Nate was cheating."

"You never proved he was, and even if he was, you said *once* with this guy. It looks like it's turning into something more than that. You aren't falling for him, are you, Monica?"

"No, don't be ridiculous," Monica said, even though she had become quite fond of him. "We have fun when we see each other, that's it."

"How about him for you?"

"No. I don't think so."

"Are you sure?" Tabatha said.

"Yeah. I'm pretty sure."

"Then it should be pretty easy to break off."

"I guess," Monica said. "If I was ready to do that."

"Do you still love Nate?" Tabatha asked. "Still think your marriage is worth saving?"

"Of course I do."

"But you're willing to give up all that you have with your husband, regardless how rocky things are right now, for this other man?"

Monica took only a moment to think about that. "No. I'm not."

"That's exactly what you'll be doing if you get caught."

Monica appreciated what her friend was trying to do. But Tabatha wasn't in Monica's shoes, so she truly couldn't understand.

"Then I'll make sure and try not to get caught when I'm with Lewis tonight," Monica said, smiling.

When Lewis's front door opened, immediately upon seeing Monica, he took her in his arms and gave her a long, passionate kiss.

"What was that for?" Monica said, when the kiss was over.

"I missed you," Lewis said, taking her hand and leading her toward the stairs.

"You just saw me yesterday."

"That's a long time." Lewis was unbuttoning his shirt as he climbed the stairs, Monica starting to undo her clothes as well.

It was a beautiful evening, so they made love outside on Lewis's deck. She was worried that someone would see them. She gazed out at the old buildings in the distance around them, and wondered if anyone stood behind their windows watching them.

As Lewis kissed her neck, and slowly finished undressing her, he reassured her that the buildings were vacant, abandoned, that nobody would be paying attention to her but him.

And that was exactly what he did, making her body feel so much pleasure that tears came to her eyes.

The way he made love to her, it was more than just the act of having sex. Every now and then she would open her eyes to see him staring almost lovingly down at her. Just below her own moans, she could hear him whispering things in her ear, but was never able to make them out.

Afterward, as they lay, their bodies intertwined on his bed, she wondered what those things were, and just what the look he often-times gave her meant.

Monica also couldn't stop herself from thinking about what Tabatha said. She wondered what her husband was doing that moment, wondered what he would do if he could see her lying with this man the way she was.

Then Monica told herself she would not think those things. Tabatha was just jealous of what Monica was experiencing now, regardless of what she said, and she would not let her talk her into giving it up.

"Hey. You okay?" Lewis said, bringing a finger to her forehead and rubbing the furrowed space between her eyebrows. "Is something bothering you?"

"Just hungry," Monica lied. "Let's go out and get something to eat."

They went to a small restaurant in Chinatown. It was far enough from Nate's office that Monica felt comfortable in not worrying whether she risked getting caught by him. Besides, it was only a few minutes past 7 P.M., and she knew he was still in some office or pricey restaurant doing business with his client.

Monica and Lewis were seated at a booth, Lewis's back to the door, Monica facing it. They had already ordered, for it was not busy. Only one other couple was dining there tonight.

"Excuse me if I'm mistaken," Lewis said, reaching across the table and taking Monica's hands in his, "but were there tears coming from your eyes earlier?"

"And why would you have thought that?"

"Because I was giving it to you so good, that the only way you could express yourself was with tears."

Monica laughed. "Baby, if anyone was shedding tears it would've been you," Monica said, briefly looking up, her attention taken by someone walking by the storefront's slightly smoked window.

"Baby, I've never shed a tear in my life. I'm a real man," Lewis said, beating one of his fists into his chest.

"Okay, maybe you weren't shedding tears," Monica said, looking up toward the window again. "Maybe there was just an owl perched somewhere above us, because I kept hearing someone crying out, 'Whooooooo, whooooooo! It feels so good! Whooooooo!'" Monica said, mocking Lewis making agonizing faces of extreme pleasure.

"No I wasn't."

"Yes you were," Monica said, and then all of a sudden, her eyes deceived her, telling her brain that she had seen something that she knew she couldn't have. It was Nate. It couldn't have been, but she saw him, walking past the front window, toward the door of the restaurant.

Her heart automatically started pounding in her chest.

The front door opened, a tiny bell ringing above it, and Monica thought she was going to die right there. There was a crosshatched wooden partition that separated the front door from the restaurant, so she didn't think she had been seen.

She still didn't think it was him—it had to be someone that looked just like him—till she heard his voice.

"Yes, pickup for Kenny."

And then Monica was sure. She started whipping her head around, her eyes huge, looking for a way out. But running across the restaurant would surely get her spotted.

"What's wrong?" Lewis said, seeing her strange behavior.

"Shhh!" Monica whispered loudly. "Don't say anything!"

Her eyes were focused keenly on the front door, when she heard her husband ask, "Do you have a rest room?"

"In back of restaurant," Monica heard the owner answer.

Now Nate would see her for sure, Monica knew. He would turn the corner any moment now and see her. She looked around desperately, one final time, then all of a sudden dropped under the surface of the table. She didn't know what good that would do, for there was no tablecloth.

The only way her husband wouldn't see her was if he walked by and didn't even glance in her direction; otherwise, she was as easy to see as Lewis was, sitting above the table's surface.

"Monica!" Lewis whispered.

She quickly struck him in the shin, and thought her cover had been blown, but she watched as Nate slowly walked through the restaurant. It was unreal to Monica, as she crouched below that table, sweating, trembling, watching her husband only twenty or so feet away from her.

He would turn, she knew it. He would turn any moment, see her, and she would be found out. But he never did. He pushed through the men's room door, and Monica quickly popped up from under the table.

"We gotta go!" she said, grabbing Lewis's hand.

"Why?"

"That was my husband that just walked by," she still whispered. "We gotta go!"

"No. Just stay."

"No! He'll see us!"

"He won't. I promise!" Lewis said. "Trust me."

"Stay if you want. I'm leaving."

Just then, Monica heard the bathroom door swinging open, and once again, she had no choice but to retreat back under the table.

Again Nate walked by, his eyes facing directly forward. And again, Monica knew she would be busted.

Amazingly enough, he walked by once more without spotting her, paid for his food at the front of the restaurant, then Monica heard the tinkle of the bell as Nate left.

The movement of Lewis's legs let her know he was checking to make sure he was gone, and then she heard him say, "All right. He left."

"Are you sure?"

"Positive. He's gone. You can come up."

Monica slowly raised herself up, on Lewis's side of the booth now, sitting beside him. She fell next to him, feeling drained, as though she had just physically exerted herself. Her chest was heaving, her body still trembling nervously.

Lewis put his arm around her, comforting her. "So that was him," he said.

"Yes," Monica said, feeling beads of sweat still forming on her brow. "That was him."

41

Nate's car sat in the parking lot of a convenience store, him slumped inside it, staring at the clock, waiting for it to change from 9:59 P.M. to 10:00 P.M. At that time he punched numbers into the cell phone he was already holding in his hand.

"Hello," Nate said, when the phone was answered. "Is this a bad time?"

It was Lewis on the other line.

When Nate finished work this evening, he didn't feel like being bothered with Tori telling him what he should be doing about the private investigator, or asking him what entree they should serve at their wedding reception, so he decided he wouldn't go over there tonight.

Instead, he would get carry-out from somewhere, and maybe eat it in the park, enjoy the evening's weather, and do some serious thinking.

After the Chinese man behind the counter told him it would be five more minutes, Nate had asked where the rest room was. He directed him to the rear of the restaurant. Nate headed back there, and upon turning the corner, immediately he saw Lewis sitting at one of the booths.

Nate was about to go over, talk to him, but Lewis caught sight of Nate as well, and quickly waved him off, frantically pointing down at the table.

Nate directed his eyes forward, and walked straight to the men's room. Inside, he no longer had the urge to go, and just stood before the mirror, his hands resting on the corners of the sink. He lifted his head to look at himself.

He didn't know if it was his wife under that table, hadn't seen her with his own eyes, but what other reason would Lewis have to divert him from coming over there?

Nate raised his head, looked sadly at himself, and asked his reflection just what in the hell he was doing. Putting his own wife in a situation that had her ducking under tables, hiding in between some man's legs like some on-the-run street ho. Why? And was it worth it?

At first, that question was so much easier to answer, but now . . .

Nate turned on the faucet, splashed cold water in his face, snatched a paper towel from the dispenser, and dried off.

On his way out, he didn't dare look in Lewis's direction, although he caught a glimpse of him out of the corner of his eye. The boy was sitting straight up in the booth, his hands dropped beneath the table.

Nate wanted so badly to look back, to see that it was his wife there, but he continued walking, grabbed his food, and left the restaurant.

"No, it's not a bad time," Lewis said, interrupting Nate's thoughts.

"Where's my wife?"

"She left here ten minutes ago."

"That was her at the restaurant . . . under the table, wasn't it?" The thought still pained Nate some.

"Yes."

"Why did you have her out like that?" Nate said, anger in his voice. "If she hadn't seen me first, you could've ruined everything."

"I didn't know you were going there. We just went out to get something to eat. How was I supposed to know?" Lewis said in defense.

The boy was right, Nate knew, but it did nothing to relieve his anger with him. "Was she shaken up?"

"Yeah. She thought you saw her."

"Did you convince her that I hadn't?"

"Yeah. I did," Lewis said.

"Did she say anything about not seeing you anymore?"

"No, but—"

"There is no *but*," Nate interrupted. "I've put too much work and effort into this thing to let it go now. You do what ever you have to do to keep her seeing you until I can get it documented that you've slept with her. Do you understand?"

"Yes."

"That is . . . if you haven't already slept with my wife."

"No!" Lewis quickly objected.

"Are you certain? Because you were supposed to tell me before you even tried."

"Yes, Mr. Kenny. I'm certain."

"Good. There are some things I have to look into, then I think we'll move forward, let you do what needs to be done, so we can end this mess."

When Nate got home, it wasn't quite eleven o'clock. He walked in the door to find his wife sitting up, reading a novel on the living room sofa.

He glanced up at her, still trying to imagine her under that table, then looked away. She would normally be in bed by now, and if not asleep, watching TV. But he knew she was sitting up, wanting to quiz him to see if he really had seen her tonight.

"How was your day?" Monica asked, looking up from the book.

"Like every day," Nate said, walking toward the stairs. "But I feel sick. I must've gotten hold of some bad Chinese food."

"Can I get you anything?" Monica called to Nate, but he was already halfway up the stairs and didn't bother responding.

In his office, he pulled off his suit jacket and tie, pushed back in his chair, and turned his fluorescent lamp to low.

He thought about how things were now with his wife. How because of his plan, he barely spoke to her, never touched her anymore, and treated her as though he didn't love her, had never really loved her.

What was worse was, she treated him the same way now, and it wasn't any plan of hers that had her treating him this way.

Because of his behavior toward her, she no longer tried to entice him to have sex, never touched him when they were in the same room, never kissed him good night like she used to, and always slept with her back to him.

He had to believe that part of the reason she was responding to him like that now was that the affection she used to have for Nate might now be going to Lewis, and he didn't like the thought of that.

No, Lewis hadn't slept with his wife yet, but they were sharing a lot of time together, and Nate was sure that they had probably kissed. That man's hands had probably been up Monica's shirt, down her pants, if for no other reason than for Lewis to try to inch closer to the point where she would allow him to have her.

Nate saw those images flash across his brain, and he threw his hands to his eyes, as if to stop himself from seeing them.

He pressed the butts of his palms into his eye sockets, until he nearly felt pain, and no longer saw the images.

He could still end all of this right now, Nate thought, glancing at his desk phone. He could call Lewis, tell him everything was off, and still possibly salvage his marriage. It wasn't too late.

But no, he told himself, lifting his briefcase from the floor and setting it down on the desk before him. He had good reason to start all of this, to have carried it as far as he had, and he just needed to continue on.

Nate popped open the case and pulled out the list of private investigators' numbers Tori had compiled for him. He sat there, staring hard at it, and decided it was what he must do. In the morning, he would call, and finally start the ball rolling.

It was noon, lunchtime, and the morning had been so busy that Nate hadn't had the opportunity to make his calls to the investigators, even though he had taken the list out and placed it in his top desk drawer, ready when he did get a moment.

A knock came at his door. It was opened, and Tori walked in, carrying a wide brown envelope in her arms. She closed the door behind her.

"Yes, Tori. What is it?" Nate said, not taking his attention away from his work.

"You don't want this to go forward, do you?"

"What?" Nate looked up at Tori.

"You must not want this to happen, do you? I ask you if your wife was sleeping with this guy yet, and you say no. I give you the numbers to some PIs, and you don't call them. Meanwhile, your wife is out there traipsing about town, having sex with this man you hired, and you're sitting up here as though everything is just fine."

"You don't know what you're talking about," Nate said, standing from his desk. "And I'm tired of—"

"Oh, I don't," Tori said, opening up the envelope she was holding, and tossing the contents onto Nate's desk.

What was spread out in front of Nate was photos of his wife and Lewis. Photos of them walking hand and hand in the park, hugging just outside his door, laughing, walking out of a movie theater. Then there were the other photos, the ones Nate could not believe, no matter how hard he stared at them. Those were the pictures of Lewis fucking his wife.

"They like to screw on his deck," Nate heard Tori saying, as he continued to stare angrily at the photos. "Seems by the big smile on her face that she really like that, hunh?"

Nate didn't say anything. Couldn't, he was feeling so much rage. He just reached out, further fanned the photos, so he could see all of them.

"Oh, and that one there, him all stretched out over that deck chair, your wife blowin' him. Now, he seemed to like that. Did you know your wife gave head like that?" Tori said, as though all of this was a joke.

"How did you get these?" Nate said from behind clenched teeth, his head spinning, pounding with fury.

"Since you weren't hiring a PI, I knew someone. I had him follow your wife and that guy, get the pictures. I got them back today. Now you have what you need to file for divorce."

"You had my wife followed?" Nate said. And he knew that she had gone too far. "What if they had seen him?"

"But they didn't."

"But what if they had! What if she would've seen him, and picked up on what was happening, somehow got Lewis to tell her everything. Do you know what you put in jeopardy?"

"Nate, I only did it for us," Tori said, her voice a little more timid.

"There are tens of millions of dollars at stake here, and you think you're going to decide to take control of this because you don't like the pace at which it's moving. You're going to fucking have my wife followed, tail her as though you have the right!" Nate said, yelling, grabbing the photos, waving them furiously about in his fist. "You throw them in my face, rub my nose in this shit as though it's going to push me into activity."

"Nate, I thought—"

"You thought! You thought!" Nate yelled, walking from around his desk. "Who told you to think? Who is paying you to think? You aren't anything more than a damn secretary, and you do this!"

Nate turned his back on Tori.

"Get the fuck out of my office. You're fired."

"What!" Nate heard Tori practically scream. "You're firing me!"

"You heard what I said."

"I need this job," Tori said, walking around Nate's desk so she could face him. "How am I supposed to live?"

"I'll make sure you receive a more than adequate severance package, and a personal recommendation that will get you on at any firm you want. I just don't want to see you in my office ever again."

223

"I could always sue you."

"Yes, you could. And you might even win. But if you don't, you'll get nothing from me, and I guarantee, no one in Chicago will ever give you another job. Your choice."

"Then what about us? Are we still getting married?"

Nate turned his body to fully face her. "No," he said. "You won't have to be worrying about that either."

42

The next afternoon, when Lewis picked up his phone to call Monica, he knew how important it was that he convince her to see him. If he did not, there would be the chance that, like Mr. Kenny said, he could lose her. And if that happened, he would lose the job, the money that came with it, and any chances of getting his daughter.

He still hadn't devised a way to get custody of her, but he knew it would be a hell of a lot harder if he didn't have a job, or the money he was making right now.

When Monica picked up the phone, she didn't sound as bad as he thought she would.

"So you're okay?" Lewis asked.

"Yeah. I'm fine."

"Did you talk to your husband last night?"

"Yeah, and he didn't see us."

Lewis paused. "Will I see you tonight? I really need to see you tonight."

"Yeah. I really think I need to see you, too."

43

Nate stood in the elevator where he lived, as it carried him up to the sixty-fifth floor. Countless times after he had seen those photos, he had picked up his office phone with intentions of calling Monica, but there was nothing to say to her.

He had set her up to sleep with this other man, and she had done just that. He just wished he had time to prepare himself, so when he finally saw evidence, he wouldn't have been so shocked.

That was why he explicitly told Lewis to tell him when he was planning to try to sleep with her. But he disobeyed him.

After all that Nate did for him, after all the money he was paying him, the boy couldn't even follow simple instructions, and that infuriated Nate.

When the elevator doors opened, Nate stepped off and headed toward his door. It wasn't even 8 P.M. yet, but he couldn't stick around the office another moment. He wondered, upon walking in the door, seeing his wife, would he be able to cover the fact that he knew about her and Lewis? He wondered, would he be able to fight the urge to throw open his briefcase, pull the photos out, and push them in her face, force her to see the filth that she participated in?

But again, he had to tell himself, if it wasn't for his efforts, she never would've done it.

Nate opened the door, stepped in, and called out for his wife.

"Monica."

There was no answer.

He remembered when there was a time when he would call her, and only a moment later, he'd hear her feet padding across the floor upstairs, and then he'd see her smiling face in front of him, giving him a hug, telling him to sit and relax so she could make him a drink and start preparing dinner.

Now there was just silence.

He walked into the kitchen, took out a short glass from the cupboard, filled it with a little scotch, brought it up to his lips, then kicked it back. He set the glass down hard on the counter, and was thankful for the burn on his palate, the tiny jolt he felt in his brain. It helped him calm down, if only the slightest bit.

He wondered just what Monica was doing, wherever she was, and one of the images from the photos flashed across his mind again. Nate shut his eyes tight, quickly poured himself another drink, kicked it back. He looked over at the clock. A little after 8 P.M., it read. She was with him, Nate knew.

Nate poured himself one last drink, brought the glass to his lips, and thought that he still couldn't believe his wife had been with that man; the photos had to be a lie.

He tilted the glass back, letting the alcohol spill into his mouth, and decided there was only one way to be certain. He would go over there and get the proof for himself.

❧

When Nate circled around the front of the place he was renting for Lewis, he saw both the Cadillac Escalade and his wife's Cooper parked out front.

Nate parked half a block up, and walked the distance back to the house. He stood out front on the walk, just before the stairs, staring up.

He thought about reaching into his pocket, calling Lewis from his cell phone, but decided not to.

He climbed the stairs, wondering if either his wife or Lewis was looking out one of the windows, seeing him approaching. He felt vulnerable for some reason.

Nate stood outside the door, wondering should he even continue with this. He knew what could be going on in there, so why did he have to see with his own eyes? He should just go home, deal with his wife when she came in.

Nate turned, thinking that might be best, when he heard a noise. He stopped there on the top stair, and listened. Again he heard it, and realized it wasn't a noise, but a scream. A scream from a voice— his wife's voice.

It was faint, muffled by distance, doors, and windows, but he knew his wife's cry.

Nate spun around, quickly sank his master key to the place into the door, and as quietly as he could, pushed it open.

Immediately, he heard another cry. This time louder. It was coming from upstairs. Nate stepped in.

He walked across the hardwood floor, heading toward the stairs. He was about to mount the first when, again, he heard his wife. This time it wasn't just a scream, but words.

"Fuck!" He heard her say. "Shit! Fuck me! Fuck me!"

Nate quickly reached out and grabbed the banister, needing to steady himself at the sound of hearing what was going on.

"You like this. You like this dick!" And that was Lewis, obviously, Nate thought. He looked up the stairs. His first thought was to grab something, a fireplace poker or something, run up to that room, and beat the man bloody to near death. But no, that wasn't part of the plan.

He thought about turning, just leaving, but something inside him wouldn't let him, was actually forcing Nate slowly up those stairs. He had to see this.

On the second floor, he pressed himself up against the hallway wall leading to the bedroom.

He heard them even clearer now, but not just the screams and the shouted words, but each moan, pant, and heavy breath.

It sounded as though his wife was getting beaten, sounded as though she was enduring heavy blows, but that couldn't be the case, because as Nate inched closer to the partly closed door, he could hear her asking for more, begging, telling Lewis how much she loved what he was doing to her.

Just outside the door, Nate felt himself wanting to vomit, but he suppressed that, and the fingertips of his left hand slowly gave the door a push. It opened, giving him a view to the bedroom. But they weren't in the bedroom, but on the deck, outside the bedroom patio doors, where Tori said they liked to screw.

He saw them there, and he wished he hadn't, for what he witnessed was his wife's body thrown over the deck's banister like an old rug, Lewis behind her, grabbing a fistful of her hair, pounding himself into her, both their backs to Nate.

It wasn't real, Nate told himself, as he walked out in plain sight, right through the middle of the bedroom, and stepped up to the glass of the patio doors.

It wasn't real, he kept telling himself, as he placed a hand up against the glass, but he knew it was; his eyes, his ears, his heart told him that.

He stood there, witnessing this man he hired from the street, fucking his wife, pulling at her hair, grabbing at her body, her ass, her hips, manhandling her in a way that Nate would never do, and he realized all this was happening because he planned it that way.

Nate lowered his head, was just about to turn and walk away, when all of sudden, for what he believed no reason at all, Lewis looked over his shoulder and caught sight of Nate watching.

Lewis didn't stop as Nate thought he would, didn't cower, try to cover himself, or the fact that he was fucking Nate's wife. But what he did was continue. Continue pulling at Monica's hair, continue forcing himself into her, but harder, still looking over his shoulder at Nate, a sick smile on his face.

"You like that dick?" Lewis said.

"Yes!" Monica moaned.

"Say you love that shit!" Lewis yelled, yanking at her hair like she was some animal at his service.

"I fucking love it!"

"That's right," he said, smacking her ass, then winked at Nate.

It was all Nate could stomach. He had to leave.

44

After Monica and Lewis were finished making love, they lay out on one of the patio reclining chairs, looking up at the stars. Monica was quiet, and by the look on her face, he knew she was deep in thought.

"What are you thinking?" he asked.

"Nothing."

He knew she wasn't telling him the truth. From the moment she walked into his house, even when he had called her earlier at the store, he knew that something was bothering her.

"Can I get you something?" Lewis offered.

"No. I'm all right."

Things had changed just that quickly between them. She had always seemed carefree before, but after the incident in the restaurant, Lewis was telling himself, she was probably wondering if this was worth continuing. At that very moment, she was probably comparing him to her husband. If he allowed her to do that for too long, Lewis knew the decision she would make.

Mr. Kenny had too much on him. With the history they'd had, the fact that she had loved him, and not to forget, she was still his wife, she would most definitely decide in his favor if Lewis didn't give her a reason not to.

"I was thinking," Lewis said, shifting some so he could look into Monica's eyes. "I know we've only been seeing each other for a couple of weeks now, but I think this is good. Don't you?"

"Yeah, sure," Monica said, not seeming as committed as Lewis.

"Not that I'm wishing anything bad on you, but I'm just putting something out there. If things don't work out with your husband, I think you and me should actually see how much we can make of this."

Monica immediately looked away, which Lewis knew was a bad sign.

"I know you like me. I know you care for me, Monica."

"Yes I do, Lewis. But—"

"And we have nothing but good times together."

"That's true, but—"

"And you wouldn't have started seeing me if there wasn't something wrong going on at home."

"There were things wrong at home, but that didn't give me the right to start seeing you." Monica squirmed out from under Lewis and pulled herself up from the recliner. "I should've never agreed to this."

"What do you mean?" Lewis said, quickly standing himself. They both stood naked on the outside deck.

"If my husband would've caught me yesterday," Monica said, as if she was seeing the moment in her head, "if he would've seen me, I don't know what I would've done. I felt so ashamed hiding under that table like that. Yeah, we were having some problems. He was ignoring me, but what should I have expected? There were serious things he was going through, things that I haven't told you about. How else should I have expected him to act? But instead, I think of only myself, go out and sleep with another man. I shouldn't be seeing you anymore, Lewis."

"If that's the case, why did you come back?"

"To say good-bye." Monica turned around, about to step back into the bedroom.

"Monica," Lewis called.

She turned.

Lewis walked up to her. "I've never met anyone like you before. You believe me when I tell you that?"

Monica nodded her head.

"I thought we were really good together, and I guess it was stupid of me to think it, but I thought there could've been some kind of a future for us."

Monica looked in Lewis's eyes, appearing on the verge of tears. "If things were different, then maybe there would've been." She leaned in and gave him a hug. "Good-bye, Lewis."

45

When Nate stumbled in from the bar he had gone to after seeing his wife with Lewis, Monica was sound asleep, as he figured she would be. She was on her back, the blankets pushed off her. Her nightgown was slightly raised, showing the smooth skin of her thighs.

An image flashed in his mind from earlier, and he wanted his wife that moment. He wanted her to scream for him the way she had for that bastard Lewis.

He stood there, over the bed, in semidarkness.

His head was spinning softly from the few more shots he had at the bar, and he focused closer on his wife's body. Nate dropped his hand down into his trousers, grabbed himself, and started stroking. How he wanted her at that moment, and he would've taken her, but nothing was happening. He pulled harder, stroked faster, but there was no response. He knew it was those damn pills, but something always told him that if he really wanted to have sex, he would be able to override the effects. He found out he could not.

He tried another twenty seconds or so, then disappeared into the bathroom, flipped open the medicine cabinet, grabbed the prescription bottle that was still half full with pills, and poured them down the toilet.

He raised his face, looked himself in the mirror, and asked himself, had he made the biggest mistake of his life?

❦

The next day, after work, Nate walked in his house at what used to be his normal time, sometime after 6 P.M.

Earlier at work, Tori was replaced with a temporary secretary. There was no way the woman could adequately fill Tori's shoes, but it was enough that she answered the phones and directed the important calls to Nate.

"Phone call for you, Mr. Kenny," the temp secretary told him over his intercom.

"Who is it?" Nate asked.

"It's a Tori Thomas."

Nate was about to tell the new woman that he wouldn't take her call.

"She says it's urgent."

"Put her through, then," Nate finally said.

When her call was put through, the first thing Nate said was, "I don't want to hear anything about us, or you getting your job back, because it's not going to happen."

Tori didn't speak for a moment, then she said, "We need to meet."

"No we don't."

"Yes we do," Tori insisted.

"For what? Everything I've wanted to tell you, I've said. There's nothing more."

"We still need to meet. And just because I haven't, don't think I can't make things really difficult for you. Your wife doesn't know about the game you've been playing with her, but I can fill her in on everything, including me and you," Tori threatened.

"I'm not worried about that. You have no proof. It'll be your word against mine, and just who do you think she'll believe?"

"I don't know. You wanna find out?"

Nate conceded, and told her he would get back to her when he was able to find time.

Now, he walked through the living room of his house, checked the fridge, but he wasn't hungry. He stopped in front of the TV, thought of turning it on, but decided not to.

He pulled the knot out of his necktie, and thought a long hot shower would do him good. It was still early, and he figured his wife was still out with Lewis, so he might as well find something to do with himself.

Nate mounted the stairs and started up, thinking about just what he should do with the situation now. The deed had been done, and he had witnessed it with his very eyes.

There really was no longer a need to hire a PI, for Tori had done that work for him. Nate had the photos locked tight in his office safe.

He hadn't spoken to Lewis yet because he just wasn't sure how he was going to proceed, but also because he didn't know how to speak to him without feeling an anger so deep that made him want to literally kill the man.

Nate climbed the final stair, putting him on the second floor, and decided that he would call him, thank him for his services, and try his best not to strangle him. At that time, he would start filing for divorce.

Nate walked past the nursery, thinking of walking in there, for it'd been weeks, but told himself it was still sloppily painted black, and going in there would do nothing but depress him more.

He continued past that room, to his bedroom door. As he walked in, he was surprised to hear the shower running in his bathroom. Stepping just inside the doorway, through the lightly frosted shower glass, he saw his wife's naked body. He watched her fuzzy image lather, scrub herself, smooth her hands all over her body, her behind, her breasts, in between her legs, and Nate felt himself growing in his pants.

The sensation was almost alien to him, for it had been so long since he had experienced it, and he almost forgot that he had stopped taking the pills, flushed them all down the toilet.

Nate pulled the untied necktie out from his collar, dropped it on the floor at his feet, and slid off his suit jacket. He didn't know just what he was doing, or why. His movements weren't inspired or dictated by thought, but the throbbing in between his legs. He wanted his wife right now, and as he pulled his T-shirt over his head, undid his belt buckle, and let his pants fall to the floor, along with his underwear, he told himself he was going to have her.

He stepped out of his shoes, pulled off his socks, was right in front of the shower, about to pull back the shower door.

His wife's back was to him, so she hadn't seen him approach, and she all but screamed when the door was opened behind her. She whipped around, holding her scrub pad up to her chest as if she was trying to hide her entire body behind it.

"Nate!" she practically screamed. "You scared me."

Nate didn't say anything. Just stepped into the shower, then looked at his wife up and down, lust heavy in his eyes.

Monica must've read that look, dropped her eyes down to the massive erection jutting out before him, and said, "You can have the shower. I'm finished."

She made a move for the shower door, but Nate threw his arm across it.

"No, you're not."

"Yes, I am, Nate. I'm going to turn into a prune in a minute."

"Then you'll just be a prune."

Monica looked at him, smiling sheepishly. "Stop playing, and let me out of here," she said, trying for the door again.

Nate blocked her attempt again, and said, "I'm not playing." He reached out, grabbed her with heavy hands, and spun her around in the shower, the water crashing down on both their heads.

"Nate!" Monica cried out, trying to pull away from him. "What are you doing!"

Nate didn't hear her, was overtaken by his lust for her. He wrapped his arms around her waist, still trying to spin her while not slipping on the slick, wet shower floor.

He managed to get behind her, and even though she was still fighting him, he had managed to press her against the shower door. Her entire front half, the side of her face, her full breasts, was pressed to the glass.

She was slick with soap and water, but Nate had a grip around her hips, pulling her ass into him. He grabbed himself, stiff as he could ever remember being.

"Nate!" he heard Monica cry. "What are you doing?"

He slid himself into his wife.

She continued to struggle as he sunk himself as deep into her as he could go. The pleasure was so intense that he no longer paid attention to her cries or her struggling. He focused on the feeling, on how long it'd been since he had felt her like this, how good it was to him that very moment.

Nate let out a moan, as he grabbed tighter on to her soft behind, and then, surprised, he heard his wife moan with him.

He felt her push herself further back into him, felt her open up for him.

She looked over her shoulder at him. "Does it feel good?" she asked.

"Yes," Nate could barely say. "It feels good."

❦

Half an hour later, Nate lay in bed with his arms around Monica. He felt close to her, felt her warmth, could feel her faint heartbeat through her back. He breathed in the scent of her hair, kissing her on the neck.

"I didn't mean to hurt you in there," he whispered in her ear.

"You didn't. It felt good. You just surprised me. It's been so long, I didn't think you wanted me anymore."

That moment, Nate felt compelled to tell her everything that had been happening, everything that he had done.

"No. I could never stop wanting you," he said, and pulled her closer.

Later, after Monica had fallen asleep, Nate lifted up his head, looked over at the clock, and then down at his wife. It was 11:25 P.M.

He leaned in over her, pushed her hair away from her face, and kissed her gently on her cheek.

Nate quietly pulled himself from bed, grabbed his bathrobe off the hook on the back of the bathroom door, and left the bedroom, looking back over his shoulder at his wife before leaving.

Downstairs in the living room, Nate pulled the cords on the blinds, parting them to look out on the city. He stood there, inches away from the glass, thinking about what just happened, and how he truly felt about his wife. He loved her. He had always loved her, even after she told him their child had died; even after he had caught her in that lie, and found out that she would never be able to give him children, he had loved her.

He was angry as hell, bitter, and resentful. Those negative emotions must've masked his true feelings for his wife, had him thinking differently about her, but the true feelings had always been there, as they were right now.

So what did that mean to him? he asked himself. Was he just to scrap all the work he put forth to place his wife in a position where he could divorce her and not be penalized? Yes, he thought, smiling a little, feeling happy that he wouldn't have to go through hurting her like he thought he would. And now, that meant that he could call up Lewis, tell him his services were no longer needed, because he was claiming his wife again. He would also tell him to hand back over the Cadillac, the other belongings, and get his ass out of his town house.

Yeah, Nate thought to himself, smiling wider, feeling content. It would be a nice moment for him.

He would do all those things, and everything would work out just fine between him and his wife, Nate thought.

But what about children? The issue that started all of this, what about that? It would have to be resolved, he knew, and regardless of what he did, or how deeply he felt about his wife, he knew that that issue would have to be taken care of in order for them to make it.

The next morning, Nate came downstairs, dressed for work, and found Monica wearing an apron, and setting the table for breakfast.

"Have a seat, Mr. Kenny," Monica said, cheerfully, pulling his chair out.

Nate took his seat, and received the kiss Monica leaned over to give him on his lips. She grabbed the morning paper off the chair on the other side of him, opened it up, and placed it in his lap.

"There you are, sir," Monica said. "Breakfast will be ready in a jiffy."

"Someone's feeling good this morning," Nate said.

"That's because I had a wonderful time last night," Monica said, spooning eggs onto a plate for her husband.

"And I had a wonderful time, too." Nate smiled.

Monica brought Nate's plate over, set it before him, and sat on the opposite side of the table, staring at him, a content smile on her face.

Nate lifted some of the food on his fork to his mouth and was about to eat it when he stopped, noticing Monica. "What?" he said.

"I love you, Nate."

"Well, I love you too, baby," Nate said. "But I know you're just saying that because I gave you some good sex last night."

"Okay, yeah. It was the sex. How about we do it again tonight? Do you have to work late?"

And there it was. Normally, Nate knew, his wife would've been with Lewis. But he realized now, that had to be only because Nate was making himself unavailable, rendered himself incapable of fulfilling his wife's needs. But now that he was back, her need to see Lewis was obviously gone. If there ever truly was one.

"No," Nate said, looking forward to putting the huge mess behind him. "I don't have to work late again."

46

All during the first couple of hours at work, Monica couldn't stop smiling.

"All right," Tabatha finally said, walking over, carrying half a dozen suits. "What's going on with you?"

"What are you talking about?" Monica said, still smiling.

"You had that stupid grin on your face since you walked in here this morning. Is your face stuck like that, or what?"

"You aren't glad to see me happy?"

"Yes. Very glad, but if you'd like to see me happy too, you'd tell me why you keep on smiling."

Monica quickly glanced around to make sure no customers could overhear her, and then she said, "Tabatha, last night was wonderful!"

"I told you, you need to stop seeing that man. It's just bad—"

"It wasn't Lewis. I was with Nate. We made love last night, and it was fantastic."

"What happened?" Tabatha said. "I thought you said he couldn't."

"I don't know what happened. I was taking a shower, and he surprised me, came in with me, and . . ." Monica shook her head, smiling more and blushing a little. "This morning, I made him breakfast. He told me how much he loved me. It was like having the old Nate back again. I don't know what happened."

"Wow," Tabatha said, trying to figure it out herself. "Maybe he had been abducted by aliens."

"After last night and this morning, it's almost like I can't even remember what that new Nate was like. All the times he ignored me, and treated me badly, it's like it's all been erased, and that made me feel guilty as hell. I felt like confessing to everything at breakfast this morning."

"Tell me you didn't, girl. Please tell me you didn't do that."

Monica thought about this morning, after they had both finished eating, and were just staring across the table at each other.

"Monica, you all right?" Nate asked her.

"There's something I really feel I should tell you."

"What is it?"

"Over the past few weeks, you've been treating me differently. You wouldn't talk to me, wouldn't touch me, and you were hardly ever home." Monica looked away from Nate, down at her plate, swallowed hard, then looked up at him again. "I was lonely and—"

"Monica!" Nate stopped her. "Whatever you're about to say, I don't want to hear it."

"What do you mean?"

"I did treat you badly, I admit that, and whatever you did in retaliation to that, or to get you through that, you did because you needed to. But as long as that's done, as long as it's over, then I don't need to hear about it. Okay?"

"Okay," Monica said.

Tabatha looked at her with shock in her eyes. "Do you think he knew what you were talking about?"

"I don't know."

"It sounded like he did."

"He couldn't have," Monica said, thinking back. "No. He doesn't know. His reaction would've been a lot different. He wouldn't have been that calm about it."

"Then everything is fine with Nate," Tabatha said. "But what are you going to with Lewis?"

"I ended it with him the other night."

"Then that's that. Everything really is cool."

"Not really," Monica said, looking concerned. "He's been calling my cell phone nonstop, saying how much he misses me, that there's still a chance for us."

"What are you going to do?"

"I'm just going to try to ignore him from now on. Hope he gives up."

"And if he doesn't?" Tabatha said, sounding grave.

"Then I don't know what's going to happen."

47

Lewis held the phone to his ear as it continued to ring. After Monica's recorded message started playing, Lewis angrily hung up the phone.

He had been calling her for the last day and half, leaving messages, and she had not returned any of them. He had to assume that she was seeing his number on her caller ID, and simply ignoring it. But why would she do that?

He knew Monica was having second thoughts about him when she felt she was almost found out. But when he mentioned the chance of the two of them being together, Lewis could've sworn he saw her give the proposal a moment of thought before telling him there was no chance.

He picked up the phone again, dialed her number, then quickly hung it up before it had a chance to ring through.

She probably thinks I'm stalking her or something, Lewis thought to himself. If the situation were reversed, and there was some woman that had called him a zillion times over the course of a couple of days, after he had ended it with her, he would probably think the same thing.

That had Lewis thinking, asking himself, just why was he behaving the way he was? Why was he trying to get hold of her, after she had told him that she was done with him?

It was the job. He would miss the money, his new lifestyle, he tried to convince himself, but Lewis knew that wasn't the real reason.

Part of it was that he was introduced to what a wonderful woman Monica was, and then to know that the man she was going back to, the man that she thought loved her, really didn't.

Mr. Kenny didn't deserve a woman like that. After everything he did to try to rid himself of her, it just didn't seem right that she would end up with him.

And then there was the undeniable fact that he had feelings for her. Was it love? Lewis wasn't certain, but he thought about the woman damn near every moment of the day, missed her when she wasn't around, felt like a better man when she was, and couldn't imagine her not being in his life in the days ahead. Something just told him that they were supposed to be together, and that's what had Lewis glancing at the phone yet again.

He picked it up, but this time dialed Selena's number instead of Monica's. There was no answer.

Lewis had stopped by there the other day, banged on the door, but she wasn't home. He had planned to go back, but there were things that he had to take care of to prepare for the repercussions he was sure he was going to face since Mr. Kenny walked in the house and saw him with his wife.

Lewis was surprised that the man hadn't called him yet, cursing him out about the fact that Lewis hadn't informed him that he was now screwing Monica.

The man was outraged, and as Lewis continued pounding his wife, he could see that in his face, in his eyes, as Mr. Kenny stared at him through the patio glass door.

It was all quite funny to Lewis. The man never liked him, Lewis knew, treated him like a child, like he was some brainless idiot off the street. But he gave Lewis instructions and the tools to have sex with his wife, so he shouldn't have been surprised when it was actually happening.

The next morning, Lewis went to the bank, withdrew all the money that was there, before Mr. Kenny decided to do something like close the account. There was a little more than $13,000 there, and Lewis had it given to him all in hundred-dollar bills.

He didn't know if Mr. Kenny would try to take back the money he had paid him, but that just seemed like the type of man he was.

Lewis wondered if he even knew what was going on, whether he was aware that his wife had ended things with him or not.

Lewis looked down at the phone again, and decided he might as well find out.

He grabbed the phone and dialed Mr. Kenny's cell phone number.

When the phone was answered, Lewis said, as if he had just made the discovery, "Mr. Kenny, something's happened. Things aren't going well. Your wife—"

"I realize something has happened," Nate said, his voice surprisingly calm.

"She told me that she didn't want to see me again," Lewis said.

"Did she?"

"Yes."

There was a long pause before Nate said, "How long have you been fucking her?"

"What did you say?"

"You heard what I said, and don't tell me that was the first time, because I have photos. I have proof that it was before then. How long?"

"I don't know," Lewis said, his voice low. "Something like a week, maybe a couple of days more. But Mr. Kenny—"

"No. There's nothing more you have to say. I need to speak with you, face-to-face, discuss these matters. I'll call you back with the time and the place."

48

It was 10 P.M., later that night, and Nate pulled his Mercedes onto an empty lot surrounded by abandoned buildings. There he saw a pair of illuminated headlights. He drove over.

He parked some ten feet from the truck the headlights glared from, got out, and started walking toward it.

Almost at the same time, the driver of the truck stepped out and started in Nate's direction.

Nate had called Lewis back an hour after he had spoken to him, and said, "Meet me on the empty Sixty-third Street lot, three blocks west of Stony, at ten o'clock."

"But Mr. Kenny—"

"Just meet me there, and we'll talk about everything then," Nate said, hanging up the phone.

Now Nate, with a briefcase in his hand, stood face-to-face with Lewis in the center of the lot, both their cars still running, their headlamps directed at them.

"Mr. Kenny, I don't know what happened," Lewis said, speaking first. "I haven't spoken to Monica in days, and I was just trying to find out what was going on."

"You don't have to worry about that anymore, Lewis," Nate said, opening his briefcase, pulling out a plain brown envelope, packed tight, and handing it to Lewis.

"What's this?"

"It's your last week's pay. But because you've done such a good job, I've doubled it. There's ten thousand dollars in there. Thank you for your help."

"What do you mean, my last week's?" Lewis said, looking bewildered.

"It's over, Lewis. I have what I need. We've accomplished what we've set out to."

"Mr. Kenny, I don't think we're done yet. You were supposed to get pictures taken, weren't you? You never told me that was done."

"That's nothing that you need to worry about. Your business now is to start packing your things and vacating my property in the next three days. Leave the Cadillac in the garage, the keys to it and the house on the living room table. The cell phone you can keep if you like, I will just have it transferred over to your name. Good night, Mr. Waters," Nate said, turning and starting to walk away. "And have a nice life."

"No!" Lewis said, loudly.

Nate stopped abruptly on the graveled pavement beneath him. He slowly turned around to face Lewis again. "No, what?"

"No, the job is not over," Lewis said.

"I just told you it was."

"Then I'm not ready for it to be. You might not want to hear this, but I've developed feelings for your wife," Lewis said.

Nate took a moment to reply, then simply said, "So?"

"So, I know she has feelings for me too, and I've decided that I'm going to continue seeing her whether you like it or not."

Nate looked at the man as though he had lost his mind, and then could do nothing but start laughing boisterously.

"And just what makes you think she'd want to continue seeing you? You have no money."

"I have the money you gave me," Lewis said, holding up the envelope.

"You're a nobody."

"You wife didn't think that when she was screaming my name,

248

yelling out how much she loved what I was doing to her. You remember that. You heard her, didn't you . . . Nate?"

This was the first time the boy had dared to call him by his first name, and Nate couldn't determine which angered him more, the disrespectful talk of his wife, or him addressing Nate in that manner.

"You can do what you want, but you'll be doing it from the street, because you're no longer able to go back to that house. As of this moment, I'm evicting you."

Now Lewis was laughing. "Sorry, Nate. I've been kicked out of too many places to know that I have rights. I need at least ten days' notice, and without that, I'm not going any damn place."

"Fine," Nate said. "Then you'll walk back there. Give me the keys to the truck," he said, holding his palm open.

"Take them from me."

Nate sized the big man up again. He looked around them, and there was nothing but empty lot, and vacant buildings surrounding them. There was no way he was going to stand out there and fistfight this guy, even though Nate felt confident that he had a chance at taking him. He would not stoop to his level. He didn't have to. Nate had everything going for him, and this character had nothing. The best thing Nate could do at that moment was just get rid of him. Give him something that would make him go away forever, and then Nate could go on living his life with his wife without interference.

"So, this is how you want to play it. Taking the gloves off, hunh?" Nate said. "Then I'll play. What do you want?"

"I told you what I wanted. Your wife."

"Besides her. You hold ten thousand dollars in your hand. Add that to the fifteen I've already paid you, that makes twenty-five. I'll equal that, giving you an even fifty, if you just forget about all of this and disappear."

"I can't do that."

"If it's a woman that you want, I know of one that you'd love. Her name is Tori, and she used to work for me. She's very attractive, and—"

"Nate, Nate, Nate," Lewis said, pacing in front of him, his arms crossed over his chest, shaking his head. "You aren't getting me. What I want is Monica, and you don't have enough money to give me to make me change my mind."

At that point, Nate had had enough. He quickly placed himself in front of Lewis, their faces inches apart.

"Now you get something straight. I stood here and tried to play your little game, but understand, you do not want to fuck with me! I have more power, and know more people, than your high school diploma could ever allow you to understand. So if you like the wonderful feeling of standing erect on two good legs, and want to continue to enjoy it, you'll do as I say, and leave."

"Is that a threat, Nate?" Lewis said.

"Take it however it best serves you."

"Come after me, and I'll tell Monica everything," Lewis threatened.

"That would hurt you as much as me, if not more. Do you think she'd want to be with someone who took money to try to fuck her? Good luck, but I think you know better than that. Lewis, be a smart kid, take the offer and run. Otherwise, you're going to find out that you were nothing but a toy that my wife played with, until her real man came back."

"We'll just see about that," Lewis said, turning and walking casually back to Nate's truck with Nate's ten grand.

49

When Lewis woke up the next morning, he reached for the phone and dialed Selena's number because he needed to see his daughter.

The phone rang, then the call was sent to voice mail.

Lewis angrily left a message.

"Selena, where in the hell are you? I'm coming to see Layla. If you get this within a half hour, call me back."

Lewis slammed the phone down, then jumped out of bed, pulled some clothes out of his drawers to wear today, then went into the bathroom to clean up.

When he stepped into the shower, he found that the water was freezing, and regardless of how many times he fidgeted with the knobs, it didn't get any warmer, prompting Lewis to run downstairs and turn all the burners on his stove on.

Nothing happened. The gas was off.

Maybe the pilot, Lewis thought, walking to the door that led to the basement, opening it, and clicking on the stairway lights, but no light came on. He clicked it on and off a number of times, but still nothing happened.

He thought about changing the bulb, but then something else came to mind.

Lewis walked over to the kitchen light switch, tried that. Nothing. He yanked open the refrigerator door. No light, no cool air, no power.

He ran through the house trying every light switch, appliance, and TV set. There was no power.

It had to have been Mr. Kenny behind this all, Lewis thought, angrily. And if the gas and electricity was off, he knew it would only be a matter of time before his phones were turned off as well.

Then all of a sudden, something even more disturbing came to his mind. He abandoned the idea of showering and ran upstairs, slid into his jeans, socks, and shoes as quickly as possible. He grabbed his shirt, threw it on as he raced down the stairs, out the house, and to the garage.

Mr. Kenny was going to shut everything down, Lewis now knew, and take everything from him, and he just prayed that he wasn't working so fast that he had already gotten around to taking the truck.

Once at the garage, he quickly slipped the key into the lock, and threw the door open.

To his relief, the truck was still there.

Lewis went to the house, locked it up, took off in the direction of Selena's place.

When he arrived, he jumped out of the truck and almost ran to the door, he was so eager to see Layla.

He knocked on the door, and realized he was feeling strangely about everything that was happening now. Yes, he had the money that he had gotten paid, but $25,000 wasn't buying him a home. He was jobless now, would have to go back to cutting hair, and he knew that wouldn't be enough to get his daughter away from Selena. At this point, he had no idea what was going to happen.

Lewis was about to knock again when the door opened up a crack, Selena peering out at him.

"What you doing here? You ain't call," Selena said.

Lewis noticed that something seemed strange about her.

"I did call, but you ain't pick up the phone."

"I was busy," Selena said, her words slurring together.

Lewis looked closer at her, and he realized something wasn't right. She looked odd, her eyes barely open, looking as though she hadn't even had enough strength to hold her own self up.

"Where's Layla?"

"She in here. She sleep."

"I want to see her. Open the door," Lewis said.

"Why?"

"Because I said I want to see my daughter!"

"I told you she sleep!" Selena said, practically screaming.

Lewis gave her another long, hard look, definitely not liking what he was seeing, then all of a sudden he was pushing himself in the door.

Selena tried to close it before he could force his way in, but he was far too strong, and Selena ended up almost falling, stumbling backward away from the door as it opened.

Lewis stood just inside the apartment, was about to head toward the bedroom, when his attention was caught by what was spread out across the coffee table.

A belt, a cigarette lighter, a hypodermic needle, and the bent, burned tablespoon.

He raced over there, grabbed one of the items, and held it up.

"What the fuck is this?" Lewis yelled, holding a tiny plastic vial in his hand, a white stone in it. "I said, what the fuck is this!" He stormed over to Selena, grabbing her arm, shaking her, as he held the vial up just before her eyes.

"You gonna wake the baby," Selena said, almost oblivious to what was happening right in front of her, her entire body covered in sweat.

"You fucking doing drugs again!" Lewis yelled. "This where all that money went?"

Selena didn't answer him, just tried to look in his direction, her head rolling about limply on her neck.

"Answer me!"

"I needed something," Selena said, her words sounding just above a whisper. "I needed something to help me do what I had to do to get my money."

"I told you you should've never started fucking those men!" Lewis said, saddened, almost feeling sorry for what Selena had reverted to.

But he couldn't let that get in his way. She had done what she said she never would again, and Lewis knew that he could no longer deal with the woman, and definitely not let her continue to raise his daughter.

Lewis pushed Selena away from him, and ran into the bedroom.

Lewis grabbed Layla out of her crib, carried her back into the living room, preparing to take her.

"Do what the fuck you want, but you ain't doing it to her," Lewis said, heading for the door.

Before he could reach it, Lewis heard a shrill cry from behind him, and then felt Selena on his back, clawing, grabbing for their child.

He quickly spun, swung his arm out, managed to push her off him. She fell to the floor, but immediately got back to her feet, started running toward him again.

"Give me my baby! You ain't taking my baby!" Selena cried, as she swung wildly at Lewis, clawing at his arms as he tried to protect Layla from her wild swipes.

"You going to hurt her!"

"Give her to me. I'll call the police, throw your ass in jail! Give her to me!" Selena screamed, continuing to fight for the baby, no matter how much Lewis tried to push her away. Then she managed to get her arm around Layla's leg, started pulling at her.

"All right! All right," Lewis said, giving the baby to Selena, so the child wouldn't get hurt.

Immediately, Selena calmed down some, taking Layla in her arms, kissing her all over her face and head.

Lewis looked on painfully. "I'm coming back to get her," he said. "I swear. I'm coming back."

❦

"Now! I need for you to go get her now!" Lewis said to the social worker at the Department of Children and Family Services.

After leaving Selena's, he ran back to the truck, called information, got the address, and sped over there as fast as he could.

Lewis followed behind a portly woman, holding a stack of folders, walking quickly down a hallway filled with young mothers and their children of all ages and ethnicities.

"Mr. Waters, I wish we could help you right away, but you'll have to speak to a social worker," the woman said, over her shoulder.

"I'm speaking to you. This is an emergency."

The woman stopped, turned to Lewis. Only then could he tell just how haggard she was. "You see all these women, and their children around you. All of them have emergencies. But first they had to see a social worker."

❦

Lewis waited three hours, but finally he was seen. He answered every question they asked.

Yes, the child was his. Yes, his name was on the birth certificate. No, he did not beat the mother, nor the child. It went on and on for almost an hour.

"Will you go out and get my daughter?" Lewis finally asked, after the social worker had completed the questions and the paperwork.

"We should be able to get someone out there tomorrow, the next day the latest."

"My daughter can't wait that long."

"Mr. Waters, there's nothing more that we can do. We will get out there as soon as we can."

50

It was half an hour till the end of Monica's shift, and she had gotten her purse, set it under the store's counter, preparing to go. She pulled her cell phone out to check what calls she may have missed, and when she looked at it, she immediately called Tabatha.

"What?" Tabatha called from across the store.

"Just come here. I want you to see this."

Tabatha came across the store, and up to the counter. Monica passed her the cell phone.

"Fifteen missed calls," Tabatha said.

"And they're all from Lewis."

Monica took the phone back from her, started punching numbers.

"What are you doing, calling him back?"

"No. I'm going to delete the messages."

"Don't you think you should listen to them first?"

"No. I don't want to hear anything that man has to say," Monica said, pressing the phone to her ear. "I just wish he would leave me alone."

But just then, Tabatha turned toward the door of the store and said, "I think you're wishing for a little too much."

Lewis was walking in, and he did not look like himself. Gone were the suits he always wore, replaced with jeans and a T-shirt. He wasn't smiling, looking carefree as he had always appeared in the past, but seemed anxious, worried, almost frantic, as he came quickly over to Monica.

"Monica, I need to talk to you."

"Lewis, you can't be here," Monica said.

"Look, it's really important. I have to talk to you. I need your help, and I think there are some things that you should know about."

Tabatha stepped in front of Lewis. "She told you she ain't got nothing to say to you, so you might as well turn around and walk up out of here."

Monica pulled Tabatha out from in front of Lewis. "I got this, Tabatha. You aren't understanding me," she said to Lewis, looking toward the door. "My husband will be here any minute to pick me up. You have to go."

"I just need a minute."

"Call me."

"You ain't been returning my phone calls. Why should I believe you when you say that you will now?"

"All right," Monica said. "I promise. But, Lewis! I told you, I don't have have time for this. Just please, go!"

"Make sure, because I have to talk to you."

"Okay. Just leave," Monica said, preparing to push him out the door, when the store's door opened again. This time it was Nate walking in.

Monica froze, her heart seeming to stop, and although she was lucky enough to escape the last close call the other night, she knew she would finally be found out here.

"Hey, Nate," Tabatha quickly said, as if everything was normal.

"Hi, Tabatha," Nate said, walking in between Tabatha and Lewis, and giving his wife a kiss on the cheek.

Monica just stood there, her body trembling, her head starting to feel light.

"Baby, you okay?" Nate asked.

"Yeah, yeah," Monica said. "It's just been a long day. Just ready to get out of here. Come on, honey. You ready?" Monica said, grabbing her husband's arm, and attempting to pull him toward the door.

"Hey," Nate said, his attention all of a sudden drawn to Lewis. "Are you going to introduce me to your friend?"

Monica opened her mouth, but found herself speechless. She looked desperately to Tabatha, who, thankfully, quickly grabbed Lewis, snatching him beside her, and said, "Oh. This my new man."

"Really," Nate said, looking him over head to toe. He extended his hand. "I'm Nate Kenny. Pleasure to meet you. And you are . . ."

"His name is . . . Luther. Luther," Tabatha said, turning to Lewis. "This is Monica's *husband*, Nate."

Nate continued to hold his hand out for Lewis, which he finally took.

"Nice to meet you, Luther," Nate said.

"Yeah, you too . . . Nate," Lewis said.

"Okay," Monica said, tugging on Nate. "We're going to get out of here. So see you, Tabatha, and Luther."

"Oh, and hey," Lewis said, before Monica was able to pull Nate out the door. "Maybe the four of us can get together sometime." Lewis stared directly into Nate's eyes. "I'm sure we probably have a lot in common."

Monica didn't know what the hell that was about, but she dragged Nate out of there before he had a chance to respond.

51

Even hours after Monica and Nate left the store, it seemed she couldn't get past the event that happened with Lewis.

"You sure you feeling all right, baby?" Nate said.

"Yeah, I'm fine," she said. "Just some stuff on my mind, and like I said, it's been a long day."

"Then we don't have to eat out tonight like we planned. Let's go home so you can relax, and I'll go out and bring something back. How does that sound?"

"Perfect," Monica said, smiling.

When they got back home, Nate took Monica upstairs to their bedroom, and insisted that she take it easy. He told her that when he returned, he would bring dinner up to her on a tray.

As Nate descended the last stair, and stepped onto the main floor, his attention was focused on his wife's purse, sitting on the dining room table.

He stepped over to it, looked over his shoulder to make sure his wife wasn't behind him, then unzipped her bag, reached in, and took her cell phone.

Once in his car, Nate flipped the phone open, and saw that Lewis had been trying to call his wife. His number was there countless times. He seemed to be desperately trying to reach her, and considering that Nate had found Lewis there at his wife's store, he figured the man was probably planning on telling her everything.

Nate looked down at the phone again, noticing it was in silent mode. He switched the ringer on, and was startled when it immediately starting ringing.

It was Lewis's number.

Nate took the call.

"Monica!" Nate heard Lewis say. He sounded desperate, frenzied. "There's something I have to tell you."

"The warnings I gave you just weren't enough, I'm assuming," Nate said. He could hear the gasp that escaped Lewis's lips. "Lewis, why don't you just leave my wife alone."

"She's going to find out."

"I'm not going to tell you again," Nate said, starting to feel an anger and hatred for this man, greater than he'd ever felt before. "Leave her alone!"

"I can't do that."

"Fine," Nate said. "Have it your way." Nate closed the phone, got out of the car, and with all his force, slammed the phone to the ground, where it broke apart. He bent down, grabbed the two shattered pieces, walked over to a sewer drain he spotted and dropped them into it.

The boy had to push his hand, Nate thought. He didn't want to, but now he had to get serious.

Half an hour later, Nate stood in front of the door to his brother's house, waiting for Tim to open it. When he finally did, Nate said, "I need to talk to you."

"Come in," Tim said, holding the door open.

"No. Come out. I don't have a lot of time."

Tim stepped out the door.

"Pull it all the way closed," Nate said.

Tim looked at Nate oddly for a moment, then reached back and pulled the door shut. "Now, what is? You don't seem yourself."

"She was having sex with him, Tim," Nate said.

"How do you know that?"

"I have photos. I have proof. And I saw it, Tim. I walked in on them, and I saw them having sex with my own eyes!"

Tim lowered his head. "Aw, dammit, Nate," he sighed, shaking his head. "But isn't that why you hired him?"

"That's beside the point. Some things have happened, and me and Monica are doing better. We've been talking, and—"

"You told her?"

"No. But we've been talking, and we've had sex, and I realized how wrong I've been. I think we can make it work."

"Then just tell the guy that he's fired. Tell him it's all over."

"I've tried that, but he said he has feelings for Monica, and that she feels the same. The man has lost his mind," Nate said, frustrated. "He says he's going to continue seeing her whether I like it or not."

"You need to tell her, Nate. You need to come clean, get everything out in the open, because it's not going to get any better."

"That's not going to happen. I won't expose myself like that, when things are as fragile as they are right now. We have a chance, but if I tell Monica what I've done—"

"Then what are you going to do?"

"I've tried everything, but nothing has worked. So now, I'm going to need your help."

"What kind of help?" Tim said, reluctantly.

"Forceful help."

"I don't exactly know what you're talking about, but the answer is no," Tim said. "If you're talking about beating this man up to make him leave Monica alone, I won't do it."

"Tim," Nate said, grabbing on to his brother's arm, "this might be the only way."

Tim pulled away. "No! You approached him with this ridiculous scheme to sleep with your wife, and then when he's successful, and actually enjoys it, falls in love with her, which is something you should've realized could've happened, you want to beat the hell out

261

of him. No. I will not do this for you, Nate," Tim said, turning away, about to walk in the door. "I will not."

"I'm asking you. As your brother, I'm asking you, Tim."

"You don't know what could happen. He may really get hurt. Or you. Or me. Just come clean like I said, then you won't have to do this. I urge you. It's the only right thing to do."

Tim turned, pushed the door open, ready to walk in.

"How many times have you not been able to pay your mortgage, Tim?"

Tim froze.

"I busted my ass to build the company that I did, and now that I'm trying to save that, you won't even help me," Nate said.

"You are not using that against me. Besides, this has nothing to do with your company, or you helping me out. It has to do with your plan backfiring on you. A plan that you devised because you were too much of a coward to tell your wife how you really felt. And now that things aren't working the way you wanted, you're still too much of a coward to tell her the truth. I'm not helping, Nate."

"Fine, Tim," Nate said, disappointed. "If that's the way it is between us. Fine." He turned and headed down the steps.

"Why don't you just tell her?" Tim called. "She has a right to know. Just tell her."

☙❧

When Nate got home, he served his wife her food, then sat on the edge of the bed.

"You know what?" he said, placing a hand to the side of her face. "I think you should take the day off tomorrow. What do you think about that?"

Monica looked up, and to Nate's surprise said, "I think you're right. I could use a little time away."

"Well, if that's the case, why don't we make it a real vacation? Tomorrow, I'll book us some reservations for the Bahamas or something, and we'll leave the day after. We'll take a week or two, just get away, and do it like we used to. What do you say?"

"They'll kill me for taking off at such short notice."

"If they don't like it, quit. You never needed to work that job anyway."

Nate smiled when he saw that his wife approved of what he said. "Okay, let's do it."

52

It shouldn't have to be this way, Nate thought, feeling his heart pound in his chest as he crouched in the bushes, looking at the three men dressed in black crouching around him.

Nate's brother, Tim, had let him down, didn't want to help Nate do what had to be done, regardless of how many things he had done for his brother. But Nate wouldn't let that stop him. The next day, from work, he made a number of phone calls to men who were acquainted with other men that for the right amount of money would help Nate do what had to be done.

When Nate spoke to them over the phone, he told them to wear black, and meet him at the location Nate specified. From there, they would drive to the house Nate had provided for Lewis, and that's where they were now.

They had gotten out of the van that the men had driven, and had quickly moved to the bushes that bordered the side of the house, crouching low.

Nate did not know these men's names, didn't want to know them. All he knew was that they were big, evil-looking, had all spent a stint in prison for breaking one law or another, and had nothing against physical violence.

They sat out in the bushes just long enough to verify that Lewis was indeed in the house. Nate had seen him pass by one of the windows, and that was all the information he needed.

"I have the key to the place," Nate said to the men, crouching in front of them. "We'll walk right in and do it there. Is everyone ready?"

One man grunted "Yeah," the other two nodding their heads silently.

"Then let's do this," Nate said, and pulled down over his face the ski mask that was rolled up on his head, the other men doing the same.

They were just about to leap from the bushes, when Lewis's front door opened.

"Hold it!" Nate whispered loudly, holding out his arms for the men to stand back.

They silently watched as Lewis closed the door, locked it, and descended the stairs. He stepped out onto the walkway, and then made a left.

Nate's wide eyes peered through the black ski mask at the men, then quickly gave them the signal to converge.

All four men sprang out of the bushes, and raced quickly and silently down the street at Lewis. By the time Lewis had heard the men behind him, they were already on him, had clubbed him over the head, knocked him down, and were dragging him into a nearby alleyway.

Lewis kicked and swung with all he had, but was no match for the four big men that had him by each limb, dragging him across the ground. Once in the narrow space surrounded by buildings, he was released.

Lewis tried jumping to his feet, but before he could, he was kicked in the face. Lewis's lip split in half, blood spraying out from the wound as his body whirled and fell over from the force of the blow.

He rolled over on his belly, lifted himself up to his hands and knees, spit out the quantity of blood that had accumulated in his mouth, and then looked up, seeing the four men in black clothes and masks standing around him, the light from the streetlight above splashing down across their broad shoulders.

"Why you doin' this?" he said.

The only answer he received was all the men closing in around him, kicking him in the ribs, on his back, in his face, stomping down on his head, his hands, his legs, till Lewis seemed very close to dead and could not move at all.

When the beating was over, the three men that Nate hired stepped back, allowed Nate to walk forward, look down on Lewis's body. It lay there on its stomach, its arms and legs stretched out, and pointed crookedly in every direction. The clothes that weren't torn from Lewis's body were saturated and stained with his blood.

Nate used the toe of his boot like a shovel, slid it up under Lewis's shoulder, then flipped him over.

They had beaten him pretty badly, Nate thought upon seeing his face now. One of his eyes was swollen, his lips were split, and blood was spilling out of both corners of his mouth. The beating was worse than he had realized, and he almost felt sorry for the boy, but like Nate said before, he just wouldn't listen.

Nate was about to turn, walk away, when he saw Lewis's good eye start to open.

Nate kneeled down over him, brought his face very close to Lewis. "This is what you get when you refuse to listen. Stay the fuck away from my wife, or next time you'll end up dead," Nate said, peeling back his ski mask.

Nate stood, then walked away.

53

Monica sat watching TV, thinking the vacation idea that her husband had come up with was a good one. They needed time together, away from all that was happening around them. Not only that, it would give things between her and Lewis time to cool off.

Monica took a sip of the glass of wine she was drinking from, and picked up the remote to do a little channel surfing, when the phone rang.

"Hello," she answered.

"Monica, is Nate there?" It was Tim.

"No. I'm sorry, Tim. I—"

"Do you know where he is?" Tim said, sounding anxious.

"No. He said that he had some follow-up business with that client he had been working with."

"I need to talk to you."

"Okay. What about?" Monica said, starting to feel a little worried, because of the tone of Tim's voice.

"Not over the phone. We need to meet. Okay?"

"But, Tim. Maybe I should—"

"Monica," Tim interrupted her. "Trust me. We need to meet. I have something very important that I need to tell you."

"When?"

"Now. Meet me now. Come down, I'm waiting outside your building in my car."

Tim drove west for twenty minutes before stopping on the side of a dark side street. He threw the car in park, then turned to her.

"Monica, what I'm about to tell you is shocking, but since he wouldn't tell you, I felt I had to."

"Since who wouldn't tell me?"

"Nate knows you're cheating, Monica. He knows about everything."

"What are you talking about, Tim?" Monica said, feeling as though she had to be dreaming.

"He knows that you've been seeing that man Lewis, knows that you've slept with him."

Monica's mouth fell open, her eyes ballooning. She tried to speak but couldn't. When speech did come back to her, she could only say one word. "How?"

"Because he set the whole thing up. He hired him, paid him, and told him everything he needed to know to get next to you."

54

Lewis was left there in the alley after he was beaten. He did not move, couldn't move for some time after that.

He hadn't known where they had come from.

He was going to walk to the phone on the corner to try and call Monica again, and then someone was on him, throwing him to the ground. He tried to fight them, but there were too many, and all he could do was curl into a ball, try to protect himself as best he could, hope that he didn't get seriously hurt.

Afterward, he lay there, falling in and out of consciousness. Then, when he finally felt able, he pulled himself up from the pavement, staggered the block home.

He went to the garage, thankful again to see that the truck was still there, fell into it, and somehow got himself to the emergency room.

There, the doctor had told him that nothing was broken. He was bruised all over. His left eye was swollen shut; cuts, scars, and scratches were all over the rest of his face and body. His ribs were badly bruised, and he could hardly breathe without pain, so they had to be taped.

The doctor gave Lewis a prescription for some pills, told him to stay in bed, rest, and move around as little as possible to avoid the pain his ribs would cause, but Lewis could not do that.

269

This morning he got back in his truck, drove to the phone on the corner, and called DCFS to see if anyone had gone out to pick up his daughter.

"Mr. Waters," the social worker he had spoken with told him, "I'm sorry, but I told you we'd get out there as soon as we were able."

Lewis slammed the phone in her face, realizing he would have to take care of the situation himself.

Half an hour later, Lewis parked in front of Selena's apartment. He quickly, and as carefully as he could, lowered himself out of the truck, and walked toward Selena's door.

As he got closer, he increased his pace, because he thought he heard his child crying.

Once closer to the door, he realized it was, indeed, Layla. Lewis banged on the door, yelling.

"Selena. You in there? Open the door."

No response, just the persistent crying of his daughter.

"Selena! Open the door!" Lewis said again, pounding as hard as his injured ribs would let him.

Still nothing.

He looked quickly to his left, to his right, as if for something that would help him get in the house.

He moved in front of the window, looked through, and past the partly pulled-back bedsheet that covered the window. He could see Selena's leg stretching from the sofa, her foot resting on the floor.

What the fuck is she doing in there? Lewis asked himself. Why won't she answer the door?

Lewis yelled into the window. "Selena!"

Again, nothing. But Layla cried even louder, recognizing her father's voice.

Lewis grabbed the steel bars that covered the window, gave them a tug as if he could pull them away.

Then he thought, Try the door.

He moved in front of it, wrapped his hand around the doorknob, and turned.

The door opened, and his daughter turned to see her father, her eyes pink and puffy, her face covered with tears.

She was lying in her mother's lap, there on the sofa, but Selena wasn't holding her.

Selena was slumped back into the sofa, her head thrown back, her mouth slightly agape, her eyelids slightly parted, as if lazily staring at something on the ceiling.

Layla turned back to her, pulling on her mother's tiny tank top, as if trying to get her to pay attention to the child.

But that was not happening, Lewis noticed, rushing over to his daughter, because Selena's legs and arms were stretched out wide, a belt looped loosely around the biceps of her right arm, a syringe stuck, and dangling from the vein just below it.

Lewis stood over her, brought his face close to her nose, her lips, and listened intently.

He heard nothing, felt no air against his cheek. He slapped her lightly a number of times.

"Selena. Selena! Wake up!" he ordered.

Layla started screaming, staring up at her father, as though she knew exactly what was going on. As though she knew that her mother had accidentally overdosed on drugs and was lying there dead.

"Selena!" Lewis said, grabbing her by the shoulders now, shaking her, tears coming to his face.

He shook her till his ribs felt as though they were pushing through his skin, and when he let go, when her body fell limp and lifeless back to the sofa, he knew that she was gone.

55

Last night, Tim had told her everything. He told her that Nate had planned this entire affair. That he did it because Monica could not have children. That, as opposed to being a man, and just telling her the truth, he behaved as a coward, went through all of that just to get her to cheat on him, so he wouldn't have to lose any of his precious money.

The man was even taking pills to make him impotent, he wanted to divorce her so badly.

After she was given the news, she wanted Tim to drive her to Nate's office so she could kill him.

"He said he'd seen the two of you," Tim said last night.

"What do you mean, he said he *saw* the two of us?" Monica said, wondering when the shocking information would just stop coming.

"He saw you having sex. On the deck, outside of the town house."

All Monica could do was drop her face into her hands, shake her head.

She felt dirty, filthy, and wondered how Nate could've seen them, and she not see him.

And then she remembered the position she was in, thrown over that railing, screaming how much she loved what Lewis was doing to her.

She almost let herself feel sorry for Nate, but then she immediately stopped that emotion from surfacing. He was the one that planned all of this. Obviously, he didn't care that his wife was getting fucked right before his eyes. He had wanted it.

It was all too much for Monica to absorb. "Take me back," she told Tim.

"What are you going to do?" Tim said, starting the car.

"I don't know. But thank you, I guess," Monica said.

When she got home, Monica could only imagine where her husband was, because he was not there.

She waited up for him for an hour, then forced herself to sleep, knowing that if he had come in while she was awake, she probably would've attacked him.

After waking up the next morning, lying in bed, pretending to be asleep, turned away from Nate as he prepared for work, she was glad that she hadn't said anything to him yet. It was best that he not know she knew, until she decided just what she was going to do about all this.

She continued to lie there, trying to find out just what that would be, when she felt her husband lean over her.

Monica quickly closed her eyes.

Nate kissed her on the cheek. "Good-bye, sweetheart," he whispered in her ear, thinking she was still sleeping. "I love you."

Monica wanted to spring up at that moment, curse him out, then scratch his eyes out, she was so angry, so hurt at what he did to her. She just remained lying there, her anger all of a sudden turning to pain.

She felt the tears coming, thinking about just how much he really couldn't have loved her. All that he had done over the past three weeks, all that he had said, everything was done to rid himself of her.

She hated Nate that moment, but realized it wasn't just Nate that was a part of this, wasn't just Nate that ran around professing his love for her, lying to her. It was Lewis too.

After her husband had gone, Monica jumped out of bed, grabbed the phone. Lewis was always telling her how crazy he was about her, had even mentioned that she should leave her husband for him.

What the hell was that about? Monica thought, quickly punching in Lewis's phone number.

It was about Nate paying him to say those things, things that Monica was foolishly starting to believe. Not saying that it would've made a difference if it was all true, she just couldn't believe that someone would do something like that.

Monica received the same message regarding his phone's disconnection she had gotten the last time she called him, and only then did she remember.

She slammed the phone down, and after only a moment of thought, she started grabbing clothes to throw on.

She raced to Lewis's house, telling herself that she would not just let him disappear, shut down shop after the mission had been accomplished.

She needed to face him, tell him how low-down, how disgraceful a man he was.

She hoped that was all she would do, feeling how intense her anger had become. She hoped she would not lash and lunge out at him, try to physically hurt him as much as he had emotionally pained her.

Monica pulled up outside Lewis's town house, ran up the stairs, and started banging on the door.

It took him longer than it should've to answer, but Monica continued banging relentlessly, yelling out his name.

"Answer the door, Lewis! I know you're in there!"

She saw movement behind the curtain, heard the door being unlocked, and she prepared herself to let him have it the moment he showed his face.

When that finally did happen, Monica couldn't believe what she saw.

Lewis stood in front of her, his face swollen, bruised, and busted. A patch covered his left eye. Purple and deep red splotches painted his face. Both his cheeks were swollen to twice their size, and his bottom lip was split down the middle.

Monica couldn't speak a word. A gasp escaped her lips.

Lewis limped back, held the door open for her to enter through.

Monica walked in, but stopped just in front of Lewis.

"What happened?" she said, softly, sadly.

"Just come in, please."

Monica stepped further in.

Lewis closed the door.

"Have a seat," he said, wincing some as he walked a little closer to her.

"I'm not here to have a seat. What happened?"

"I don't want to talk about that right now."

"Why not?"

"I just don't," Lewis said quickly, almost angrily.

It was a bad time, Monica thought, to be bringing this to him, but just because he was in obvious pain, that did not discount everything he had done to her. The beating he had obviously taken probably had something to do with it.

"Then I have something I need to talk to you about," Monica said, feeling her anger slowly starting to return to her.

"No. Not before I tell you something."

"What?"

Lewis appeared as though he was about to speak, stopped himself, swallowed hard, then finally said, "Someone has been paying me to sleep with you."

"What!"

"Yeah. Just sit down, and I'll tell you."

To Monica's shock, Lewis confessed to everything. He told her that it was him that had wrecked her husband's car. That was how it all started, Lewis said.

He told Monica that her husband was threatening to sue him, throw him in jail, if he didn't go along with what he had planned, even though Lewis didn't want to do it at first.

"At first," Monica said.

Lewis told Monica how he saw the photos, how he became attracted to her that very moment, how it wasn't an act when he was trying to get to know her, or when he acted so sincere when he made love to her. Lewis confessed that he had fallen for Monica be-fore they had even made love for the first time.

"Then after you saw your husband in the Chinese food place, everything just fell apart," Lewis said, speaking slowly, his head down as he sat on the edge of his living room chair. "After that, I don't know what happened. Things must've gotten better between the two of you. He told me everything was over, and even though I told him I didn't want it to be, that I was in love with you, he said it was."

"In love with me?" Monica said, surprised by his admission.

"I wasn't sure it was that, until just this moment. But yeah, Mon-ica. I love you."

Monica could not respond. After all this man had done to her, now he was telling her that he loved her.

"Do you have any feelings for me?

"You have no business asking me that. After what you did. After taking money—"

"It wasn't just to sleep with you. I needed that money."

"For what!" Monica said, raising her voice. "Did you need money that damn bad that you were willing to ruin someone's marriage for it!"

Lewis just sat there, looking apologetically into Monica's eyes.

"Answer me, motherfucker! Well, did you?" she screamed.

"Yes," Lewis said, his voice very low, and then all of a sudden, the sound of a baby crying could be heard from upstairs.

Monica whipped her head in that direction, then quickly looked back to Lewis. "What was that?"

"The reason why I needed the money."

56

Nate was happy with himself. He was certain that he had taken care of the situation with Lewis. Unless the man had a death wish, he would heed Nate's warning and leave his wife alone from now on.

Early this morning, instead of going to work, he went by his travel agent and picked up the two tickets to Barbados.

But that wasn't why Nate was proud of himself. At that very moment, he was sitting in the office of a Mrs. Wolcott, from the True Home Adoption Agency.

After Nate had gotten out of bed, and Monica was still sleeping, he scoured the living room and dining room till he found the folder of information Monica had shown him.

When he went to the agency this afternoon, was greeted by Mrs. Wolcott, and taken back to her office, the first thing Nate said to her was, "Is this boy still available?"

He was holding up the photo of the little infant boy Nathaniel.

He had told Mrs. Wolcott who he was, that his wife had come in some time ago, looking to adopt, and this was the boy she was interested in. Mrs. Wolcott definitely remembered Mrs. Kenny, had Nate fill out some paperwork, and said, "I'll be right back, find out if he's been adopted yet."

As Nate completed the final page of the three forms, he was hoping, praying that the child was still available.

His wife would be so happy, so surprised and excited if Nate came home and told her that they would still be able to get him.

He laid the pen down when he was finished, and couldn't believe it, but found himself starting to get excited as well, and really began to look forward to the idea of this possible adoption.

Nate didn't know why he wasn't open to this earlier, instead of going through everything that he had put himself through.

Forget it, he thought. Just be happy that it wasn't too late to save his marriage, and he still had the opportunity for this to happen.

When the door opened, and Mrs. Wolcott came back in the office, she wore a huge smile.

"Mr. Kenny, little Nathaniel is still available."

57

Lewis brought Monica upstairs to see the baby. She was a beautiful, chubby, brown-skin angel, with curly black hair all over her head.

When Monica and Lewis walked into the room, from behind the bars of the crib, Layla immediately stopped crying.

When they walked closer, Layla reached up and out for them.

"Can you pick her up? It hurts when I . . . my ribs," Lewis said, placing a hand against his side.

"Lewis, I can't."

"Please. I want to take you somewhere."

❧

They went to where Lewis used to live.

"The Ida B. Wells projects," Lewis said, looking out from the passenger seat of Monica's car while holding Layla in his lap. "I lived there with Layla's mother, but she's dead now."

"Dead?"

"Found her early this morning."

"This morning!" Monica gasped.

"She overdosed on something. I don't know if it was by mistake, or on purpose. But I know she wasn't very happy," Lewis said, still looking out that window. "I don't know. Maybe she's better off where she's at now."

When they pulled up back in front of the town house, Lewis said, "Can you come back in? I want to give you something."

Monica waited in the living room, holding Layla, as Lewis walked out of the kitchen with a brown envelope in his hand. He held it out for her to take.

"What is it?" Monica said.

"It's the money that your husband paid me. I took some out to give to Selena so she could take care of my daughter, and I paid her rent up for the rest of the year so she wouldn't have to think about that. But this is all of what's left." He held the money out to her again. "Here."

"Why are you giving this to me?"

"Because I don't want it. Because it was wrong for me to take it. And . . . and like I said, I love you, was hoping you'd forgive me."

"Forgive you!" Monica said, wanting to blow up, but the baby was still in her arms. "You thought that?"

"I was with Selena because she got pregnant, and I ain't want her aborting my child. I stayed there because of Layla. She was the only reason. Selena wasn't a good woman, don't ever think I had one. But you . . . you're everything I could ever want," Lewis said, walking closer to her.

"Your husband didn't want you because you can't have children, and like a fool he paid me to be with you, not realizing that you're so beautiful, you're so wonderful, that I could've fallen for you."

"Lewis, you shouldn't be saying all this," Monica said, feeling herself softening only slightly by his words.

"Yes, I should. Because when I walked into the place and saw Selena dead, I realized we only got one life, and my child shouldn't have to live it without a mother," Lewis said, looking directly into Monica's eyes.

"What are you trying to say?" Monica said, feeling a zillion different emotions racing through her, from flattery to rage. That this

280

man could think that he could do what he had done to her, and believe that . . . that . . .

"I want us to be together. It ain't right, and I'm sorry that it happened to you, but the fact is, you can't have children, and you're
holding one right now that needs you. I love you, Monica," Lewis
said, walking up to her, wrapping his arms around her, his baby in
between the two of them. "I think you've known that for a little
while now. I don't think there's any other way for us to be, but together."

It was a cute little family hug, Monica thought, feeling herself becoming even more angry, thinking that he could use his child, and
the fact that she couldn't have any, to cover up for all that he had
done. How dare he? How fucking dare he!

"Take her," Monica said, pushing Layla toward Lewis.

"What?"

"Take her!"

"Why?"

"Because this is not my child, and you're not my man, and the
only reason you're saying any of this is because you're broke, and you
need someone to watch after your daughter."

"That's not true, and you know it!"

"I don't care," Monica said, hurrying to the door.

"So what are you going to do? Go back to your husband, when
you know he doesn't want you?"

Monica didn't respond, just reached for the doorknob.

"I love you!" Lewis said.

Monica turned the knob, flung open the door.

"We need you!"

And then Monica paused; just for a second, she stopped, before
stepping out of the house after hearing what Lewis had said to her.
They needed her. Out of nowhere, a million images flooded her
brain, of the three of them together, of Monica raising that child, of
Monica being a mother. A mother! Then she stepped out of Lewis's
house and slammed the door behind her.

58

When Monica heard the front door of the penthouse opening, she was pulling the zipper closed on the huge suitcase she had quickly filled with as many clothes as she could, upon returning home.

When her husband entered, he had a huge smile on his face. He closed the door, actually skipped down the two stairs into the living room, practically ran over, hugged her, kissed her, and said, "Baby, I got surprises for you!"

Monica just stood there, leaning against the back of the couch, stupefied at how he could've orchestrated all that he had, and now could pretend that none of it had ever happened.

But then she started thinking as she had been doing while she stuffed her clothes into the suitcase, preparing to leave Nate for good. He did plan everything, set her up to cheat on him, but neither Nate nor Lewis held a gun to her head, forcing her to be unfaithful.

She could've turned Lewis down. She could've been stronger, dealt with the fact that Nate had been treating her badly, waited till things got better. But she didn't. She committed adultery, and wasn't that as bad as what her husband did? Wasn't it worse?

Besides, he would be the one that would have to live with knowing that she was with another man, would be the one that had seen her with that man. And considering the way Nate was smiling, practically bouncing with excitement before her right now, he seemed as though he would be okay with that. All she had to do was not mention the fact that she knew.

Nate reached into his suit's breast pocket, whipped out an envelope.

"Two tickets to Barbados, one of our favorite spots. I even got us a suite at the Mirage Hotel, the room facing the north shore. What do you say about that, honey?"

He was proud of himself, had no clue that she knew what he had done.

"That's good, baby," Monica heard herself say, still wondering what good it would do to expose her husband for the coward he was. She would tell him that she found him out, they would divorce, she would get money from him—that was, if he couldn't prove her affair. And then what would happen? Where would she be then?

But if she said nothing, she would still have her marriage, still have her husband, and things would go back to the way they were.

Monica felt herself leaning in the direction of just keeping quiet, letting everything just blow over, and then fade away. But what would happen once Nate started wanting a family again? That was what sparked everything, and she knew that the same thing could happen once more, regardless of how much he tried to pretend that her being unable to have his children didn't bother him.

That moment, Monica realized she couldn't stay with him, and she opened her mouth to tell him that when Nate said, "I have another surprise for you."

Again, out of his breast pocket, he pulled out some folded papers, and held them out for Monica to take.

She just stared down at them.

"Go ahead. Take them."

She grabbed the papers, unfolded them, and immediately she recognized the writing on the letterhead. "True Home Adoption Agency," it read.

"What's this?" Monica asked, looking up at Nate.

"I went there this morning to see if little Nathaniel was still available. He was, baby. And I started the process. Mrs. Wolcott said there shouldn't be any problem at all with us getting him," Nate said, more excited than Monica could remember ever seeing him. "We're going to have our son!" He threw himself at her again, hugging her tightly. "Aren't you happy?" she heard him say.

"Yes," Monica said, the word kind of seeping out of her lips. And she was actually happy, but there was an underlying sadness accompanying that, because now her decision was so much harder to make.

But she kept telling herself, all she had to do was just keep her fucking mouth shut and everything would be perfect.

Nate leaned away from her, still grabbing her by the shoulders, the huge grin plastered to his face. But when she looked up at him, Nate was looking strangely back at her, and said, "Baby, what's wrong? Why are you crying?"

Monica reached up, felt tears on her cheeks that she hadn't realized were there.

"I know, it's because of all of this, the vacation, the adoption, us getting back on track," Nate said. "I understand, sweetheart, because from now on, things are going to be perfect between us."

He let go of her, reached down, and grabbed the handle of her suitcase, and said, "I'm going to take this down to the car with my bags, because we should be heading to the airport. Are you ready?"

That was the question that Monica still couldn't answer. Tears began to stream down her face even harder now, because she knew if she told him, she would retain whatever dignity she had left. She would be letting him know he wasn't able to just treat her anyway that he chose, lie to her, just because she couldn't have his babies. She was so much more than just a reproduction machine, and she would receive so much satisfaction in telling him just that.

But what would she have after that? Nothing. That's why Monica said, "Yeah, I'm ready."

"Good!" Nate said, cheerily, and started dragging the bag toward the door, as Monica watched.

She watched the man that she would spend the rest of her life with, the man that had gone through the trouble of booking their vacation, and gone through the trouble of going back to the adoption agency to secure the child that Monica knew she could one day love. But as she continued watching him, she realized that he was also the man that went through the trouble of finding pills that could render him impotent. He went to the trouble of paying some man, setting him up in a home, so Monica would fall for him, sleep with him. She remembered how Nate had told her that he had thought about divorce when she walked in the nursery to find it painted black. She remembered how he left her standing there in the living room naked, when she wanting nothing more than to just be acknowledged by her own husband. And then she remembered the evil look he gave her when he woke up, and found her trying to make love to him. She could even hear the words he had spoken to her—"Why would you want me to come in you? What good would come of it?"—as if they had just been said.

She knew then what her decision had to be.

Nate pulled the suitcase up the two stairs, reached out, opened the door, and was about to step out when Monica said, "Nate, wait!"

He turned. "What is it, baby? We'll be late for the airport."

"We aren't going to the airport."

"What?"

"Nate," Monica said, wiping tears from her face. "I know about what you did. I know about it all."

Nate released the suitcase, and it was clear to him that the game was over.

59

Three weeks later, Monica stood at the checkout counter of the grocery store and watched as the cashier quickly scanned the groceries she was buying. She kept an eye on the steadily growing total, making sure that she would be able to cover the amount with what was in her checking account.

"That'll be fifty-two fifty-six," the woman said.

"Food is getting expensive, hunh?" Monica said. "Can I write a check?"

"Sure."

Monica wrote the check, and jotted down the amount in the back of her checkbook, quickly balancing it, seeing that it was going to be tight the rest of the week till she got paid again.

After the bag boy packed her cart with her groceries, Monica wheeled the cart toward the exit of the store. It had started pouring again, so she opened her umbrella, and covered herself.

Monica quickly pushed the cart across the slick parking lot, and stopped at the back of the '91 Saab she was now driving. She popped the hatch, then was about to load the car when someone stepped up behind her, startling her.

"Times ain't like what they used to be, when you're no longer married to a millionaire," a woman's voice said.

Monica spun around. "Who are you? And what did you say to me?"

The woman was wearing a long raincoat, a plastic scarf pulled over her hair, tied under her chin. She extended her hand. "My name is Tori Thomas. I used to be your husband's secretary. You mind if we talk?"

Monica glanced up at the clouds. The rain had started falling harder.

"If you help me get these in my car."

Tori helped Monica quickly throw the bags of groceries in her car, and they both hurried around and jumped in, slamming the doors.

Monica turned to Tori. "Now, what is it you want to talk to me about."

"You were a hard person to find. I've been looking for you."

"Looking for me for what?" Monica said, starting to lose her patience.

"I don't know if you knew this or not, Mrs. Kenny, but me and your husband were having an affair."

Monica didn't speak a word, move an inch, didn't even bat an eyelid.

"Mrs. Kenny," Tori said, "did you hear what I just told you?"

"Yes, I heard," Monica said, thinking that she should've been shocked, but she wasn't. She should've been hurt, felt betrayed, and for the news that was just given her, she should've wanted to confront her husband, scream and yell, and demand he tell her how he could do such a thing to her. But Monica had already been through that, felt all those emotions, so all she could say now was, "So why are you telling me this now?"

"I would've told you sooner, but like I said, I had to find you first."

"You found me, and I really need to get home before my ice cream melts, so if there's nothing more you have to tell me—"

"There is," Tori interrupted. "I know how much your husband hurt you, but he hurt me too. He was going to marry me, after he divorced you. I was going to have his children, but that never happened. He fired me, after he made those promises to me."

"Am I supposed to feel sorry for you?" Monica said, feeling anger all of sudden. "Get out of my car!" Monica said, reaching over Tori, trying to push her door open.

"Mrs. Kenny, please! Just hear me out. There's a reason I'm telling you all of this."

Monica calmed herself, leaned back into her seat, and listened.

"After he fired me, I called him, and told your husband I could still make his life difficult. I told him I needed to meet him to talk. He agreed."

"So."

"So, when we met, we had sex one last time. I had him explain to me why he couldn't continue seeing me, why we couldn't still get married."

"I still don't understand what all of that has to do with me."

"I was videotaping everything we did, everything we said," Tori said, smiling. She dug into the large purse that hung from her shoulder, and pulled out a brown padded envelope, the size of a videocassette. "I have it all on tape, and it's yours."

Monica received the tape that Tori handed to her. "Why are you giving this to me?"

"I figure you're going through your divorce right now."

"That's right," Monica said.

"And I also figure that Nate probably won't have to give you a thing, since he can prove that you had an affair with those photos he has of you."

"You know about those?" Monica said, shocked.

"I'm the one that had them taken, Mrs. Kenny."

"You had them taken. You're the reason why I won't be entitled to anything, but you're trying to give me this tape. Exactly what is it you want?"

"Exactly what I hope you want," Tori said. "He can prove you cheated with those photos, and now you can prove he cheated with that tape. I'd imagine that they would be offset by each other, and then the proceedings would go on as if it was a normal divorce, and you'd get everything that you're supposed to get."

"I see," Monica said, everything starting to come together for her now. "And you'd want some of that, I suppose."

"What I want most is to know that that worthless man won't get away with this without losing a chunk of everything he holds so dear. But yes," Tori said, a sly smile spreading across her face, "I do want a little something for my efforts."

"How much?"

"Just ten percent," Tori said.

"Five percent."

"Seven and a half."

"You've got yourself a deal," Monica said, reaching out and shaking Tori's hand.

Epilogue

Two months later, Monica was heading north on Lake Shore Drive, heading in the direction of her new million-dollar town home, which sat in the South Loop, when she saw the Pershing Road exit coming up.

She thought for a minute, smiled, then shook her head, telling herself the idea was foolish. She told herself to continue on driving; then, at the last minute, she cut the wheel of the 2004 Jaguar sedan, and made the exit.

It took a little effort remembering all the turns, but moments later, Monica found herself pulling up in front of the Ida B. Wells apartment that Lewis said he would be living in.

Monica parked the car but left it running, trying to find the nerve to shut it off, jump out, and go up there and knock on the door.

But why would she do something like that? she asked herself. Maybe because she was lonely? Maybe because she never really got Lewis out of her system, or that she felt a little sympathy for him, knowing that he was probably going through hard times?

Monica probably would've been in a similar situation if it hadn't been for Tori giving her that tape. Because of it, Nate was forced to give her what she would've been entitled to if they had gone through a normal divorce.

To say that it was a ridiculous amount of money was the understatement of the year. Considering Nate had married Monica before he had started his business, and her lawyer argued that she was instrumental in its success, Monica was entitled to half.

When Nate heard that, he started coughing, practically gagging, and Monica thought he was going to fall to the floor that moment, and just die.

She decided that she didn't need that much. She took a fourth, and a percentage of the stock.

She would never have to work another day in her life, if she chose, but she knew she would get back out there and do something when the time was right.

Till then, she had all the time in the world, and nothing to do with it.

Monica looked out her window again, toward Lewis's door. She thought about his daughter, Layla. She wondered how she was doing, and Monica wondered what kind of mother she would've been to that child, if she had taken Lewis up on his offer.

She told herself to stop being ridiculous.

Lewis was a gorgeous, beautiful, caring person, who could take care of his own child. And even if he couldn't, he probably found some eager woman to do it for him by now.

All of a sudden, Monica saw Lewis come out, pushing his daughter in a stroller, and when he looked up, he saw her, stared her right in the eyes.

Lewis smiled.

Monica blushed.

He waved for her to stop, and she did.

Monica got out of the car, smiling, leaving it running, and happily ran over to Lewis and Layla. She wasn't sure what would happen for the three of them, but she had a good feeling. A really good feeling.

About the Author

RM Johnson is the author of *Dating Games, Love Frustration, The Harris Men, Father Found,* and the #1 *Essence* bestseller *The Harris Family.* He lives in Chicago.